Jamaal's INCREDIBLE Adventures in the BLACK CHURCH

Myron J. Clifton

Jamaal's Incredible Adventures in the Black Church

Copyright © 2022 by Myron J. Clifton

ISBN: Paperback: 978-1639453917
eBook: 978-1639453924

All rights reserved. No part of this publication may be reproduced, distributed, or transmitted in any form or by any means, including photocopying, recording, or other electronic or mechanical methods, without the prior written permission of the publisher or author, except in the case of brief quotations embodied in critical reviews and certain other noncommercial uses permitted by copyright law.

This is a work of fiction. Any resemblance to any persons, living or dead, places, or events are either products of the author's imagination or used in a completely fictitious manner for the purposes of telling these stories.

Cover design by Katya Lerner/Buzzword Consulting
Interior & EPUB design by Sharon K. Miller/Buckskin Books
Editing by Robin Martin/Two Songbirds Press

Printed in the United States of America

Writers' Branding
1800-608-6550
www.writersbranding.com
orders@writersbranding.com

Contents

Dedication

This book is dedicated to the churchgoers who never give up the faith no matter what they see or hear.

"The Bible is right, somebody's wrong."
- My grandfather

"Don't believe everything you read."
- Unknown

Prologue—Sixteen years ago

Meredith and Gerald drove in silence, the rain providing the only conversation other than the gospel music that was so low Meredith could only hear when the choir sang the loud parts. Meredith was grateful not to hear the music because she was in no mood to hear. Her day was already shittier than she had ever imagined a day could be. She was doing her best to ignore her husband sitting next to her, and her God, who was all over her mind and heart.

"Meredith, I just want to say—"

"Not now, Gerald. Not now." Meredith reached down with her left hand and increased the volume to the car stereo, her wedding ring with its big gems catching the light from an oncoming big rig's headlights. She left her hand there and looked at her ring, prayed silently to God, hummed the refrain now playing loudly through the speakers, and kept her hand there, ensuring her husband would not lower the volume, forgetting for a moment that he could change it directly from his steering wheel.

Meredith was what her late grandmother, Exie B., referred to as a "tough young-old broad, like me." Meredith loved her grandma for her bluntness and insight. Nothing came easy, Exie had often said, and Meredith had learned to not be bothered by hard things: roadblocks, racism, or cheating men like the husband sitting next to her.

"Just drive. Don't talk. Don't sing. Just drive, Gerald. Your voice is the absolute last thing I want to hear." Meredith's voice was calm, harsh, and included an unsaid demand to shut the fuck up.

Gerald acquiesced and drove on.

Meredith silently prayed to God for guidance. Then, she cursed God for forcing such a heartbreaking lie on her. Her husband was supposed to be a man of God. Meredith's training fought her heart as she tried to figure out what went wrong and when. She refused to accept that she was at fault—she was never going to be a woman who blamed herself for her man spreading his seed around the community. She fought back negative self-talk, applying the advice of so many books and so many online self-help gurus. She understood that this was necessary for loving herself.

She had tried to share in bible study what she had been learning about self-reliance and positive self-talk by linking both topics to scripture, but the bible study group had no interest, frequently shutting her down and saying, "All you need is the bible," "The bible is right, somebody's wrong," and, "If the bible was good enough for my mother, father, grandparents, then it is good enough for me."

So, after trying with earnestness and excitement to convince her group to apply the words of others in their bible studies, she was forced to give up when Gerald had shown up and, after the discussion was mostly over, had stood to talk and "say a few words." His "few words" turned into a sermon that challenged her self-help words and advice and countered them with scripture taken out of context. The bible study group became excited—cheering on their pastor in front of their first lady.

She knew she had lost that battle. Meredith felt so hurt and betrayed. She told Gerald later that night when he was asking for sex that he had made her feel "like shit" at church so she wasn't about to fuck him, purposely and pointedly cursing at him because she knew he hated it.

Soon after, she opted out of teaching bible study entirely, feeling she was being judged and betrayed by the women she had thought were her close circle of friends. All her friends were now church members, her circle having closed over the years of being first lady.

She never told Gerald the real reason. And he never asked, and that is what hurt her most.

Meredith saw they were approaching the hospital and her heart sank. It was real now, not a rumor—Cousin Jean had confirmed it with the phone call.

Gerald had cheated on her, and now the ultimate outcome—a baby—was before her, waiting to mock and maybe even destroy her. Meredith inhaled and readied herself for hurt her life could not have prepared her for: attending the birth of her husband's child by another woman.

Meredith pushed down bad feelings toward the baby because it wasn't the baby's fault. She had taken to reminding herself of this every time she thought about the baby being born.

But she couldn't help it because of the hurt, shame, and overwhelming sense of betrayal. Gerald was the only man she had ever loved. Despite having experimented with her fair share of men before falling in love with Gerald, soon after marrying him she had fully dedicated herself to him, his church, and his preaching career, slowing her own career aspirations so she could be the best first lady and pastor's wife.

She remained quiet as Gerald pulled into the parking lot at the hospital. She turned the music down as he slowed to take a ticket and search for a parking space. Meredith watched him without looking directly at him. She told herself to slow her breathing and focus on centering her emotions and feelings, just like Rev. Melissa Tipton, the author of the book *Slow and Center,* taught in her seminars and weekly podcasts. Meredith had been listening to them with religious fervor.

After he parked the car on the second floor of the hospital parking garage, Meredith got out, refusing to wait for Gerald to open her door as he had for the entirety of their marriage. Meredith knew she would never again allow Gerald to pretend to be chivalrous.

Her shoes thudded softly as she walked through the garage, into and out of the elevator, and then finally through the large glass sliding doors of the hospital. Meredith was an impressive figure who commanded a room in that certain way a tall, dark, Black woman could. In heels, which Meredith was always in, she was easily six-feet tall while her commanding presence made her at times seem twelve-feet in all directions. She was forty but could easily pass for thirty. Meredith was striking with sharp features, full wide cheekbones, and a full nose that made her smooth face look regal whether with or without makeup, but today she had on stunning purple lipstick that matched her handbag and accentuated her smooth, shiny skin.

She wore royal purple from head to toe: her dress was form fitting, showing off her curvy thickness and fit calves. Her hair was a dark wig that was contoured to her face in a sharp angle on the left side that seemed to point to her beautiful purple lips and mouth.

It was the mouth that she knew Gerald feared today of all days.

Meredith was unafraid and, like her grandmother had taught her, not easily intimidated. She was comfortable in who she was, regardless of the audience, but today of all days she knew her inside emotions would betray her calm, determined exterior.

Today's audience were hospital staff too busy to notice her, so Meredith walked on, already aware of the floor and room number where the baby would be delivered. Meredith walked on with determination, ignoring Gerald's slower, more deliberate pace. She glanced at the children's drawings that hung on the walls that led to the elevator. Drawings made by young children who were treated in the hospital and who sent their drawings that each said “thank you” in ways only little kids can say—with rainbows, dogs, trees, and happy suns in the upper corners.

Meredith didn't wait as Gerald followed her across the shiny hospital floor, his steps less certain but still preacher aggressive, as Meredith liked to refer to his walk. His steps were familiar, Meredith took note, as they reached the waiting area and took a seat.

The steady hum of the vending machine and the occasional overhead announcement paging an employee were the only noises in the waiting area. The room was decorated with more drawings from kids on one wall and pictures of groups of excited and celebratory hospital staff surrounding joyful mothers cradling little swaddled bundles of babies.

Meredith took note that most of the mothers were Black and most of the care staff were white or Asian. Probably Filipino, Meredith noted, recalling the story her grandmother had told her about many Filipinos who came to America after one of the wars and, to secure citizenship, went into nursing.

Meredith watched the doctor walking down the hallway and knew what she was going to say. Her shoes thudded purposefully as she approached in a pencil skirt, eschewing the traditional white scrubs.

"Good afternoon. You're the family of Deborah Andrews? Dr. JoAnn Del Rosario."

Meredith stood, and as she did, Gerald reacted and looked up from reading his old bible. Meredith had noticed that Gerald hadn't turned pages in the past hour. His coffee was cold and his breathing slow. Meredith had sat in the same spot for now going on three hours since arriving at the hospital.

"Hello, Dr. Del Rosario. I am—"

"I am Pastor Gerald Ferguson," Gerald interrupted, as he thrust his hand out to shake Dr. Del Rosario's hand.

The doctor ignored Gerald and reached for Meredith's hand. "And you are?"

"Meredith. I'm Meredith, thank you, Doctor."

"You're the mother's…" Her words hung there, tempting.

"What is the news, Dr. Del Rosario? Is the baby, okay?" Meredith was never one for small talk or talking around issues. She folded her hands in front her as if she were about to bow her head in prayer.

"The delivery is risky at only six months but—"

"But nothing, Doctor. You're a doctor who delivers babies, right? You will deliver the baby. God will make it so; of that I am certain. You need to be certain, too. Don't take your negativity back into her room."

"Meredith, what is your relationship to the mother?" Dr. Del Rosario asked again.

Meredith looked to Gerald, her eyes ablaze and poorly hiding the pain her face betrayed.

"Sister." The word came out strained, Meredith's voice cracking from holding back her tears. "I am her older sister," she continued. "My husband here …" Meredith's right hand was outstretched, and her pointing finger accusingly directed JoAnn's attention to Gerald, "is the baby's father."

The word father came out forceful, like an accusation but one that could not be refuted or denied. Gerald had passed the point of denial.

"Does that answer your question, Doctor?" Meredith hated hearing her voice crack and she hoped Gerald didn't hear but knew damn well he did, which further infuriated her.

"Well, yes. Thank you. I will share with my attending nurse, and then—"

"Then go deliver her baby, Doctor." Meredith had redirected her gaze to Dr. Del Rosario. "Please."

"Of course." Dr. Del Rosario lightly touched Meredith's arm then turned and walked away, her heels forcefully thudding down the hall.

"Meredith."

Gerald's deep raspy voice caught Meredith's attention as his hand tried to hold hers, but she deliberately, quickly, pulled her hand away.

"Do not, Gerald. Just... do not." Meredith turned away, her heels signaling her displeasure as they thumped away from the nurse's station before finding a resting place midway down the hall where she sat on the small, cushioned bench. There was room for two and Meredith sat far on one end, ensuring that she and Gerald would not touch.

Meredith felt Gerald sit down, her edge of the cushion rising slightly. She ignored him, knowing he would lean his head back and pray, as he always did when visiting church members who were hospitalized.

The hours passed and at some point, Meredith was remembering falling in love with Gerald and how happy her younger sister, Deborah, was for her. Deborah was always happy, Meredith reminded herself. How could she have done this? Was this why she hadn't visited in nearly six months?

Meredith saw the doctor before hearing her. She was walking toward where she and Gerald had now been sitting, ignoring each other. Meredith was satisfied to keep things that way, while Gerald attempted to speak every twenty minutes only to be steadily rebuffed.

"Good evening, Meredith," Dr. Del Rosario said softly as she reached Meredith and Gerald. A young woman accompanied the doctor and stood slightly behind her to the right. "This is Dr. Zoey," Dr. Del Rosario continued. "She is observing me for the next few months. She'll soon graduate—we are a teaching hospital, as I am sure you're aware."

"That's nice. It's nice to meet you, Dr. Zoey. What about my sister and her baby, doctors?" Meredith asked.

"Thank you for including Dr. Zoey. Your sister—"

Gerald spoke up, interrupting the doctor and causing Meredith to look at him with an angry, exasperated look.

"My wife is… concerned for her sister. I'm sure you understand. I apologize for her directness. What can we expect?" Gerald's deep voice, which usually carried power, was soft. Anyone who knew him would have been surprised by his hesitancy and lack of certainty as he spoke to the doctor. But not Meredith. She knew his pensiveness was covering his guilt.

"We've got her stable at the moment, but she's hemorrhaged very badly and lost a lot of blood. We are treating her as best we can right now and will update you when we are able," Dr. Zoey answered.

Meredith looked to the younger woman and nodded. "Thank you, Dr. Zoey."

"Wait, I want to hear from you, Dr. Del Rosario, not a college student. No disrespect, young lady." Gerald spoke forcefully, more so than he had all day, and this reminded Meredith how he felt about her sister and his baby.

"Sir," Dr. Del Rosario began, her body now facing Gerald. "Dr. Zoey is excellent at what she does or she would not be here. I am here supporting her, not the other way around."

Meredith knew she would like to get to know this JoAnn Del Rosario if the circumstances were different. But as it now stood, she never wanted to return to this hospital once the baby was born and she knew her sister was safe.

"The baby, a boy, was delivered successfully and is in the NICU. I feel confident he will be okay, though certainly he will need to stay here until we are assured he can live on his own and he is healthy."

"My sister?" Meredith's directness had returned.

"We are monitoring her every minute and will continue to do so until we know she is going to be okay. I am sorry we do not have a more definitive answer for you right now. Just please know we are doing what we can, and our goal is the same as yours: a healthy baby and a mother to care for him." Dr. Zoey spoke at length for the first time.

Meredith considered her and her words. She accepted that her sister's life was in danger, but the younger doctor's words comforted her, against her instincts.

"Thank you, Doctor." Meredith finally offered, watching the doctors turn away before Gerald spoke, trying to reassert himself to a group of women not impressed by his title, station, or gender.

"Thank you, Doctor. I will attend to my wife now. God bless you and may He work through you to save the life of the mother and child," Gerald said with painful supplication.

Part One—Revival Season

CHAPTER 1

SUNDAY

A time to be silent and a time to speak ~ Ecclesiastes 3:7

At sixteen, Jamaal was selected to become his uncle's official driver. His uncle had announced that he was so busy that it would be nice to have a driver so that he could clear his mind, prepare sermons and speeches, and just relax before arriving at an event, wedding, or funeral. The church agreed, and Uncle Gerald chose Jamaal, as he always intended. It was an important position that involved more than just driving, but also doing errands and such for the pastor. When Uncle Gerald arrived at his office, Jamaal would quietly take a seat at the back of the office, and his uncle-pastor wouldn't make him go into the sanctuary. Jamaal humbly accepted the paltry twenty-five dollars a week "offering" the pastor's care committee allotted him, and, as he was trained from a life in church, he didn't complain about "the Lord's blessing."

Jamaal did not yet have his driver's license, but his uncle told him not to worry because if he was in the car, he could take care of any police officer who happened to stop them.

"I hope so, Uncle-Pastor Gerald. I don't want to get shot."

"Ain't no cop shooting my nephew. But also, don't act a fool."

+++

Jamaal pulled into his uncle's parking space.

“Okay,” Jamaal said as he straightened the car and hoped they'd never have to test or prove his uncle's words.

Being his uncle-pastor's driver gave Jamaal access to things he neither sought nor wanted.

Jamaal entered his uncle's office and took a seat on the big leather sofa that sat on the far wall, just beneath the framed pictures of Marcus Garvey, Malcom X, Martin Luther King, Barack Obama and, recently added by the women's committee after a complaint from one of the young women in the office, Kamala D. Harris.

“We need a big offering, today, deacons. We've been low for a few weeks now. I need y'all to get it together,” Pastor Gerald said. He was marking up his sermon, which he still hand-wrote. The paper was heavily marked up, which signaled to anyone who knew him he was changing the focus of his sermon to something or someone that had caught his attention since he had first conceived it.

“You worry about your sermon, Pastor. We will take care of the money,” one of the elder deacons responded.

Jamaal imagined that Pastor Gerald pretended to ignore his deacon but had made a mental note of his insolence.

“We will start off praise with “I Am Praying,” then move to more up-tempo “Be the Praise,” and we will finish with “My God, What's Up?” the choir director said.

“No, we will not sing that fake gospel song, Dwayne.”

“I know you don't like it, Pastor, but our young folk—”

"Not today. Leave that junk for tonight or during the revival. Not Sunday. That's all I'll say."

"I believe the children are our future—" the choir director started singing.

"I don't believe you are the future of my choir if you continue singing songs that belong in the club on Saturday night but not in church on Sunday morning."

Jamaal chuckled to himself at his uncle's joke.

The leadership team continued talking about the morning service, song choices for praise and for the choir, prayer lists, and finally how much money they needed to raise today to ensure revenue targets were met before the big event scheduled to start the following week. Jamaal sat quietly, like a fly on the wall, listening to the same discussion the church leaders held every Sunday. They were like a sports team in the locker room before a game, reviewing their game plan, in-fighting, trying to win the coach's favor, and, finally, reaching a type of consensus that allowed the team to execute.

Jamaal liked feeling invisible during the pre-church meetings and just about every other meeting he attended. He had long learned to sit quietly and observe the world around him. He did it in school, at home with his Aunt Meredith and Uncle Gerald, and with friends and cousins. Some called him quiet or introverted, but he didn't think he was either of those things. He knew he liked to observe, learn, think, and watch. He didn't always listen to the words, though that was primarily what he did, but watched the facial expressions, mannerisms, and hand movements while he studied what people were wearing and how they moved. He would later study group dynamics and traced his interest in that subject back to these moments in his uncle's office before church.

"Let us pray before we enter the Lord's sanctuary. Come over, Jamaal."

"Okay, Unc... Pastor." Jamaal corrected himself to follow his uncle's explicit directive to respect his title at church and around church folk.

"Grab a hand. Let us pray."

Jamaal hoped no one grabbed his hand, but like every week his hand was grabbed by someone, today the oldest deacon in the church, and Jamaal cringed when the old man and his soft sweaty hand grabbed his.

"And may the Lord bless and work through us as we..." Jamaal heard his uncle-pastor drone on in a prayer that lasted way too long and caused Jamaal's mind to wander and imagine the sweaty hand that was holding his was sweating holy water.

"Amen," the pastor finally intoned, looking up with the satisfied look pastors have when they're convinced they've just finished talking to God.

"Amen, Pastor," the deacons and church mothers said in unison, with the harmony of a well-rehearsed choir.

Jamaal wiped his hand on his shiny church pants and drifted backwards, allowing the group to leave the office, single file, behind his uncle-pastor in what he heard his uncle-pastor refer to as "the processional" which, to Jamaal, sounded odd because his uncle-pastor also used the word when he was officiating funerals.

Once everyone was out, Jamaal turned off the desk lamp, then urinated in his uncle's private bathroom before leaving the office and locking the door with his own key to the private space.

Right before the final prayer, Jamaal rushed out of church so he could make it to the men's bathroom before everyone else because there were only two urinals, but also because there was only one small mirror and if he didn't get there first, he'd end up in line behind all the older men—and the old men—who took far too long and got on Jamaal's nerves.

All the young and old men were primping in anticipation of the after-church ritual of talking about the service that just ended, eating, sharing stories of the past week, and talking about the week ahead. There was always fundraising—Jamaal loved the homemade ice cream one of the church mothers sold for one dollar a cup every Sunday.

But it wasn't all about food and fun; it was also about young men and women and older men and women, flirting in the name of the Lord.

Jamaal ate his ice cream while standing off to the side, carefully avoiding the young children running about, ignoring the admonishments of any and every adult yelling at them to slow down and stop running. Admonishments like this never worked on any kid anywhere, and they weren't working on this day. As Jamaal chuckled, a little boy ran into him causing his ice cream cup to toss up a big dollop that landed smack dab on top of the boy's head, which caused the boy to shout loudly and, subsequently, the little girl who was chasing him to point and scream her pleasure. This, in turn, caused three of the church mothers who had been talking conspiratorially between themselves to simultaneously shush the little girl, while one of them roughly wiped the boy's head and face with a handkerchief she had whisked out of her overlarge designer purse that matched her designer scarf.

"Are you ready for tonight, Jamaal?"

Jamaal turned to see Sister Julie standing to his right. As he turned toward her, he accidentally looked straight to her breasts. Jamaal snapped his head up, looking Julie in her eyes. She smiled at him.

"Yeah."

"I hear this evangelist is really good, pulls a big crowd, and brings in big money."

"Yeah."

“You will be here every night. I will too, I think. Right?”

“I guess, yeah.”

Jamaal moved his ice cream cup from one hand to the other, and then back again. Then he looked down and realized the mistake he made as soon as he looked up and was looking straight at Sister Julie's breasts again. He quickly looked up into her eyes where she had been waiting to look at him.

“You're a funny young man, Jamaal. You're getting good-looking, too. See you tonight.”

Jamaal realized he had been holding his breath and finally let the air out and reflexively lowered his shoulders.

Once the week-long revival began, a city-famous evangelist would be preaching at his uncle's church every night for a week. Folks were excited. Services would be held every night, with two services each on Saturday and Sunday—day and night. Jamaal dreaded these events. They were mostly about separating members from their money while the evangelist reiterated that they were all sinful and the only way to get God to even hear their prayers was to give him, the evangelist, money. His secondary message was how sinful women were and are. The church was mostly women, but all the ministers, preachers, and almost all the evangelists were men who preached about how sinful women are, how they cause men to sin and lose their way, how almost all the problems with men and the Black community at large was mainly due to women not being faithful enough, or prayerful enough, or obedient enough to their husbands. But some of the worst attacks were directed at young single women who were constantly reminded that sex outside of marriage was sin.

And now, with this evangelist in town, he would have to hear it every day.

“Jamaal! Let's go, son.”

Jamaal saw Uncle Gerald standing next to his car—a late-model grey sedan that had a red stripe on the side and a REV G license plate that was framed by small alternating crosses and fish.

Jamaal hurried to his uncle's car, and they drove slowly through a stream of churchgoers who talked to his uncle through the window of the car for another twenty minutes.

+++

Feeling full of his aunt's early dinner, while his aunt and uncle watched the news in the front of the house, Jamaal crept to his room to lie down and recharge his energy. Looking up at his ceiling, he wished he could lie in bed for the rest of the day and night, just relaxing and enjoying his own company in silence.

Church and church people were draining to Jamaal. He felt the same after school and always looked forward to just lying on his bed staring at the ceiling and doing nothing and thinking nothing. But it was hard for him not to think.

Jamaal was certain people were having sex and were not married, judging by the conversations he listened to while in his uncle's church office. He hated the two-faced message about sex and resented being forced to listen far too often to what he would grow up to call "messy theology."

Too soon, Uncle-Pastor Gerald was yelling, "Jamaal! Let's go!" Jamaal rolled his eyes then closed them before finally rolling off the bed. Jamaal was moving deliberately because he didn't want to go. He finished tying his tie and exited his room, walked down the hall, through the kitchen, and out to the garage where Gerald waited in the car. He started talking as soon as Jamaal got in.

"I hope the evangelist delivers a good sermon. He wanted me to guarantee him ten thousand dollars this week, but I told him he needed to raise the money. If he preached well and the folk liked him, they'd bless him, I told him. If God wants to bless you, he will."

Jamaal listened. He rarely commented on these conversations except when he wanted to be a smart ass.

"Besides," his uncle continued, "he's good-looking, so that'll help, and his wife ain't coming, so I'm sure he will be blessed in other ways."

Jamal chose not to talk and hope his uncle changed the topic.

"He will have his pick of the cows and get all the milk he wants."

Jamaal internally shook his head while wishing he had left with his aunt earlier. Unlike morning service when she went late, when there was a revival and visiting evangelist, she went early to help set up and make sure all the women officers, ushers, and kids were where they needed to be, when they needed to be. She was in charge, and no one had better cross her. Jamaal admired and feared his aunt. She was one hundred and forty pounds of fire and energy, and she was petty when she had to be. He wasn't the only one who feared her.

Jamaal brought his homework, all the kids did, so he could do some while church was going on. The kids weren't allowed to leave the services and do homework—God was more important, they'd been taught and chastised—so they sat in the back of church during services trying to concentrate and complete homework assignments.

So, there they sat, three rows of kids, ages one through seventeen, each with reading, writing, and arithmetic materials, some siblings, many cousins, and all family, learning lessons from school and God simultaneously. Or rather, God first, school second.

"How much homework you have, Jamaal?" Penny asked. Penny was always reading for pleasure in addition to her required reading, and tonight she was reading one of the Harry Potter books, Jamaal could tell, even though she attempted to hide the book inside her geometry book.

His uncle had proclaimed Harry Potter to be a demon and the books to be from the devil. Never mind Jamaal had read them and had gotten his copies from the church library.

Jamaal could tune out the sermon but still couldn't concentrate due to the little kids who had stopped even pretending to do homework and were playing—climbing over and crawling under the benches, bumping into Jamaal's legs every couple of moments.

The evangelist, Preacher Jesse, had just been introduced by his uncle, so Jamaal decided to take a seat in the sanctuary and away from restless kids. Picking up his things, Jamaal made his way down the far right aisle to the front of the church and sat down, ignoring the looks of the members who always stared when anyone walked in late and especially when walking all the way to the front of the church because doing so was seen as breaking an unwritten rule about being an attention hog. Jamaal simply wanted to get a seat where he wouldn't be bothered by the kids but also so he could be left alone in general. Sitting in the front of the church was often a good place for quiet time, Jamaal had learned.

The evangelist was now at the dais and saying his hellos to folk he knew from the last time he came around. Jamaal listened, observing the way the evangelist, like his uncle and most preachers, spoke quietly and deliberately when they began talking, sounding almost tired, or weary, as they liked to say.

Jamaal watched the evangelist work the podium; his skills evident by the way the church members were responding to his every word, how he slowly sipped water, and how he looked solemn and concerned as he prepped them for what would be a hellfire of a sermon of the type he was known for.

Jamaal was absently thinking the evangelist looked to be in his late forties, medium brown-skinned, taller than his uncle, and with his hair short, wavy, and styled in the old style like Cab Calloway.

"I was going to start preaching, but I see Sister Wanda over there and I wonder if she will sing a solo before I preach?"

Jamaal watched the performance that always played out in just this fashion, with the preacher appearing to be surprised to see a woman in the audience that he knew was there all along and that he had specifically requested be there to sing for him. He had chosen the song she would sing as well. But it played out because everyone expected it to play out. Ritual was important in church just like it was everywhere else.

The song was a slowly building toward its rousing crescendo had the members and the preachers, including the evangelist, on their feet, clapping, waving handkerchiefs, and yelling at the singer to "Go on!" "Let God use you!" "You better sing that song!" And, simply, "Sing!"

Jamaal watched it all, noticing that most of the energetic feedback was coming from those sitting in the front half of the church, while the back half looked on with faces that were impassive and purely in an observation mode, comparing it to the emotional distance like those in a mosh pit and those at the back of a concert.

Sister Wanda returned to her seat and her pre-song persona of sitting stone-faced, immovable, and furiously patting her face with a little round powder-puff thing. Jamaal wondered what that thing was actually called.

Now thirty minutes into the sermon, Jamaal's mind had wandered. He thought the evangelist was droning on, and he knew it was going to be a long goddamned week of listening to him preach pretty much the same message every night, though he would change the scriptures that backed his messages. Jamaal was deep in his thoughts, so he didn't at first notice the evangelist had stepped down from the pulpit and stood right above him.

Jamaal was used to this act when preachers would focus the congregation's attention on a person the preacher decided needed extra prayerful attention. Jamaal also knew preachers would do it when they wanted to prove a point or to purposely make someone uncomfortable because the preacher was told something of the person's recent sin.

Jamaal realized, with no little bit of pain, it was his turn. He hated this and usually avoided this type of nonsense because he was experienced enough to know where to sit, when to move, and when to get out of the main sanctuary.

Not tonight, though. His daydreaming prevented Jamaal from paying attention and before he knew it the evangelist was now standing just a few feet away from him and, as best Jamaal could now determine, the evangelist was addressing him directly.

"GET UP," the evangelist yelled into the microphone. The speakers were turned up too loud, as usual, and the music was extra loud and as a result, the evangelist was screaming. And he was screaming at Jamaal while the entire church looked on.

Jamaal tried to sort out what the evangelist had said just prior to yelling at him to get up, but he found no help in his memory.

"GET UP!"

Glancing around Jamaal saw faces looking back at him, expectant faces, some with wide eyes as if their eyeballs could physically lift him out of his seat.

Jamaal was stubborn, though, and the pressure being exerted on him by the evangelist and some church folk annoyed him. And he didn't like the evangelist because he was loud, his hair was too greasy and now dripping with sweat, and he had spittle on the corner of his mouth that needed to be wiped away. Or knocked away. Either was fine, Jamaal decided.

"SATAN YOU WILL NOT WIN TONIGHT! GOD IS IN THIS HOUSE, AND I REBUKE YOU IN THE NAME OF JEEE-SUSSSS! JEEE-SUSSSS!!"

The church cosigned and amened, clapped, and encouraged the evangelist in calling out Satan.

All eyes were on Jamaal as the evangelist's voice dominated the sanctuary, bouncing off the walls, tambourines, drums, wigs, and the church organ, but not off Jamaal who ignored it all.

Jamaal wasn't certain that there was a Satan, and why, if Satan did exist, he would be in this little church at this very moment. But if, in fact, there was a Satan, he decided that he looked just like the loud-mouthed, sweating, greasy evangelist yelling at him to get up.

"LOOK AT SATAN! LOOK AT THE DEVIL! HE SEEKS TO DESTROY AND CAUSE OUR YOUTH TO DISOBEY! THE DEVIL IS A LIE! HE IS A LIE! STAND UP! STAND UP! STAND UP!"

Jamaal sat.

He had decided that nothing on the planet would make him stand. He hated the moron yelling at him and drawing all the church's attention to him. He looked around at the members staring at him—many of them who knew him to be a quiet person who kept to himself and liked to be left alone.

He could see their expressions, and some were expectant, some angry like the evangelist, and still others showed what Jamaal thought looked like unhelpful, concerned faces.

He saw some of the other kids in the back of the church, their attention also drawn to the spectacle playing out between Jamaal and the evangelist.

Most were pointing and laughing, homework having been long since tossed aside. But most had wide unbelieving eyes that showed surprise and fear and, Jamaal decided, relief that it was him and not them at the end of the evangelist's unrighteous attention.

Then he saw his aunt.

Jamaal knew Aunt Meredith understood him more than any adult. That she knew he was beyond stubborn, and normally she'd yell at him because of it, but Jamaal knew, too, that she was protective of him and all her nieces and nephews, and all church kids.

He met her eyes, and he knew she knew: Jamaal wasn't budging.

She got up from her special *Pastor's Wife Decorated Chair That You Better Not Think of Sitting In* and walked over to Jamaal, gently resting her soft hand on his shoulder.

"Jamaal," she said quietly, as she hunched over.

"LOOK AT THE PASTOR'S WIFE LET GOD USE HER! GOD IS BLESSING THE PASTOR'S WIFE RIGHT NOW!" Jamaal heard he evangelist's big mouth shout, the sound reaching into Jamaal's head like a giant gong.

"Jamaal, do it for me. Stand up, baby, and this will stop."

Jamaal just stared at her. He looked at his uncle sitting there in the pulpit in the Pastor's Chair That You'd Better Not Even Think of Sitting In and saying nothing. His uncle's face was impassive, showing no disapproval, approval, or understanding. It was all a show to him, Jamaal thought.

Jamaal wanted to punch the loudmouth evangelist in his loud mouth.

"Jamaal, get up baby," his aunt said again, her voice stern but soft, imploring but not demanding.

Jamaal stood up. He didn't want his aunt to be embarrassed. But he didn't want the stupid evangelist to think he won, either.

"LOOK AT GOD, LOOK AT GOD, LOOK AT GOOODDDDD!!!!"

The evangelist moved closer to Jamaal and stared straight into his eyes. Jamaal met his stare and silently told him, "Go to hell, loser."

"WE WILL PRAY FOR THIS YOUNG MAN, AND PRAY THE DEVIL AWAY, AND PRAY THE SIN AWAY!!"

Jamaal stood up, turned around, and walked straight out. He knew his aunt would not try to stop him. He knew there'd be hell to pay later, but he'd had enough of the evangelist's nonsense. The walk through the rows of wooden folding chairs seemed to take a long time. Long enough for Jamaal to see shocked faces of the older people, surprised faces of the young folk who were around his age, and the laughing faces of the younger kids who found the scene unbelievably funny.

It was only the first night of the revival. Jamaal knew it was going to be a long week.

Monday is going to suck, but at least I get a ride to school, Jamaal thought, as he dozed off sometime after one in the morning.

CHAPTER 2

MONDAY

How long shall I put up with you? ~ Matthew 17:17

Jamaal could not quite place the intermittent thumping that was working to sort itself into a pattern and fading out before it did. Then it was back, and it was sorting itself into another pattern. Slowly, awareness forced its way in, pushing the much-needed sleep far away and replacing it with an old-school church music solo being banged out by his aunt on the old piano that sat in the corner of the living room.

Jamaal groaned and slowly turned over, hopelessly pulling the large red and green quilt—made by his uncle's church-women's sewing circle, led by his Aunt Meredith—over his flat pillow that was already atop his sleepy head.

Jamaal knew it was hopeless. The piano was used to torture him, he liked to tell people in secret. The flat pillow and the heavy quilt failed to block the sound of Aunt Meredith's relentless playing. And they failed to block the heat from Aunt Meredith turning on the heater and setting it to eighty-five degrees because, as Jamaal heard too many times: "This is my house, and I will not be cold, and I pay the bills so mind ya business and stay warm."

On worse mornings she would also loudly sing church songs, so Jamaal was minimally thankful that today she wasn't singing. Jamaal loved his aunt's singing when she sung at church but hated it at seven in the morning.

He knew it was time for him to get up for school, and Aunt Meredith was now belting out her second church song, so Jamaal pushed the quilt and blanket off his head and torso as he sat up and wiped his eyes.

Jamaal was seventeen, lean, and with a small stomach he could push out far enough that it looked distended. He had had a recent growth spurt that put him on the cusp of the golden land of six-feet tall. He was a solid five-ten, and finally taller than both his aunt and uncle. He kept his hair short, which satisfied Uncle Gerald, even though he complained whenever Jamaal asked for haircut money, which he did every two weeks.

Finishing his shower and now standing naked in front of the mirror, Jamaal checked his muscles knowing they hadn't grown because he didn't do anything to make them grow. He was newly dismayed by what appeared to be stretch marks just above his tailbone.

“Why, God, have you forsaken me, goddammit,” Jamaal said, as he moved his finger inside the thin groove that was, without a doubt, a stretch mark.

“Damn.”

“Get out of the mirror, Jamaal, and come eat your breakfast.”

Jamaal jumped at his uncle's husky preacher's voice, and then he quickly put on the old-man deodorant his uncle insisted Jamaal use (because it was the what he used to woo his aunt), dressed, and then, as he quickly walked-ran down the hall, grabbed the doorknob to his bedroom and slammed the door.

He knew a closed door would never stop his aunt or uncle from entering his room whenever they felt, because, as Uncle Gerald loved to say, "There will be no drugs or alcohol in our home."

Jamaal neither smoked nor drank but his calm protests and request for privacy went nowhere and the inspections went on.

Jamaal sat next to his uncle at the kitchen bar over which his aunt handed his uncle his plate first—as was the house rule—and then Jamaal his plate.

Jamaal inhaled the goodness on his plate: seasoned potatoes, two fried eggs, sliced avocado, three thick slices of bacon. Two slices of toasted wheat bread were on a small plate and there was a thick pat of melting butter on the top slice. A small glass of orange juice was on the left of the toast. Uncle Gerald had coffee instead of orange juice.

"I like my coffee black like I like my women, Jamaal," Uncle Gerald volunteered every time he drank coffee around Jamaal.

His aunt's cooking, Jamaal often thought but seldom said aloud, was "magical." Jamaal started by mixing his eggs with his potatoes, then crunching up two slices of bacon and dropping them on top of the eggs which were on top of the potatoes. Jamaal then mixed all the pieces together before taking his first bite.

"Boy, you work as hard mixing your food as your aunt does preparing it."

"It is all going to the same place so..." Jamaal paused long enough to take a sip of his orange juice, his mouth still full of food.

He ignored his uncle who was staring at the side of his head, eyes wide, as Jamaal continued chewing.

“I see you're loving the deodorant. I knew you would. It will get the ladies' attention. Just like I got your aunt.”

“Shouldn't you be going to church by now, old man, instead of telling Jamaal them lies?” Aunt Meredith crunched a slice of bacon as she walked away.

Jamaal made note of the fact that Aunt Meredith seldom ate while sitting down. She nibbled as she cooked and when she did sit, her plate had no more food than what a young child would have. Unless that young child had a plate made by Aunt Meredith, in which case the plate would be as full as any grownup's plate.

“Let's go.”

Jamaal watched Uncle Gerald as he finished his coffee, picked up his old leather briefcase, kissed his Aunt Meredith, and headed toward the garage door.

“The only time he speaks softly is when he is ready to leave,” Jamaal mumbled to himself as he ran to his bedroom, quickly put his shiny church shoes in his backpack, ran back down the hallway, briefly stopped in the kitchen and finished his orange juice before pivoting to the garage door.

“I'm coming!” Jamaal yelled as he opened the garage door. Uncle Gerald was backing out. The car braked, and Jamaal got in and slammed the door before hastily putting his seatbelt on.

“A person is either early or they're late, Jamaal. I tell you every day to be early. Try it sometime,” Uncle Gerald said.

“Can you wait for me just one time, Uncle?” Jamaal asked, exasperated, and breathing hard.

"The bible says: They that wait upon the Lord shall renew their strength. The bible does not say: They that wait upon Jamaal, son." Uncle Gerald answered. "Tomorrow, you take the bus."

Fourth period English always dragged on the longest, as staying up too late the night before, his teacher droning on about the rules of essay writing or the details of the latest required book they were reading, combined with wanting a nap, made the class particularly difficult. A little piece of paper hit Jamaal right on the cheek and stuck there. "I hate you, Kevin, I really do," Jamaal said, flicking the spit-wad off his cheek as Kevin failed to suppress laughter and drew the attention of Mrs. Hannigan. She gave him the stare she seemed to reserve mostly for Kevin.

"And you, too, Jamaal." Mrs. Hannigan had now directed her ire at him. "I'm sure you both behave at your uncle's church, so I expect the same respect here. This here classroom is my church."

"Yes, ma'am," Jamaal replied, louder than he needed to.

"And you?" She looked at Kevin who Jamaal saw was still trying not to laugh. Jamaal followed his eyes and saw that the spit-wad he had flicked off his cheek had landed right on the tip of Kevin's sneaker.

Jamaal tried not to look Kevin in the eye but the urge to not look wasn't as strong as the urge to look and once he did, all the laughter in his body gushed out simultaneously with Kevin's own laughter.

"To the office. Go. GO!" Mrs. Hannigan yelled as she waived the book she was holding—Catch-22—toward the boys as they exited the room in a jumble of sneakers, elbows, laughter, and flailing backpacks.

+++

“That lady just likes to pick on us, Jamaal.” Jamaal and Kevin were outside church waiting for services to begin and were trying to get to the extra homework Mrs. Hannigan had assigned.

“She probably does pick on us but not today. That spit-wad got us in trouble, punk.”

“Jamaal.” It was Auntie Meredith. “You and Kevin help me put the folding chairs out downstairs; we'll need them after services when folk get dessert. Then when church is over you can put them away. And don't make those faces; just be glad this is the lightest punishment you'll get at church. Pastor Gerald wants you both to apologize in front of the church tonight.”

“Dang.” Kevin mumbled while Jamaal just silently shook his head and exhaled.

“Don't you 'dang' me, Kevin, and don't you shake your head at me, Jamaal.”

The boys followed Auntie Meredith downstairs and began loudly unfolding the folding chairs, sliding them across the floor and causing more noise than necessary but which always seemed to follow teenagers doing chores they did not want to do.

“Watch where you push those, young man. You need to pick them up and walk them over to where they need to be, instead of taking the lazy way out.”

Jamaal looked up to see the loud-mouthed evangelist who had humiliated him last night. The man looked mean, Jamaal thought as he rolled his eyes and bent over to pick up the chair at his feet. As he did though, another came sliding toward him, followed by Kevin yelling, “Incoming!”

The evangelist's face expressed what Jamaal, somewhat perplexed, thought was disgust, but it didn't last long, so he turned and walked away.

Chairs set up to Auntie Meredith's satisfaction, the boys went back to the rear of the church to do homework in between talking about Mrs. Hannigan kicking them out of class and wondering in whispers whether the loudmouthed evangelist had it in his mind to harass Jamaal again.

"Kevin, let me borrow your pencil since you're not going to use it." Jamaal snatched Kevin's pencil from his friend's lap.

Jamaal let the pencil slack in his hand as he zoned out staring ahead, and church began. Jamaal had a "looking route" he followed when sitting in back of the church and staring ahead. He looked first to the faux stained-glass windows—there were six of them; three on either side of the building. They reflected the days preceding Jesus's crucifixion on one set of windows, then the crucifixion and subsequent resurrection and ascendancy to Heaven on the other set and side of the church. Jamaal liked to count the number of colors within each windowpane. Then he counted the chairs and number of people sitting in each aisle, then the numbers of women and men—there were always many more women. The counting helped Jamaal focus but also calmed his mind and helped him relax.

"Gimme my pencil back," Kevin said, snatching the pencil from Jamaal's hand, causing Jamaal to yank his hand backwards exaggeratedly.

The friends laughed loudly, and an usher just as loudly shushed them. But other than that, and the normal high-volume preaching of the loud-mouthed preacher, church passed uneventfully.

Aunt Meredith joined them in the car on the way home, though, and something had struck her the wrong way because when his Uncle Gerald made a comment about how the church women were responsible for that night's big offering, she replied, "Yet women are the cause of all sin in the world, huh?"

Jamaal tried to think what it might have been that made her set to go off on her husband, but nothing in particular stood out. Never mind about that, though, because the car ride was going to be memorable, he could tell. She was on fire.

"You know it is just a refined hustle covered in religious piety, salvation, and guilt trips, especially for women, Gerald." Auntie said with a tinge of anger in her voice as she watched her favorite reality show, Real Church Wives of Black Pastors.

"Most things that could be considered 'fun' are also considered 'of the world' and therefore not 'of God' and strangely enough, a lot of that crap is directed at us, Gerald. Makeup, wearing pants, dancing, dressing cute, sex, and abortion. Y'all just figure out more and more ways to keep our hard-earned money in the church and in the hands of you and your little preacher friends."

"Alright, Meredith, let's talk about something else, okay?"

"Oh, now you want to stop talking, eh, preacher? No. Let me finish, I'm on a roll."

Jamaal chuckled. Auntie was really laying into Uncle Gerald. One of the rare times she criticized the institution of the church. At least in front of him.

"All sex is sin. Women need to obey their husbands. Domestic violence is ignored with the only responses alternating between 'pray for them both' to 'she needs to stay with him and remain prayerful.' There is little care for abused children—if the police didn't get involved—or other social issues. The answer was always: prayer, stop sinning—especially girls and women—and give more money to the church."

"That's enough!" Uncle Gerald's voice boomed in the room.

"No, it's not. It's never enough if preachers ignore the sin of their preacher friends who abuse girls AND boys, Gerald. And you know what I am talking about. Just like all those preachers having all those babies with women who are not their wives. Now I will stop."

"Meredith. Please. Let's talk about this later. In private. Please."

Jamaal sensed that something had just passed between them.

"Whatever, Gerald."

"This is why we don't all ride home from church together! It might be the last time," Uncle Gerald said.

CHAPTER 3

TUESDAY

Therefore, love is the fulfillment of the law ~ Romans 13:10

Jamaal was tired. Church on Monday night had lasted until eleven-thirty, and then his uncle lingered and talked to members and the loudmouth evangelist until midnight while Jamaal and his aunt waited outside in the car. They hadn't arrived home until twelve-thirty. Jamaal never finished his homework and didn't have time to do it in the morning. He had to be at the bus stop no later than seven-thirty which left no time to do it at home. His aunt and uncle, both tired from the night before, were sleeping in.

Jamaal sat on the bus about midway back and next to the window. The bus was an older model city bus, not a school bus, because the city did not have school buses.

Jamaal looked to see if the emergency glass, behind which a little red hammer hung, was intact. It had become fashionable at school to have key rings that included the little hammers. Jamaal wouldn't take one himself, but he had a habit of checking each bus to see if one of his classmates had taken it.

The little hammer was gone, and the glass case was shattered—the city had recently stopped replacing the glass and stolen hammers.

The smell of perfume caught Jamaal's attention and he swiveled his head to see a girl he had seen on the bus before. She was a senior and athletic and Jamaal had imagined that he would one day have the nerve to speak to her. He found himself sitting right next to her on this foggy Oakland morning.

Jamaal stared straight ahead and thought that maybe he was holding his breath. He had run for the bus and prior to seeing her, he distantly recalled breathing hard.

“Hi,” Jamaal heard himself say, much to his own protest.

“Hey,” Jamaal heard her say back.

Jamaal wondered if by her answering it meant he should say something else.

He looked out the window and, though it was foggy, it wasn't too foggy to see the homes pass by as the bus made its way through the last neighborhood before it would, as the kids called it, “hit the hills.”

A few minutes later, as the bus made its way up the hill, it began to slow, its old engines straining against the steep hills with a full bus of kids. After a couple of minutes, the bus stopped and, just as the driver did every day, he stood and faced the kids and told them all to get off the bus.

And as they did every day, the kids whined, groaned, cursed, and laughed at the driver as they did what the driver said and exited the bus because they knew two things to be true: The bus could not make it up the hill if they were all on it, and two, the driver wouldn't drive until all kids were off the bus.

Jamaal decided to run up the hill, thinking he would show the pretty girl he was also an athlete. He was certain she was watching him, impressed.

Once the bus reached the top of the hill, the students, who were already there and waiting, got back on, most in the same seats they were in before getting off the bus.

And, like before, Jamaal was holding his breath as the pretty girl again sat next to him.

"Hi again," Jamaal heard the pretty girl say.

"Hey again," he answered.

"Do you have a name?" she asked.

"Yea."

"And?"

"Oh. Jamaal."

"Hi Jamaal. I'm LaTonya."

"Hi, LaTonya."

Just then, Jamaal felt a big dollop of sweat roll down his forehead, curve and stop briefly near his inner eye, before he instinctively wiped it away.

"You're sweating."

Jamaal realized that running up the hill wasn't the best idea after all. He wiped away the sweat from his brow, shook his hand, and watched LaTonya flinch as some of the sweat landed on her cheek just below her eye.

"Ewww, boy, dang."

Jamaal sat in silence the rest of the ride to school, silently praying LaTonya would remain silent as well. She did.

+++

At church that night, Jamaal was in his uncle-pastor's office with Jesse, whom he now thought of simply as the loudmouth evangelist, Assistant Pastor Johnson, and two local preacher friends of the evangelist who had come to support him and listen to him preach. The only woman was Sister Julie, the treasurer who had been in the role for only a year, who was leading the discussion about funds and how much money needed to be raised tonight and each night for the rest of the week. Jamaal noted that though Sister Julie was trying to keep the discussion focused on finances, the loudmouth evangelist interrupted her time and again, repeatedly starting his story over until he had everyone's attention. Jamaal had already faded to the background hoping, as always, not to be noticed, not speak up, and to just listen and watch or try his best to ignore whatever story was being spit out of the preachers' mouths.

The loudmouth evangelist was talking about sex, and Jamaal was doing his best to not listen but was failing miserably.

“I knew I was gonna screw her the moment I placed my hand on her head and blessed her with the oil; her whole body was shaking and—I know one thing about church women,” he continued, “when they shake when you touch 'em with oil, they'll shake later when you touch 'em with something else!”

Jamaal listened as they laughed, and he looked over to see the loudmouth evangelist pushing and pulling on Assistant Pastor Johnson's shoulder, as the two men continued laughing even after others had stopped.

The loud-mouthed evangelist then told more detail of his late-night activities. Jamaal tried not to hear, but the loudmouth evangelist was living up to the nickname Jamaal had given him. Before long, Jamaal had heard each of the preachers talk about their own affairs with women in his uncle-pastor's church and other churches. Normally his uncle-pastor laughed and cracked jokes, without telling on himself, but tonight he started to speak.

Though Jamaal felt disgusted, he began to listen more closely, keeping his head buried in his assigned reading from English class. He hated hearing preachers talk about women who he knew attended his uncle-pastor's church. Jamaal knew every name he heard and recognized belonged to a nice person who he thought of as sincere and devoted to God.

"Back in my day," his uncle-pastor started, "I could preach all night, and then screw all the rest of the night. I could do revival preaching for two straight weeks; as long as there were pretty women in the church, I'd preach every night."

"You know Sister Willoughby?" his uncle asked the group.

"Sister Willoughby?" one of the preachers asked, incredulously. "No way, Pastor!"

"Yep. Got her a few times. She hasn't always been as holy as she pretends to be now!"

They continued like that for another thirty minutes before it was time to start church.

Jamaal learned something that night and it confirmed what he had long suspected about his uncle-pastor. *He's just like the rest.*

Jamaal locked up the office and entered the church sanctuary after his uncle and other preachers had left the office. The combined choirs of three churches were singing. On their fourth consecutive song, Jamaal could see the church was uplifted, and members were singing along with the choir, women and girls were playing tambourine with a ferocity and rhythm that Jamaal envied because while he could play tambourine, he couldn't play at the level the best players mastered. So he often found himself staring at the best players, alternatively looking at their hands, faces, and the tambourine as it swished through the air in short powerful bursts before crashing into the opposing hand over and over. The drummer was banging the cymbals, his facial and hand muscles tensing as he pounded out the beats that everyone clapped and stamped their feet to. All of this matched the pace of the organist. The organist looked serious and cool at the same time as his hands and fingers worked in unison, not only to play the melody of the song, but also to play the musical interludes members required he play to facilitate their dancing, shouting, and emotional displays.

The organ music seemed simple, Jamaal knew, but watching the organist, choir director, lead singer, and the experienced choir all work in silent unison while adjusting to a look, a hand movement, a head turn from any or all of them, was a marvel. It was a level of sophisticated communication—a language, Aunt Meredith had once told him—that non-Black churchgoers cannot pick up or understand.

Uncle Gerald had once likened the communication between the organist, lead singer, choir director, and most experienced choir members to what a baseball manager, catcher, pitcher, first and third base coaches, and other coaches do between every pitch. "If you watch the manager, he will signal the catcher who looks over to him for a split second. Then the manager may send a message to a bench coach who will relay the message to an outfielder to move left or right, forward, or backward so they synchronize the fielders to the pitch. The managers will also adjust the infield according to the pitch the manager told the pitcher to throw. Or maybe the pitching coach told the catcher who then told the pitcher. It is a symphony between every pitch, every batter, and it will change pitch to pitch and batter to batter and depending on how many runners are on base.

"Our choirs," Uncle Gerald had continued, "are like that and more, because they must also keep time, keep the emotional moment where it needs to be, and keep every church member involved, not only watching."

Jamaal had loved his uncle's analogy because they both loved baseball, so hearing his uncle put it in terms he could understand made it more fascinating to Jamaal. "And Jamaal, the choir will do it for thirty minutes to an hour at a time with continuous music."

Jamaal took his seat but as soon as he did, he realized he was the only one sitting so he quickly got up and began clapping along with everyone else.

After a prolonged duration of clapping, the silent signals must have happened while Jamaal wasn't watching, because in a flash the organist slowed the music, the choir sat down, and the drummer stopped banging on the cymbals.

Jamaal was near the front of the church and as the music finally came to a stop, he watched and listened as the choir began singing one of their "cool down" songs. The organist played quietly as the choir sang sitting in their seats and slowly swaying in unison in a planned choreography that appeared spontaneous.

He watched the choir director's face and saw the earnest expression as he worked to match the moment, the music, and his choir, his face sweating and his hands swaying slowly along with his body. The soloist, Dani, shapeless under her light purple robe, had a beautiful voice, though she was what the older members called "masculine," and his uncle and the other preachers simply labeled "lesbian."

Jamaal watched the soloist sing, and his mind drifted back to another day in his uncle's office, and what he heard the preachers say about the members they thought were gay.

"Some of the singers are gay," Pastor Gerald had remarked. "I preach against it, but frankly I don't care what kind of sex folk have, to be honest."

"It is a sin, though, Pastor. We need to call it out. They need to stop sinning and be saved just like everyone else," Assistant Pastor Johnson, the most anti-gay preacher in the church, said sternly.

"Sin is sin, Reverend Johnson. I don't care if it is lying, drinking, or screwing. Gay folk are no better or worse than any other sinner."

"That's not true, Pastor. Homosexuality is an abomination and affront to God. You should know better."

"Watch yourself, preacher."

Jamaal, who had been listening to the debate while staring out the window, trying not to be noticed, turned his head, recognizing his uncle's shift in tone.

"Pastor, respectfully, you need to preach harder about the sin of homosexuality. The choir is full of them, and everyone knows there are many gay men in the church, but I am the only preacher in this room who talks about or preaches about the sin of homosexuality."

"And we will keep it that way for now," Jamaal recalled Uncle Gerald responding.

The loudmouthed preacher hadn't said a word, Jamaal had noticed.

The song ended and Jamaal let his memories of that conversation ebb away. He wasn't sure what to make of all of that anyway.

When the singing finally came to an end, the soloist took her seat next to Katherine who was one of the lead singers and one who was among the best and so good that she too was often called to sing a solo prior to the pastor's sermon. Jamaal knew from conversations overheard in the pastor's office that Dani and Katherine were best friends, roommates, and the two were inseparable.

Jamaal wasn't certain where the thought came from, but at that moment he realized that the two women were a couple which meant they were gay. He looked at the two sitting behind the pulpit, Dani whispering to Katherine, her mouth so close as to be touching the other woman's ear, their bodies touching as any couples would.

His uncle apparently knew, and that meant other church folk knew, too; and as far as Jamaal knew, no one seemed to care much, despite how often some preachers preached about the sin of homosexuality.

Jamaal tried to make sense of the disconnect between what they preached and what they did, but he realized he would not be able to tonight, or ever.

The loudmouth evangelist's voice shook Jamaal from his thoughts. Again, he was up at the pulpit. The pleasure that could be found in the choir's musicality was over for now.

"I HAVE A SPECIAL MESSAGE FOR FORNICATORS, LIARS, AND THE WORST OF THE WORST SINNERS IN THE WORLD—THE FAGGOTS, THE GAYS, THE HOMOS, AND THE FANCY BOYS AND BUTCH GIRLS."

Jamaal winced as the loudmouthed preacher went on. "The gays"—which he pronounced as "gaaayzzz."

Jamaal listened as the loudmouth evangelist preached about the "evils of being gay," and how "God would smite them all," and that God had "sent the AIDS" to show the gays and the world that God was not happy, and sin needed to be punished and gay people needed to repent of their sins TODAY and cast out Satan that had "given them a lying spirit that made them believe they were gay."

Jamaal looked at his uncle. He didn't know what he expected to see, but he knew the loudmouthed evangelist was going after gay people even after hearing that his uncle had said he didn't really care to press this point.

But his uncle's face was solid, unmoving, and betrayed no feelings one way or another. Jamaal turned away from looking at his uncle, recognizing that pastors like his uncle seldom registered anger or contempt when in the pulpit. They might smile now and again, and on a rare occasion laugh. Jamaal saw nothing and admonished himself for even thinking his uncle would do anything to stop the loudmouth evangelist.

"NOBODY IS BORN GAY, NO MATTER HOW MUCH THE WORLD TELLS THAT LIE," the loudmouth evangelist droned on.

Jamaal needed a break and some fresh air to get away from the pollution, so he walked out just as the loudmouth evangelist was calling on any gay person to "COME TO THE THRONE OF GOD AND HAVE YOUR DEMONS CAST OUT TONIGHT."

Jamaal could still hear the evangelist from where he stood, but most of his words faded against the cars going by and the thick cool night air. Jamaal thought about his homework and exhaled heavily knowing he would not have much, if any, time to get anything done.

"Hi," a voice said, causing Jamaal to jerk his body.

Reverend Booker, from a church just a few miles away, stood just outside the door. He was perhaps thirty or so, a sharp dresser—most of the preachers were—and he wore a gold chain with a big gold cross at the end that hung down the front of his tight shiny grey suit. He wore a purple shirt underneath his suit, and Jamaal thought his eyebrows were smoother than any person he had ever seen before.

"Hey," Jamaal replied, hating the fact his peace of being outside and away from the pollution from the loudmouth preacher was broken.

"What, you can't shake a preacher's hand?" Reverend Booker grabbed Jamaal's hand and shook it vigorously, holding it longer than Jamaal felt comfortable about. Of all the preachers who regularly visited his uncle's church, Jamaal felt that Reverend Booker acted the strangest.

And he smelled funny, Jamaal remembered after the light wind pushed the smell into Jamaal's face.

Jamaal was annoyed. He shook back just a little.

"Boy, you have some big hands!" Reverend Booker said, jubilantly. Too jubilantly, Jamaal felt.

He had stopped shaking Jamaal's hand, but he still tightly held his grip.

"You know what they say about big hands, right?"

"No, sir," Jamaal replied, his voice barely above a whisper which could hardly be heard over the loudmouth preacher, who had taken his homophobic preaching to another level of loud-mouthiness. Jamaal gently tried pulling his hand back toward his body.

Reverend Booker didn't release Jamaal's though. He was staring into Jamaal's eyes, a half-smile on his smooth angular face. Jamaal also noticed the reverend's upper lip was sweating and that made Jamaal aware of his own hand which felt moist, but he couldn't tell if it was because his own hand was sweating, or the reverends was.

Jamaal stared back and gently tugged his hand again, but again Reverend Booker held tight, letting out a slight "mmmf" as he did so.

"They say, a young man with the big hands, those big hands mean big other things. I'd like to find out if other things are big. When are you gonna let me find out?" Now Reverend Booker's middle finger was rubbing the palm of Jamaal's hand, his finger going back and forth, like the preacher was scratching him or trying to tickle him. Jamaal's unease increased by the second, and thoughts ran through his mind, from listening to the preachers' homophobic talk in his uncle's office, to the loudmouthed preacher saying the same things in his sermon, to the faces of the young men who were being singled out by the loudmouthed preacher, to the choir soloist who was called "masculine," and to his uncle-pastor who listened in his office, and then in church and said nothing to stop any of the homophobic talk.

All the thoughts and feelings Jamaal was going through were swirling around his mind so much he hadn't paid attention to the tightening grip of the preacher's handshake.

With much more force than he had used before, Jamaal yanked his hand back, this time freeing it from the older preacher's creepy, sweaty grip. Jamaal looked at Reverend Booker with confusion and anger. Reverend Booker looked back with what emotion Jamaal wasn't certain, but he knew it was neither anger nor confusion.

Walking away seemed the best option, and Jamaal turned and with a few steps was at the church door. He refused to look behind him to see if the creepy preacher had followed him or if he was still where he had left him. Jamaal knew that no matter what, he didn't want to see the man's face again, so he walked back into the sanctuary and sat down, relieved to be back in the too-warm church.

Ignoring the usual stares, and prepared to stay seated until service was over, Jamaal sat in the middle of a row that was in the middle of the church, as a way of protecting himself should the preacher want to sit next to him. Jamaal knew the preacher would not sit in the audience, and certainly not by the pastor's nephew, so he felt safe doing it.

Settling in, Jamaal could see that the loudmouth evangelist was now standing in front of the pulpit and praying while three young men stood facing him, heads down and eyes closed.

"WE ARE GOING TO PRAY ALL THE GAY AWAY! PRAY ALLLLLLL THE GAY AWAY."

Jamaal just shook his head. He shook his head a lot at the sermons he heard these days. Things he hadn't really paid attention to when he was younger—what kid did? But now that he was older, he was able to discern some of the not-so-hidden messages the preachers talk, or yell, about.

And he noticed how they'd quote the bible out of context, or mix up passages, or sometimes even invent passages that weren't even in the book.

Jamaal liked to read and had already read his bible end-to-end three times. He liked the poetic nature of much of the writing and he had come to understand that a lot of it was allegorical or a story with a lesson to be learned, and not necessarily real history. But his uncle's church taught that the bible was the absolute word of God and thus absolutely true and accurate history.

Though Jamaal believed that way of thinking was dumb, Jamaal dared not tell anyone in the church and certainly not his uncle or aunt, that he felt that way.

It was again close to midnight when church ended and, once again, his uncle lingered to talk and they stopped for a snack so, as with Monday, Jamaal resigned himself that he would not get enough sleep and not finish his homework. Again. He would need to make it all up before Friday, he knew. Maybe I can do it tomorrow night, he lied to himself.

As they pulled into their garage, his uncle put his hand on Jamaal's shoulder.

Uh-oh, Jamaal thought. What now?

"I know you heard some stuff in my office tonight before church."

"Yeah," Jamaal mustered. He wanted to go inside and go straight to his bedroom and go to sleep. He was thinking about all the homophobic talk and thought his uncle was going to somehow apologize for it.

"I let you be around me, around all the preachers, because I know you can keep my trust. You can, can't you?"

It was more a statement than a question, and Jamaal's uncle seemed as intense with him as he could ever remember.

"Yeah," Jamaal replied. *The bed is right through that door*, he told himself. *Don't say anything to prolong this conversation.*

"Look," his uncle went on, "everybody likes to screw. Everybody. Sometimes wives don't do what they should, so men go get their milk somewhere else, because there's always free milk from a cow willing to give it up. You just have to go get it. It's the easiest thing in the world because women are loose, and a little sweet talk goes a long way."

Jamaal realized this was not about the gay talk but about the other thing. He tried not to hear his uncle's words and stayed quiet, hoping he would stop talking. But no matter how he tried to ignore his uncle, Jamaal knew he could not help listening and wondering if this was leading to the sex talk some of his friends—especially Kevin—and too many of his teachers talked and joked about.

"Don't tell your auntie. All it would do is hurt her. I never screw any woman who doesn't want to screw. That's a fact."

Jamaal thought that last sentence sounded… too something. Too close. Too current. He didn't want to talk or listen anymore. And he didn't want to think about facing his auntie again in the morning, knowing what he now knew.

"Don't forget. Keep your mouth shut," Uncle Gerald said, as he opened his door to signal that the ride, the church day, and the oddly worded "confession" was over.

Tuesday sucked, Jamaal thought, as he finally lay in bed, homework undone, just after one-fifteen in the morning.

CHAPTER 4

WEDNESDAY

Your two breasts are like two fawns, twins of a gazelle which feed among the lilies ~ Song of Solomon 4:5

The loudmouth evangelist was standing right in front of Jamaal. He had come out of the pulpit to shame the members for not "giving enough to the Lord" during the first two nights of the revival.

His goal for the week, according to what Jamaal heard in his uncle-pastor's office prior to church starting, was $15,000, and they were still under $5,000, and Jamaal could see that the evangelist was mad even before he started talking.

"Look, Pastor, I need this money. You said you'd have the crowds here, and that I'd make more than 15 Gs. You need to deliver on your word, preacher man." The loudmouth evangelist was standing directly in front of Gerald's desk and his voice was carrying.

Jamaal watched and listened, wondering how his uncle would react to being reprimanded in his own office. He didn't have to wait long, as with a smile and a short laugh, Uncle-Pastor Gerald retorted.

"Maybe if you spent less time screwing, and more time ministering, you'd raise more money, fella. I know you were out again last night—

this time with Mother Mabry's daughter! That girl is only twenty-five years old, man. She's gonna kill your old self!"

"God ain't through with me yet," the loudmouth evangelist snapped back, laughing loudly. "She was a good piece of ass, that's for sure. And if it weren't for all that weed she was smoking, we coulda gone another couple rounds, too!"

"Preacher, you need to leave that weed alone. It's a sin to smoke, you know that," Jamaal's uncle said, in all seriousness.

Jamaal cringed; his uncle had missed on the greater sin committed by the loudmouth evangelist.

"Hey, it's better than those Kools I smoke. I'm trying to break my habit, but the devil won't let me. I'll quit one day," the loudmouth evangelist finished.

"Pastor, it's time to go into the church," Jamaal said from the back of the office where he sat and rarely spoke.

The room went quiet, and everyone turned toward Jamaal, faces registering surprise that the normally quiet Jamaal had spoken. Jamaal felt himself audibly gulp when he saw all the faces staring back at him.

"Thank you, Jamaal," Uncle Gerald said, half-smiling at Jamaal before he looked away along with everyone else and resumed their conversation.

Jamaal felt himself get hot as he realized how easily he was dismissed and ignored by his uncle-pastor and the rest of the folk. Jamaal resumed his favorite office habit of staring at the picture of the famous Black people while trying to again ignore the repugnant chatter. Before he could settle into the background, the loudmouth evangelist's voice reeled Jamaal back in.

"Okay, look, Pastor, I'll preach hard tonight, and then I'll raise my own money, how about that?"

Jamaal watched as his uncle considered the loudmouth evangelist's offer, his hand rubbing his chin like an old-timey villain.

"Okay," Uncle-Pastor Gerald finally said, his hands now outstretched to either corner of his desk. "You can raise your own, but just make one appeal and don't drag it out too long." Jamaal watched his uncle-pastor heading toward the exit—movements Jamaal had hoped for minutes ago.

Jamaal also stood to leave, trailing behind as always. While pulling the door shut to lock it, Jamaal nearly bumped into his uncle-pastor who had uncharacteristically waited for him. Jamaal thought his uncle-pastor's face looked more serious than it had just a few moments ago.

"Jamaal," his uncle-pastor said, as he placed his hand on Jamaal's shoulder. "Tonight, I want you to help count the money. We've raised enough money—I can see it coming in, but it's not all reaching me at the end of service. I need you to help count tonight, and when the counting is done, come into the pulpit and whisper to me how much we raised. Come straight to me, you understand? Keep that number in your head and no matter who may drop in while you are counting, you ignore them and anyone else. You have one job, count the money and tell me. Got it?"

"Yes, sir. Okay," Jamaal said, uncertain about why his uncle-pastor wanted him to count the money rather than having one of his deacons or treasury people do it.

So much for homework tonight, Jamaal thought, as he walked into the sanctuary for the start of the night's services. He had been looking forward to his biology homework; they were preparing to dissect a frog and he wanted to be ready.

Church services were uneventful, and for that, Jamaal was grateful because it allowed him to sit and daydream about maybe getting home in time to finish his homework.

The choir sang, and the church was rocking as they sang one of their more popular upbeat songs that older members would later complain sounded too secular, but who during the song were enjoying themselves as much as anyone else.

The loudmouth evangelist had preached, and the few times Jamaal paid attention, it had seemed he was preaching about giving and supporting God through giving and supporting preachers and evangelists.

Now Jamaal watched as his uncle-pastor shook the evangelist's hands and slapped him on the shoulder and back, congratulating him for preaching. Jamaal read his uncle's lips and knew he said, “a wonderful message.” Jamaal then watched as the evangelist got down on one knee in front of his seat and began praying.

He had only ever seen his uncle do that prayer move. He wondered if his uncle had told the loudmouth evangelist to copy him or something.

Jamaal's thoughts were interrupted by his uncle's words asking him to come to the front of the church and help count the money. It wasn't Jamaal's first time helping, but it was the first time he was helping during a major service such as the revival they were now hosting. But Jamaal didn't feel proud; in fact, he felt annoyed because he knew his uncle was using him to spy and find out why money was missing.

Jamaal walked to the front of the church, ignoring the usual stares anyone received when walking to the front of the church. Soon he reached the offering table, where members who marched from their seats, into the aisles, to the front of the church, would drop off their money.

Jamaal had noticed that, though many modern churches had moved away from this tradition, favoring instead passing collection plates, using mobile apps, and using autopay from member's banks, his uncle's church hung onto this old-school method of tithing. Jamaal actually enjoyed seeing the parade of members, old and young, as they brought money, checks, money orders, and coins to the offering table.

The polished wood table was inscribed along the lengthwise outer edge of the table on the side that faced the audience: ***THIS DO IN REMEMBRANCE OF ME***. The words were part of the script for communion, which the church performed every fifth Sunday. Jamaal had always thought the words conflicted but also worked well with raising money.

> THE LORD BLESSED ME TO BE HERE TODAY, AND HE GAVE ME A MESSAGE THAT I SHARED WITH YOU TODAY. I PREACHED FROM MY HEART BECAUSE GOD TOLD ME WHAT THE CHURCH NEEDED. DIDN'T HE DO IT?

The loudmouth evangelist spoke with a softer voice than he used while preaching, preferring to speak almost at a whisper, but with his mouth right on top of the microphone, he was as loud as ever.

Jamaal wished the man would shut up so they could collect the money, but he continued talking. Now, about how much money he wanted to raise.

> WE WERE A LITTLE SHORT LAST NIGHT ON THE OFFERING. AMEN. AMEN. BUT I KNOW GOD HAS GREAT THINGS IN STORE TONIGHT AND THE BLESSINGS WILL FLOW LIKE THE RIVER JORDAN BECAUSE WON'T HE DO IT?

"Amen," a few members responded.

"THAT'S NOT A GODLY AMEN, CHURCH. CAN I GET AN AMEN? AMEN?"

This time the "amens" were louder, befitting the call-and-response tradition and equally important, finally satisfying the loudmouth evangelist. Jamaal stood still behind the table as he listened to the loudmouth evangelist implore the members to now stand up with twenty-dollar bills in their hands.

"HAVE FAITH THAT GOD WILL BLESS YOU IF YOU BLESS GOD, AND TRUST IN THE WORD OF GOD AND GOD'S SERVANT."

"How is it looking, young man?" The loudmouth evangelist asked Jamaal, as the members continued walking past, dropping more money on the table even though there were two small threaded collection plates on the table, one each in front of Jamaal and his co-money counter, Sister Julie.

The loudmouth evangelist was on his third appeal for more money, and he was now imploring the congregation to "REACH INTO YOUR POCKETS, PURSES, AND WALLETS AND JUST GIVE FIVE DOLLARS MORE AND WATCH GOD RAIN DOWN BLESSINGS ON YOU—WON'T HE DO IT?!"

Jamaal just wanted him to shut up. He stared at the clock the remainder of the time, so he knew it was another twenty minutes before the man stopped begging, saying loudly that "God was pleased they had raised another two thousand dollars."

Jamaal and Sister Julie bundled all the money and checks and took it all to the small office behind the pulpit to be counted, Jamaal now fully nervous knowing his uncle was depending on him to count fast and bring the totals to him.

"I don't need you to help me count," Sister Julie said in a sharp and measured voice immediately after she closed the door to the little office.

The small office was warm and in it sat an old office-type desk, and a few pencils and pens in an old coffee cup that had a picture of Black

Jesus on it. The organist was playing a festive song that faded to the background on the other side of the closed door.

"Okay," Jamaal said. Great, he thought, this is going well already. "I'm here because my uncle told me to be. Plus, I can count really fast if you want me to help."

Jamaal looked at Sister Julie and she was looking back. He thought she was less than thirty years old, but he wasn't certain because he had learned that with Black women, it was very hard to determine their age and, according to his auntie, it was against the law to ask them.

And Sister Julie was pretty, Jamaal decided. Very pretty. She was shorter than him and her hair was short and in a style that left a strand of hair in front her left eye. She was curvy and Jamaal knew from listening to the preachers in the office that they loved how she wore form-fitting skirts and tops. Her skin was smooth and on the lighter side of brown, with brown eyes to match, and distinct features that were sharp except for her rounded cheeks.

She was, Jamaal thought again, very pretty.

Jamaal smiled an awkward weird smile that he knew was weird, but he couldn't pull it back and could only hope Sister Julie didn't notice. She was married, but her husband was "out on the streets," as his uncle-pastor told it one day in the office before church.

Jamaal knew that in the church world, his uncle's words were code for being on drugs and "living in the world" which meant he was "running with the devil" and a host of other ways of talking about drugs without having to mention drugs. And in Sister Julie's husband's case, his drug of choice was, apparently, various forms of cocaine.

"Well, your uncle needs to mind his own business because I can count a few thousand dollars without his or your interference."

"Fine with me," Jamaal said, standing to the side and thinking about the homework he wasn't doing and again trying not to awkwardly smile at Sister Julie.

"Okay, look, you count this stack," Sister Julie said, apparently changing her mind within a minute of telling Jamaal he couldn't help her.

She pushed a bunch of bills to one side of the small table, the shooshing sound filling the small room.

"Count that," she said again in a less-than-friendly tone.

"Okay," Jamaal said, and he started counting the money.

They each began counting, the only noise being Jamaal's whisper-breathing that was noticeably louder whenever he reached another thousand. Sister Julie was quick, fast, and efficient, her hands moving fast and only stopping momentarily to lick her thumb.

"Okay, I am done," Sister Julie said, looking over to Jamaal.

"Me too," Jamaal replied.

"How much do you have?" she asked him, her voice firm and demanding.

"Six hundred twenty-two dollars, and sixty-four cents," he said. "What about you?"

"Two thousand thirty-five dollars, and forty-five cents," Sister Julie answered.

Jamaal tried to be as gentle as he could as he suggested, "Let me count yours and you count mine, just to make certain we are accurate."

"Boy, what the hell are you talking about?" Sister Julie questioned angrily in that way that Jamaal knew did not require an answer but did require silence because there was something else coming.

Jamaal said nothing, as expected.

"I'm not counting any money again. Why would I? My number is correct so just put yours in this envelope and go back to church. I'm sick of this church and, yes, your uncle for not trusting me. I do this every Sunday and for this stupid revival, I am here every night counting their money! I've got my own bills to pay and my so-called husband ain't helping one bit. So what if I take a little here and there—that's what churches are supposed to do, right? Help people! Well, I need help!"

Jamaal was silent, fearing that if he spoke Sister Julie's anger would be directed at him. She went on, "Plus, it's only three hundred dollars. That evangelist is going to use the money on more whoring and smoking weed with that slut again."

Jamaal tried to breathe but was afraid to interrupt Sister Julie.

"I need it more than him, anyway! Look, Jamaal, why don't you take forty for yourself, how's that?" Sister Julie quickly separated three hundred dollars into three small stacks, then she pushed the three stacks toward Jamaal's side of the desk.

Jamaal just watched.

Sister Julie looked up after she placed the money near Jamaal.

"Nah, I'm good," Jamaal said, pleased with himself. A recent Sunday school lesson had been about Jesus in the wilderness and being tempted by the devil. Jamaal realized he was inadvertently making Sister Julie the devil in this scenario.

“Fine then. Don't take any. Just don't tell, okay?”

Jamaal noted the shift in Sister Julie's tone and words.

“Okay,” Jamaal said.

Sister Julie then stood up and took one step so that she was now standing above Jamaal who still sat in the old chair opposite her chair. Jamaal looked up and told himself not to look at her breasts but to focus on her eyes. He realized he was holding his breath again.

Sister Julie leaned down toward him, her cleavage ten inches from his nose. Then she placed a thick wad of folded twenties in her bra, pushing and positioning them while Jamaal looked. Her hand lingered there for a few seconds that, in Jamaal's world, felt like it lasted a week.

Then, she placed two more wads of folded twenties in her bra and, just as Jamaal began to exhale, Sister Julie leaned in further and kissed him on the lips, delaying him from exhaling.

Jamaal remained still, stunned, nervous, and with his lips slightly parted until Sister Julie pulled back, and stood up. Jamaal looked up and saw that she was smiling, her lips closed, and her eyes mischievous. Jamaal realized he still wasn't breathing so he opened his mouth and let out a long stream of pent-up breath. He wondered if his breath was stinky, but then he saw Sister Julie smile, so he settled his mind that his breath was just fine.

“There's more kisses where that came from. I am a bit… lonely, so when you get some free time how about you come over to my apartment and I'll give you a few errands to do, okay?”

Jamaal watched Sister Julie as she walked out of the small room behind the church with all those wadded up twenty-dollar bills comfortably stashed in her already full bra.

+++

"Did you see Sis Julie take any money?" Uncle Gerald asked as they drove home from church, his arm stretched out to Jamaal's side and his two fingers poking Jamaal on the shoulder as he asked the question, annoying Jamal to no end. Jamaal was glad his uncle didn't want to stop for donuts tonight, and he had hoped to make it home without any talking about anything, much less Sister Julie.

"Yes, sir, she did," Jamaal offered, hoping it would be enough but knowing full well it would not.

"How much?"

"I couldn't fully see," her cleavage flashed in his mind, "but it looked like about sixty dollars or so," Jamaal lied comfortably, surprising himself.

He recalled the bible story where two women both claimed a baby as their own, and King Solomon resolved the dispute by declaring, "Cut the baby in two so each woman can have half." The real mother then gave the infant to the fake mother, and that was how Solomon knew the real mother—because a real mother wouldn't allow her baby to be halved. Jamaal figured he was giving Sister Julie what she wanted, and he was giving his uncle what he wanted. He was dividing the baby.

Well, something like that, he thought, while also thinking of Sister Julie's tight blouse and cleavage.

"That's fine then," his uncle responded. "She's been doing it for some time now. If she's not taking too much I won't worry. I will replace the money she took after the revival is over."

Jamaal remained quiet, pleased his uncle was talking to himself rather than asking him more questions.

“Then I will relieve her of money-counting duties and have someone else do it. Someone who won't be stealing my money.”

“Why not now?” Jamaal asked as he pulled the car into the garage.

“She's out with the evangelist now. She may as well make and take some of his money since he's screwing her tonight,” his uncle said as he got out of the car. Jamaal turned the car off, took off his seatbelt, and let his uncle's words dangle in the musty garage that smelled of a car engine.

Jamaal didn't think about Sister Julie's breasts, cleavage, or her kiss anymore that night. And he wished he'd taken the money she'd offered. It was past midnight, and Jamaal's homework was still undone and he was exhausted. He fell asleep as soon as he turned on his side and covered his ear with his blanket.

CHAPTER 5

THURSDAY

You are altogether beautiful, my darling ~ Song of Songs 4:7

Jamaal had to be at church right after school to practice with the choir.

Jamaal wasn't in the choir, but the choir director mandated that on the last day of the revival, which would be next Sunday, all "young people sing in the choir to show the (loudmouth) evangelist the power of God in our voices."

Great, Jamaal silently huffed and puffed.

Music wasn't his thing, and he could not sing or carry a tune at all. Jamaal had been told that his voice was unnaturally deep for his age and because of it the choir director would ask him to sing tenor or bass because as he said, "We don't have enough men to sing, and your voice is deeper than most grown men's voices."

Jamaal knew he could not sing, but more importantly, he really disliked the director and knowing he would be there made Jamaal really not want to go. He had no choice because the request was made during the previous night's church service when the youth pastor made each young person stand and commit to attending the practice.

The church was momentarily quiet, and Jamaal sat in the back of the choir stand, the area reserved for tenors, usually but not always men, and choir members who were asked by the director to sit there. They had been practicing now for two hours and Jamaal was tired and increasingly frustrated.

"Jamaal, stay on key," the director shouted as they practiced a new version of an old song.

Jamaal knew he had been singing off-key the entire practice because he was not a good singer. They knew it too, but it didn't matter because as the pastor's nephew, he was expected to set an example for all the other young people.

"Focus, Jamaal. You can sing this song; your part is just repeating the same thing over and over," Dwayne implored him.

The choir director, Dwayne, a twenty-seven-year-old hustler who "got saved and found God," was still just a hustler, Jamaal and most other church members knew. But Dwayne had grown up in Pastor Gerald's church and that got him loyalty from the members no matter how awful his behavior was.

That loyalty was extended to all the members, and Jamaal had learned it was the same in other Black churches. It was both a blessing—to the poorly behaved—and a curse to the church, as those poorly behaved folks often took advantage of members' forgiveness in small and large ways that usually involved money. Dwayne was no different, Jamaal knew.

"That's better, keep it up, Jamaal." Dwayne had come to stand next to Jamaal and was now singing along with him, to demonstrate to Jamaal how to sing the part correctly, while the backup organist played.

Jamaal was uncomfortable but when he was next to him, he found himself singing on key just like he wanted. For a moment, Jamaal felt good about his singing.

Jamaal did not like Dwayne, and thought he was a punk who took advantage of his position in the church and used anyone and everyone. Jamaal recalled his uncle saying that "Dwayne worked hard not to work hard." Jamaal felt he knew what his uncle meant, but he wasn't certain of it. But his uncle's words always echoed in his head when he was around Dwayne.

"Take a break during this next song, Jamaal. We got this one," Dwayne said.

Jamaal was relieved. He sat and listened as Dwayne worked exclusively with the sopranos on a particularly difficult section of the song. He watched the backup organist as he played the same part of the song over and over, following Dwayne's lead. He was one of the best organists in the city and he was self-taught. He bragged how he could not read music, but he could play anything after hearing the music played only once.

Jamaal begrudgingly admitted to himself that he admired the organist to a small jealous degree. The man was in his early twenties, not particularly handsome but attractive in that musician wild man kinda way.

Jamaal was part of the group of young folks who used to ride with Dwayne as he led the choir to singing events and competitions in the city and surrounding cities. Following the competitions, the group would routinely spend late nights in their favorite after-church restaurants talking, flirting, and laughing.

It was during those late-night restaurant visits the organists would conspiratorially regale Jamaal and the other young folk with stories of sex, drinking, smoking, and drugs. He was the older guy with stories to tell that the young kids found fascinating, interesting, or, in Jamaal's case, as warnings to the dangers of drugs and drinking.

"Let's try the whole song now that the sopranos figured out how to sing again."

Jamaal stood up, not ready to sing and not remembering his part.

"That's okay, Jamaal. I think you're all set, hon. Sit this one out," the choir director said to Jamaal with a tone that Jamaal interpreted as caring.

Jamaal was satisfied and knew the director didn't want him ruining all the good work, even if he did say it with a gentle tone.

Jamaal watched Dwayne and thought of how his uncle was kind to him and even backed him when church members, usually women, complained.

The only scolding Dwayne got was, "So many of your women called me looking for you and complaining you screwed them and left them, it's got me wondering what you got between your legs. I might need to inspect what you got in your pants, son, so I can know why so many women want you so much."

Jamaal had just listened as usual as his uncle-pastor made light of Dwayne's sex stories.

"Jamaal! Boy, wake up!" Jamaal was caught daydreaming and Dwayne was yelling at him from behind the organ, his voice causing the other choir members to look at Jamaal.

Jamaal felt his body heat up, knowing he was the center of attention.

"Yeah, okay, sorry. Was thinking about homework." Jamaal's quick lie might have worked, but his deep voice was suddenly higher pitched.

"Go outside and get Sandy and Marie and tell them to come inside so we can work on one more song. It's our last of the night. We were terrible the other night and when we sing again on Sunday, we need to bring the shi—the stuff," Dwayne finished as the other choir members laughed.

Jamaal happily went outside. He felt the fresh air and relished it as much as he did the break from the singing and Dwayne. Looking left and right and realizing the girls weren't nearby, he decided to head to the corner store just down the street from the church.

The church elders had always warned the kids to stay away from the liquor store, but its proximity to the church meant that the church elders were always on the losing side because the kids never stopped going before, during, and after church buying snacks and candy, the stuff all kids bought if they could.

Jamaal crossed the parking lot of the liquor store and as he walked up, he saw Marie handing money to an older guy, Bobby, who was known as the corner weed seller.

"It's time to practice, and Dwayne says come inside. Where's Sandy? Let's go," Jamaal said all at once, hoping to get back to the church and away from a drug deal. He hated seeing Marie buying weed, but he knew to keep his mouth shut. He and most of the kids had learned that in the city where they lived the key to survival was shutting up and minding one's own business.

"Okay, let's go. Don't you say nothing, Jamaal? Especially to your uncle."

"Okay," Jamaal said. Then he added, "What about Dwayne? Should I tell him?" Jamaal teased and half-flirted, though he wasn't sure why he said anything at all.

Marie was seventeen, as tall as Jamaal, with dark curly hair that was spread out on both sides of her head in the way kids draw girl's hair. She had a pretty voice that, though it was soft, could get to another level when Marie was belting out church songs. She was the lead singer on many choir songs and on the Sundays when she sang, Jamaal always felt a little better about God and himself. He liked her but he didn't tell her or let her know, and he didn't know if she liked him, though they were good friends.

"Boy, he's who I'll be smoking this with, and he's who sent me down here. I don't care if you tell him," Marie responded while laughing the kind of laugh that told Jamaal he was the last to know the information she had just shared. Marie's laughter broke Jamaal's daydreaming about her.

Jamaal couldn't help thinking about Marie's laugh and how the sound of it, plus her teeth, her lips, and the way her eyes squinted, made him feel good.

Sandy finally exited the store, and she was carrying a small bottle of vodka and Jamaal thought her crooked smile made it seem like she had gotten away with something. Jamaal liked Sandy, too, because she was fearless. She was sixteen and athletic, she wore long goddess braids that framed her angular face so that she, in fact, looked royal. Her confidence most attracted him to her. But it was a different attraction than what he felt for Marie. Jamaal thought he liked Sandy because she was like a cool cousin.

"We gon' party tonight after stupid choir rehearsal," Sandy said excitedly. "I got Dwayne's favorite brand. You get the weed, Marie?"

Sandy stood so that she was now between Jamaal and Marie.

"Yep," Marie said, looking over at Jamaal. Jamaal looked back but didn't know why she looked to him so he wasn't certain if his face should change to match hers or if he should nod, so he tried not to look confused.

"Don't look so confused, Jamaal," Marie said, laughing and pushing him playfully.

The threesome started walking back to church, side by side, with Sandy still in the middle, until Marie stopped, grabbed Sandy's shoulders, moved her aside, and switched places with her.

"Sandy, I spent all my money," Marie said as they were just about at the church.

"Jamaal, you should come with us after choir rehearsal. It's time for you to learn how to get high and party. Has your cherry been popped yet?" Sandy giggled and Jamaal saw that Marie just smiled.

Jamaal didn't know what Sandy meant by "cherry popped" but he sensed it was something to do with drugs or drinking.

"I don't know. No. I guess, well. I don't know." Jamaal decided to just give up and hope either of the girls would tell him what "popped cherry" meant.

The girls laughed and each grabbed one of Jamaal's arms and they walked into church together. Jamaal thought that Marie was squeezing him tighter than Sandy and that made him feel something and think again about how pretty Marie was and how he really should tell her how much he liked her.

+++

Later that night during the revival services Jamaal sat thinking about earlier in the day when Marie and Sandy held his arms as they all walked to church from the liquor store. The feeling then was good, and the memory now was good as he halfheartedly listened to the loudmouth evangelist preach an incoherent message.

Maybe I'm not paying attention or… he's really off tonight. Jamaal stopped daydreaming about Marie and Sandy and instead focused on the preacher. After listening and watching him for five minutes Jamaal was certain the loudmouth evangelist was behaving as if he were dizzy or maybe sleepy.

This is really weird. Looking around, Jamaal could see that other members had concerned looks on their faces as well, making him believe whatever it was he was noticing, others were also noticing.

Jamaal was sitting in the front of the church and could smell a strange odor coming from the loudmouth evangelist as he preached—screamed is more like it, Jamaal thought, suddenly wishing he had sat in the back of the church– and then the preaching stopped.

Jamaal knew that preachers sometimes stopped mid-sermon as a way of drawing attention or to make or reemphasize a point. But the loudmouth evangelist hadn't been making a point, but had been sounding like a young preacher who was super nervous or just terrible at the art of preaching. The loudmouth evangelist was neither of those things, so his sudden pause caught everyone's attention for different reasons.

Jamaal watched him just stand there.

The organ was blasting preaching tunes and the drums and cymbals were loud and on the beat. Church emotions were high as the preaching, music, drums, and tambourines escalated to a swirling frenzy of music, clapping, dancing, shouting, and crying.

All the voices and instruments were in competition yet complementary in expressing of cascading religious emotions before they all reached a crescendo of unified praise of God.

But the loudmouth evangelist just stood there, frozen, completely still, looking weird and, to Jamaal's nose, smelling a way that instinctively told Jamaal that something was wrong.

The loudmouth evangelist was now sweating more than he had all week, Jamaal decided that the loudmouth evangelist didn't only smell funny, he stunk of alcohol. He was hungover and sweating alcohol odors from his pores. Jamaal had seen Dwayne act the same when he was drunk so he recognized the vacant look in the eyes, the slight wavering as he attempted to stand still, and the slurring words and occasional incoherent word.

The loudmouth evangelist was checking all the I-am-drunk-preaching boxes.

The loudmouth evangelist was mixing up his bible verses, stuttering, and losing his train of thought. It was awkward and the members sensed something was not quite right. But no one would dare saying anything against the man of God while he was up preaching.

Jamaal watched and thought maybe he should say something. Maybe pull the microphone out of his hands, hit him on the head with it, and then push his loudmouth out of the pulpit and out of the church. It was a happy thought and Jamaal felt better just thinking it, though he knew he could not do any such thing.

But his uncle-pastor could. Jamaal looked to Uncle Gerald, who had been sitting in the pulpit, his face showing nothing different than it showed any other time another preacher was preaching in his place. Then, Jamaal saw his uncle-pastor shift his bodyweight and push himself forward in his seat.

Jamaal knew his uncle-pastor had heard enough.

His uncle-pastor got up and took the microphone out of the loudmouth evangelist's hand and said, very loudly in a voice and tone that matched the volume and intensity of the loudmouth evangelist, so that there was no emotional drop off and making it seem like his uncle-pastor had already been preaching:

> **"I HEAR YOU PREACHER, AND I CAN'T KEEP MY SEAT. GOD IS CALLING ME TO PREACH, AND I GOT A MESSAGE FOR YOU."**

The members went crazy, signifying they knew their pastor was taking control because he had to take control.

Dwayne also knew, so he smoothly changed keys to match the pastor and increased the volume and intensity of his playing, pulling on the emotions rippling through the members.

Uncle-Pastor Gerald had taken control and moved the loudmouth evangelist out of the way.

The loudmouth looked for a minute like he was going to vomit up all the contents of his stomach, and Jamaal found his Aunt Meredith in the seats, met her eyes, and knew that if this preacher was sick that his Auntie Meredith would be running out of the church to throw up the contents of her own stomach. She was amazing with so many things, but was squeamish around nasty body stuff. She did not look happy at all.

But Uncle Gerald continued preaching, drawing in his church and his members. Words gushed from him and he was hunched over, sweating from his entire head and face, his pants riding up on his legs, and his suit coat flowing as he swung this way then that way showering his flock with rhymes, challenges, bible quotes, and filler words and phrases that were used to transition from one thought to the next without interrupting the flow and energy.

GOD IS A GOOD GOD! HE WALKS WITH ME! HE TALKS WITH ME! HE KNOWS WHEN I NEED HIS HELP! HE KNOWS WHEN I AM BROKEN AND NEED A BLESSING! HE KNOWS BECAUSE HE IS A GOOD AND RIGHTEOUS GOD AND I AM NOTHING BUT A SINNER! HE KNOWSSSSSSSS!!!

Everyone was on their feet, screaming, clapping, dancing, and shouting, as Pastor Gerald screamed, "God finally brought the Holy Ghost into the revival." Drawing out the "L" until he was fully out of breath and on his knees in front of the pulpit in a final performance move that delivered just enough emotional expression the preacher could stop because the energy had been fully transferred to the members who were now celebrating, dancing, shouting, and praising God in unison with the organ and drums.

Jamaal was standing, but as was typical of him, doing more watching than participating. He scanned the church, seeing familiar faces and friends, before he looked past the pulpit into the choir stands where his eyes fixed on Marie. She had moved from her usual second row position where the altos sat and stood alongside the singer who was finishing her song, and would soon move aside so Marie could sing hers.

The loudmouth preacher just sat there, red-eyed and sweating, fully disconnected from what was going on in the church. Thankfully, he had not vomited.

Jamaal watched Uncle Gerald drink from a small glass of water handed to him by one of the ushers. He was sweating, and in the next moment, the same usher handed him a handkerchief. Jamaal felt proud of his uncle-pastor as the services wound down.

Uncle Gerald had saved the revival like God saves souls.

+++

On the drive home, after a stop at the donut shop, Jamaal and Uncle-Pastor Gerald were silent, both lost in their thoughts. Once Jamaal turned the corner approaching their home, he felt his uncle's familiar poke on the shoulder, signaling that he was about to start talking. Though the poking irritated him, Jamaal welcomed the coming words, though he did not know what to expect.

"He drank all night, screwed all night, and thought he could get up there and preach the word of God. He's a young man who is showing himself to be a dummy. When I was a young man, I could do all those things for weeks on end. I had stamina in bed and the pulpit. But the difference was, I didn't drink. Never did. Drinking is sinful and can ruin a man. He had better learn his lesson. He's got three more nights here and he needs his money so he's gonna straighten up while he's here—tomorrow—or I will sit his butt down for good. He can do whatever he wants when he leaves.

“Besides, he learned an expensive lesson: Since I had to preach, I took the entire offering tonight—one thousand-two hundred. Don't mess over my church.”

“Yep,” Jamaal said, reminded of his incomplete math homework, as another night ended with no homework completed.

CHAPTER 6

FRIDAY

Now the young lady was beautiful of face and form ~ Esther 2:7

After Sundays, Friday nights were the biggest and best church nights, Jamaal believed.

More people showed up, more choir members sang, and folk dressed better than Monday through Thursday, but not as good as they would eventually dress on Sunday. Friday night church services would sometimes last until midnight after which young folk would go to dinner and be out until the early morning. It was like a party and then an after party, but just for the church crowd and for Jamaal and his friends who were generally prohibited from going to parties with non-church-going friends.

Before going out after church though, the young folk found ways to go outside of church and talk, flirt, play, argue, and do what all teenagers did—mind their own business—while annoying any adult who happened by.

Jamaal found himself outside just hanging out with his friends Kevin and Kenny and the always annoying Roy. Marie and Sandy were nearby, and Jamaal saw they were deep in conversation, though one or the other occasionally looked over toward him and his friends.

Jamaal tried to act cool and not let the girls know he was watching them, but he figured out that he was glancing over more than he realized, and not being too cool about it when Marie and Sandy began to laugh uproariously the next time he looked their direction.

Jamaal quickly turned away from the girls and back to his friends.

“Yeah, they're laughing at you, Jamaal,” Kevin said.

“So are we, you clown!” Roy added in, harsher than anyone else.

Jamaal rolled his eyes and punched Kevin in the shoulder, and Kenny joined him and grabbed Kevin around the shoulders, followed by Roy who attempted to grab them all by wrapping his arms around the group but failing to do so.

“Hit him, Jamaal. I got him for you,” Kenny grunted while holding Kevin who was trying to shake Kenny away like when a dog shakes off water, while Roy by now was left only holding Jamaal's arm.

Jamaal tried shaking his arm, yanking it, and finally when nothing worked to cause Roy to loosen his grip on his arm, Jamaal spun his body so that he now faced Roy and prepared to yell at him to let him go.

“What are you fools doing?” Sandy said loudly as she pulled Kenny off Kevin and shoved him away. Roy released Jamaal's arm.

Jamaal saw Sandy and smiled, feeling as if she had personally rescued him.

“Oh, you're on Kevin's side? I thought we were cool, Sandy?” Kenny grabbed Sandy's hand and she pushed it away, slapping it with her opposite hand.

The four had been friends since they were children and knew each other like siblings but the teen years had evolved their relationships from close friends to friends who were exploring and probing each other via constant flirtations. And church gatherings were the prime time for exploration. Roy was a relatively new member of the group, his family having joined a few years prior.

Getting together with the other young people was the primary reasons Jamaal loved church and he knew it was the same for his friends. Before church started, they could catch up, bother and annoy one another, and expend excess energy they would need to tamp down while inside the church.

"Come to the car with me, Jamaal," Marie, who had hidden from Kenny by running behind Jamaal, said, pulling on his shirt.

Jamaal followed Marie, catching up to her just as she began crossing the street to where her mother's car was parked.

Marie and her mom looked like they could be younger and older sister. Except for her mother being a little thicker around the waist, the two were almost identical about the face, hairstyle, height, voice, and smile. They were only fourteen years apart, Jamaal knew, and they loved the compliments folk generously offered to them about how they looked like twins.

"What you need from the car?"

"Nothing. I just wanted to get away from Kenny's wild ass. He's always chasing me or trying to hit on me."

"Maybe he likes you," Jamaal said weakly.

"Maybe you do, too. Get in." Marie opened the passenger door and closed the door.

Jamaal waited for Marie to walk around car and get in. He looked over to the front of the church and his friends were still running around—well, Kenny was running around and this time it was Kevin chasing him while Sandy was cheering him on. Jamaal knew Kenny had gone too far with teasing Sandy and Kevin had gone after him. Kevin would not admit how much he liked Sandy—they argued all the time—but Jamaal had a feeling the arguing was a clue to something.

Jamaal shook his head without thinking about it and he heard Marie laugh.

"What are you laughing at?" Jamaal smiled shyly.

"You, boy. You're sitting in this car with a pretty girl and you're over there daydreaming and ignoring me."

"Oh, ha ha." Marie had slid into the car seat next to him. "Sorry. I was just thinking—"

"Daydreaming." Marie interrupted. "Let's kiss."

"Okay."

Jamaal had been talking to Marie with his head turned, but now he turned his whole body, lifting his knee as he did, and placing his hands on Marie's hands so they both rested on the center divider of her mother's five-year-old GM car. Jamaal hadn't realized how soft Marie's hands were.

And he never imagined how soft her lips were.

Jamaal was in the parking lot, in Marie's car, and they were making out. Her lips were so soft, Jamaal was thinking. And her lipstick, balm, or whatever it was, was sweet-smelling and tasting.

He could not believe what was happening but at the same time he could believe because his senses were filled with Marie's aroma from her perfume, her lips, her hair, and even her breath. She smelled… wonderful.

He tried to move his hand, but Marie held him tighter and Jamaal, uncertain what her reaction meant, relaxed his hand thinking that it was Marie wanted.

Marie's hand relaxed and Jamaal felt good knowing he had done what she wanted. He decided right at that moment that not only did he like making out with Marie—it was everything he had ever imagined it would be—but he also hoped they could stay outside all night and not go back inside church.

Jamaal could tell that Marie was more experienced in kissing than he was, but he was catching on quickly. Too quickly, it turned out. Jamaal instantly felt good, then hot, and then embarrassed, hoping Marie did not notice.

Marie laughed and said, "I told you I'm gonna pop that cherry, boy. Clean yourself and get in the church," she said as she laughed while grabbing a box of tissues that rested underneath the driver's seat.

"Here."

Jamaal smiled as he took the box and watched Marie laugh her way out of the car and head back to church.

"Shoot, I did pretty good, I guess," Jamaal told himself, as he wiped the front of his pants. Jamaal exited the car and walked toward the church where Marie stood near the door waving to him to hurry up.

Church was rocking. Jamaal knew that was why Marie had waved to him to hurry up.

Most of the choir was there and they were singing the song they'd practiced earlier in the week. Marie went around back and joined the choir as if nothing was amiss. Of course, everyone in the church saw her enter the choir stand late—and Jamaal arrived just in time to see

Dwayne the organist give Marie a dirty look—and Jamaal knew that everyone saw that, too, just like he did.

Jamaal also knew that he too was getting looks because it was obvious to folk that he had arrived in church about the same time Marie did. When they were younger no one seemed to care if they were running around and playing, but now that they were older the members seemed to track their every move inside and outside church—if they could.

Glancing around quickly because he did not want to seem obvious, Jamaal met the eyes of each person he looked at. He knew he had made a mistake because every single person was looking back at him with the same disappointed expression.

There were no secrets in church, Jamaal accepted.

He sat down and focused on the music, trying to get over the guilt the members had made certain he felt.

The choir was singing and reaching one of those crescendos that seem to be the end of the song but turns out to just be about midway. And they kept singing.

Jamaal, who did not join the choir late with Marie, sat way over to the side and ignored the looks and pleas from fellow choir members, Dwayne, and a few other members to join the choir. He wasn't in the mood and no matter what anyone said or did, he'd decided his deep voice singing off-key would not be heard tonight. But in church they'd all just say, quoting the Psalmist: *Make a Joyful Noise unto the Lord. That* was the excuse for bad singers like Jamaal.

They'd all be mad at him but that never bothered him, and he was in a particularly good mood after spending time kissing Marie, and his bad singing wasn't going to be part of his night.

He noticed the loudmouth evangelist who, like Jamaal, had arrived late. He had been at church early—Jamaal had seen his car—but he was late coming into the sanctuary. And then Sister Julie walked in late too.

Jamaal wasn't the only one who noticed, either. All the folk who noticed him come in right after Marie, noticed the loudmouth evangelist and Sister Julie come in one after another.

The choir sang on for what seemed like thirty minutes because it was thirty more minutes.

Finally, they stopped, and soon afterwards, the loudmouth evangelist was up preaching. He was going on and on, again, about promiscuous women and how:

> EVE CAUSED ADAM TO SIN, THUS ENSLAVING ALL MANKIND TO EVIL. THROUGH EVE'S ORIGINAL SIN, WE WERE ALL SEPARATED FROM GOD, AND ONLY GOD'S SON COULD RECONCILE SINNERS TO GOD. EVE DIDN'T TRUST GOD'S WORD, SO DON'T BE LIKE EVE. DON'T BE LOOSE WITH THE TRUTH OR ANYTHING ELSE!! WOMEN NEED TO REPENT AND STOP LEADING MEN TO HELL AND ETERNAL DAMNATION! I AM SPEAKING THE WORD OF GOD! THAT IS WHY JESUS DIDN'T GET MARRIED! HE DIDN'T WANT OR NEED ANY TYPE OF DISTRACTION FROM GOD'S PURPOSE! SO, IF YOU ARE MARRIED, WOMEN, I AM TALKING TO YOU. THEN YOU NEED TO GET BEHIND YOUR HUSBAND AND OBEY HIM, LOVE HIM, SUPPORT HIM, AND TELL HIM THE TRUTH!!

The older church women were in a frenzy now, while many of the younger ones were, too, but they were also shaking their heads toward their friends and boyfriends which was a way of saying, "I don't agree with that part" without actually having to say that out loud. *They'd all talk about it later at the restaurant,* Jamaal knew.

Sister Julie just sat and cried though, and Jamaal noticed and wondered why she would be crying. Jamaal knew it wasn't unusual to cry during church, at any point, but something about Sister Julie crying tonight piqued his interest and made him look at and linger on Sister Julie crying for longer than he intended to.

"HEYYYY!" The sound of someone yelling close to where Jamaal stood, caused him to jerk to attention, and then move out of the way as the church usher shouted and danced right past Jamaal, continuing to the center aisle and eventually turning left and going straight toward the pulpit—the very route she spent much of Sundays and Fridays preventing other members from utilizing.

When Jamaal looked back to where Sister Julie had been sitting and crying, she was gone.

Later, when he and Sister Julie were alone to count the money, Jamaal decided to ask her why she was crying.

"I saw you crying out there," Jamaal said, trying to express concern in his tone, but he prepared himself for Sister Julie's harsh response.

Sister Julie just kept counting, ignoring his words which had drifted away to the silence of the small room.

Jamaal glanced down at the money she was counting. Her "private" stash looked like it was even more than the last private stash he saw her take.

Jamaal thought he'd better not say anything more, since she didn't seem like she was in a talkative mood.

She kept counting at a consistent pace with expertise and fluidity. Jamaal watched her count, the easy rhythm of her arm and hand movements, the repetition, and consistent pace.

Jamaal's eyes drifted away from Sister Julie's manicured fingers and her smooth arms that glistened from her wrist up to where her blouse started on her upper arm.

Sister Julie continued counting, the quiet sound of money landing on money, and the quiet swish of her movements kept Jamaal riveted.

Twenty-dollar bill, twenty-dollar bill, five-dollar, ten successive one-dollar bills, then a hundred-dollar bill that Sister Julie placed to the far right of the table then placed halfway under her handbag. There were now four hundred-dollar bills there. Sister Julie's flow started again, having barely stopped, and now she was again deftly counting the cash.

Five, twenty, twenty, ten, one, one, one, five, check, check, twenty …

Jamaal watched Sister Julie's arms still and then he allowed his eyes to drift upward until he was now looking at her blouse, which he thought was even tighter than it was the night before. He felt his face heat up like when he was with Marie. Her blouse hid breasts that were fuller than Marie's, and Jamaal could not stop staring at her.

"That's enough, young man," Sister Julie spoke as she looked up, catching Jamaal's eye as he fruitlessly tried turning away after their eyes met.

"SORRY!" Jamaal blurted out, ashamed to be caught staring and certain Sister Julie was about to read him for filth.

He found himself staring at the fire extinguisher that loosely hung on the far wall, needlessly wondering why it hung in that spot that was so far from the sanctuary but staring nevertheless since it was a better alternative to meeting what he presumed was Sister Julie's judging eyes.

“I saw you staring, Jamaal. It's no big deal. Men have been staring at my chest since I grew them when I was twelve. Preachers are the worst, including your uncle.”

“Okay.”

“But when you try to turn away so fast as if you were not staring—like you just did—then it is annoying.”

“Okay. Sorry. I was just—” Jamaal started before she cut him off.

“Because he told me I am a whore, that's why.”

“Huh?” Jamaal responded, forgetting the question he had asked Sister Julie.

“Ugh, boy, keep up. You asked me why I was crying, remember? Don't be a douche. You're too young for that.”

“Oh, yeah. I, uh, I did. Oh, that's… mean.” Jamaal chastised himself for not saying something more comforting.

“And that is why I hate preachers. And I hate that fucking preacher the most.”

Jamaal didn't think he had ever heard anyone say the “F” word in church.

“Why he say that?”

“Ignorant niggas like him don't need a reason, Jamaal. That's who he is and will always be, no matter if he's a goddamned preacher.”

"I'm sorry, Julie." Jamaal felt older using saying her name out loud without using her church title.

"He said I shouldn't have been screwing him and that I needed to get control of my life, close my legs, and seek Jesus. This muthafucka said that shit as he took his dick out of my..."

Sister Julie's voice had begun rising, her anger growing, as she told her story in the small room. The counting of the money had stopped completely, and the only sound was the church sounds from the main sanctuary that were alternately slow then fast. Jamaal knew the choir had been singing the entire time they were in the back counting the money and talking.

"Sister Julie," Jamaal said quietly as he moved closer to her, closing the already small space between them. Jamaal was quiet because he really didn't know what to say or even think, but felt his presence was worth... something.

"He said all bullshit when we finished fucking and I asked him if we can be a couple. I know I'm married, so don't fucking judge me because I need attention just like every grown ass woman. And my drug addict *so-called* husband ain't coming back, and I don't want him back anyway. I like Jesse..."

Sister Julie continued talking and Jamaal realized this was the first time he'd ever heard anyone say the first name of the loudmouth evangelist. He hated the name Jesse.

"I know he likes me, Jamaal. We've been... together... for a year. Well, every time he comes to town we get together. He never sees his wife because he's always on the road. We can be a couple if that fucker just acts right for once in his damned life."

Jamaal felt the smallness of the room and the largeness of the emotions that Sister Julie spoke with, and he wasn't certain what he was feeling but he instinctively knew his feelings were inadequate and that he lacked the words to comfort Sister Julie, if she even wanted that. Jamaal settled on the fact that above all else, he was confused, and he was okay with it because at his age and experience everything having to do with girls was confusing. And Sister Julie is a woman, he reminded himself.

"But he calls ME a whore and HE is fucking me, and HE is married too!"

Sister Julie put more money into her stack and Jamaal saw that her stack was growing with anger and her words, like she was paying herself to share her heart with him.

"That might be too much," Jamaal said and instantly regretted it.

"It's NONE of your business, child. NONE. He doesn't deserve one PENNY of this church's money."

"I agree," Jamaal said, which seemed to catch Sister Julie off guard.

"Here. You take some, then. You can go buy yourself some condoms because if you are having sex with Marie, you'd better have some protection."

Jamaal's eyes went wide, and he instantly started sweating. He stopped breathing and instantly wondered how could she know what happened tonight before church? And we didn't have sex! Well, she didn't. Wait, I didn't either, really. Jamaal's thoughts were reeling, but he said nothing.

"Look. I saw you in the car because I had to go to my car and get my folders. Hand that one to me." Sister Julie pointed to the folder that was resting against the wall on the floor behind Jamaal.

Jamaal turned and reached for the blue folder. He picked it up and handed to Sister Julie, noticing that it was empty.

"Don't worry. I won't tell anyone." Sister Julie straightened the stacks of money, making certain each stack was the same.

She then pushed the stacks closer together, then wrapped each stack with a rubber band, one after another.

"I used to be a bank teller," Sister Julie answered Jamaal's unasked question.

"Oh. That's why you're so fast. Why you leave the bank?"

"None of your business, but since your nosy ass asked, I got caught shorting my drawer."

Jamaal held in a laugh. Julie smiled and shook her head, knowing Jamaal was holding in his laugh.

"Stop being silly. It means that the money I turned in at the end of my shift was less than it was supposed to be because I was taking some and giving it to my husband to support his drug habit. Then I started giving some to the evangelist. My dumb ass got caught."

"Did you get arrested?"

"Sure did. Your uncle got me out. Kept me out, too. He's got connections with the police chief and the district attorney. The bank wanted them to charge me and if they had I would have been in prison for at least seven years, my lawyer said. He worked his magic and here I am, stealing from him, just like he suspects, I bet."

"Oh wow."

"Your uncle is a good man despite all his flaws, Jamaal. But don't tell him I said that, or else it'll go to his big head."

"I won't say anything. I promise."

"Good. Thank you."

"And you are right, he does know."

"I figured. Just like other people in the church know about you and Marie."

"Oh. Dang. Okay."

"It's church, Jamaal, there are no secrets. Don't forget that. But some of what I told you is a secret. At least for now. Please don't tell anyone about what I said, okay? I don't want any problems for the evangelist or me and I sure as hell don't want any of these nosy-ass church hoes asking me questions. Or your uncle."

"Okay, I won't," Jamaal responded. He meant it, too, since he didn't even know who to tell or what to even say after hearing all he heard from Sister Julie, just like it was when he listened to the preachers talk while he quietly sat at the back of his uncle's office.

Sister Julie put one of the stacks of bills into her handbag and then gathered the others and put them in a large yellow envelope, pausing to write something on it before sealing it by licking the folded part and sealing it by pinching it between her two fingers.

"Here. Take this to your uncle. I am going out the back door." She handed the envelope to Jamaal, who immediately looked at what she had written.

Jamaal smiled.

Sister Julie then stood up, faced Jamaal, her body just inches from his, making Jamaal visibly uncomfortable.

"You're gonna be handsome when you finish growing up," Sister Julie pressed herself into Jamaal and kissed him on the lips, then turned and walked away, her handbag swinging wide of her body, hitting the fire extinguisher, and causing it to rock slightly as a small piece of dust defied gravity and hung in the air.

Jamaal reached out and steadied the fire extinguisher, the piece of dust caught in a whirlwind before it miraculously landed back on the now steadied fire extinguisher. Jamaal's eyes followed Sister Julie as she walked down the long corridor that led to one of the exits and thought about her red lips approaching his face to kiss him.

"Stop looking at my butt, Jamaal," Julie called out from the other end of the hallway.

Jamaal turned away, embarrassed again, and wondering how sister Julie knew what he was doing.

"That was a lot." Jamaal said aloud. He'd waited a few minutes after Sister Julie was gone so that he was certain she was in fact gone.

He took a long inhale and held it before exhaling and looking at the envelope that he still held, and saw that Sister Julie had written a personal note to the loudmouth evangelist:

"I got mine—love, J"

Much later after church, at the restaurant, Marie asked him who he had been kissing on because his lips had faded red lipstick on them, and it wasn't her color.

Jamaal learned that night that not all red lipstick is the same, even if they looked the same to him, and that trying to lie about it wasn't the best strategy if you wanted your dinner date to not ignore you for the remainder of the evening.

CHAPTER 7

SATURDAY

I do not box as one beating the air ~ 1 Corinthians 9:26

Saturdays could be the best day of the week. Most Saturdays there was no daytime church, and night church didn't start until after six or so unless there was a fundraiser event, lunch, or choir practice.

And this Saturday, Jamaal noted, as he drifted off to sleep the prior night, there was nothing scheduled.

This was one of those Saturdays that Jamaal was free, and he was loving every minute. He had slept in until about nine o'clock. He wanted to sleep longer but his aunt had programmed the heater to come on at eight-thirty every day of the week.

Jamaal sat up in bed and looked at himself in the mirror across from the foot of his bed. The mirror sat atop his aunt's old-fashioned bedroom furniture that was cream color and framed swirls of teal flowers.

"You'll be handsome when you finish growing up." Jamaal repeated Sister Julie's words and finished the sentence by puckering his lips and simulating the kiss she planted on him the night before.

"Maybe I am handsome. Marie never said I was handsome. But she let me kiss her and …" Jamaal trailed off, preferring not to rehash the embarrassing part of the car event, as he decided to refer to it, and only think of the good parts.

After a big bowl of Raisin Bran mixed with Cheerios, Jamaal dressed and headed out toward the local middle school to meet his friends and play basketball. The walk to the school was enjoyable, the fog still heavy and cool, and exactly how he liked it on basketball days. And every day. Jamaal was a true Bay Area kid who grew up with fog every morning, sunshine midday, then fog in the evenings.

He steadily bounced his ball as he walked in solitude, and the rhythm of the ball pleased him as he passed the colorful single- and two-story homes of his neighborhood.

Kevin's home was just down the street, but he knew Kevin was already at the basketball court because he practically lived there. Turning the corner and crossing the street, Jamaal heard sounds that brought him true joy—the sounds of his friends playing basketball. Grunts as rebounds were fought over, smack-talking, laughter, screams, and hollering when a shot was made or missed—Jamaal loved it all.

Playground basketball was everything to Jamaal, his friends, and so many other young Black and brown men in the city who played in city parks, schools, and the streets. There weren't many driveway hoops like they'd see in the suburbs and which Jamaal would shake his head at, knowing the ease he would have shooting hoops if he had a driveway hoop.

“Bring your ass over here, Jamaal! I'm about lay some wood on you, boy!”

Jamaal ignored Roy and instead walked over to where everyone had placed their gear—backpacks, extra basketballs, drinks and bottled water, and extra shoes—and dropped his own things. Jamaal took off his hoodie and dropped it where he stood so that it landed on top of Kevin's backpack.

"Next." Jamaal said it loud enough, so his friends knew not to start another game without him and so that he could shoot around by himself on the next court while he waited for their game to finish.

"Let's go, loser, you're up," Roy called out to Jamaal.

"Whatever. You talk too much, Roy."

Jamaal rebounded his ball and then as he began walking to the court where his friends had been playing, rolled his ball toward Roy as sign of disrespect, and slapped high-fives with Kevin.

Halfway through the second game, Saturday turned into another horrible day when Roy decided he wanted to tease Jamaal about Marie, the rumor having spread after Sister Julie told one of her friends who promised not to say a word.

"I know you were mackin' on her, punk, and you know I was tryna hit that, so why you go and do that to ya boy?" Roy shot and missed, and Kevin grabbed the rebound and passed it to Jamaal.

Roy guarded Jamaal, closing the distance on him quickly as Jamaal looked to pass the ball.

"Imma still try to get with her, J-Mall. And you know she likes me anyway, loser." Roy had started making fun of Jamaal's name soon after they met.

"Shut up and take the L, Roy."

Jamaal shot and missed. Roy grabbed the rebound, laughing as he cleared the lane and turned to face Jamaal.

"Oh, you trying to cock-block me, J-Mall?"

"Man, shut up and play."

“Oh, Imma play with Marie, son.”

Roy was just a punk, Jamaal knew, so Jamaal had mostly ignored him, preferring to just nod when Roy told stories about how tough he was at school or in his neighborhood.

Roy didn't talk with Kevin the same way. No one really did. Though Kevin was quiet like Jamaal, and with his glasses looked just as nerdy, Kevin could also fight. But even more, he liked to fight, and when Roy first joined the church and tried to test Kevin, Kevin punched Roy squarely in his chest and Roy instantly regretted his decision to provoke him. Kevin had calmly told this new boy, “Don't mess with me or I will beat your ass.”

Roy had learned what everyone else knew: Do not mess with Kevin.

So, Roy had switched his antagonism to Jamaal, who was smaller, quieter, less threatening, and as the pastor's nephew, expected to have the best behavior.

“You know she just a slut,” Roy said and started laughing. “She'll mess with anyone, that's why I know she'll mess with me.”

“You talk too much. Shoot the ball, Roy, or pass it to someone who will shoot and make the shot.”

Roy faked going to his left, then went right, barreling into Jamaal who wasn't fooled by Roy's same-old fake. Roy's momentum pushed Jamaal backwards clearing the lane for a short shot from the right side of the key. The ball jangled the chain net.

“In your face J-Mall,” Roy gloated as Jamaal turned his back and walked toward the top of the key.

“I schooled you, nigga, now Imma get with ya girl and do what I gotta do with that slut.”

Jamaal stopped playing and walked over to Roy, who was still standing near the basket.

"You need to shut up, Roy," Jamaal said, now standing directly in front of Roy, their faces inches apart.

The fog had started to recede, but it was still cool, the afternoon warmth still another couple of hours away. Neither boy was sweating, though both were breathing heavily from playing. And Jamaal from nerves.

"Boy, don't you ever walk up on me unless you want to fight," Roy responded, with his finger just about touching Jamaal's left eyeball.

Jamaal didn't blink.

Roy walked away and pretended to laugh as the tenseness of the moment passed. But he kept walking to the side of the basketball court, where he picked up a baseball bat, and walked back to Jamaal. The friends had planned on playing baseball after basketball and Kevin had brought his new bat that he had from attending "Bat Day" at a recent Oakland A's game.

Jamaal stood still, watching Roy return with the small green A's bat in his right hand. By the time he reached Jamaal, Roy held the baseball bat aloft and pointed the barrel end of the bat at Jamaal's eye, just like he had with his finger. Roy didn't say anything and neither did Jamaal as the two stood there in another tense moment. Their friends seemed to be mostly ignoring them; they talked, traded basketball shots, and waited for the next game to start.

Then Roy lowered the baseball bat and started laughing as he walked away before reaching the edge of the court where he tossed the bat toward Kevin's duffel bag. It missed the bag and instead bounced and rolled on the asphalt toward the fence, a small green chip from the handle of the bat falling away.

Jamaal looked at Kevin who was already looking back at him. The two friends' expressions didn't change but Jamaal felt he knew what Kevin was thinking and he felt confident Kevin thought the same of him.

The games resumed, and the conflict was quickly forgotten by everyone as the joy of playing basketball with neighborhood friends took over the moods and emotions, and because arguments while playing basketball were as common as three-point shots. The ebb and flow of the game, the players switching sides, great defense, great shots, and bad defense and bad shots all led to nonstop jostling, arguing, and the very rare pushing and shoving which usually went away as quickly as it started.

After the final basketball game, as everyone was either chatting or gathering up their things, Jamaal stepped over a couple of the guys and kneeled in front of Roy.

The sun was fully out now and there was the warmth that foretold another day of perfect weather that was also as common as three-point shots.

“Roy, sorry about what happened. We cool?” Jamaal extended his fist.

“Yeah man, we good,” Roy bumped Jamaal's fist and offered a half-smile.

“Okay,” Jamaal said and sat down next to Roy and lowered his voice so that only Roy could hear him.

“Hey, I don't smoke weed but I know you do.”

“A little smoke is how I deal with my parents. You should try it, J-Mall.”

“Not my thing. But I and Kevin have a friend who sells individual joints if you ever want some.”

“That's not your friend, that's Kevin's friend, I bet. You too square, J-Mall.”

Kevin, hearing his name, interrupted his intense focus on his phone long enough to flash the finger toward them.

"Fuck you back, Stankston." Roy laughed at his play on Kevin's name.

Kevin pointed at Roy before turning away and resuming his focus on the phone as he began packing his duffel bag.

"Both." Jamaal responded, answered Roy's comment, and brought his attention back to their conversation.

"But do you want some?" Jamaal used the fence they were both leaning against and pushed himself up. Roy did the same, and the boys trailed behind their friends as they left the basketball court and then middle school.

"How much?" Roy was tossing the basketball between his hands as they walked. Jamaal bounced his own basketball between his legs as he walked.

"Whatever you work out with him. He's just our age and takes it from his father so he only charges a little per joint just for spending money. He don't even smoke. He just like to buy books."

"Has he heard of the library?"

"I know, right? But whatever. Do you want to meet him? I don't know where you get your weed but if you don't need a lot and want it cheap, he's there."

"Sounds good to me. Where he at?" Ray responded hopefully, as they crossed the street where they would now go in different directions.

Jamaal placed his basketball underneath his left arm where it rested on his hip. Everyone else had drifted away, off to attend to chores, or errands, before they would eventually meet up again later at church.

“Me and Kevin are meeting him later at Bancroft Park around six, before I head to church. He also sells CDs and new movies, so Kevin is getting those. Come on by. We'll be by the benches—the ones farthest from the basketball court.”

“Aiight,” Ray agreed.

“Don't be late. We gotta make it back to church on time too. The last thing I need is my uncle making me apologize in front of the church with the loudmouth evangelist in town.”

“That would be fucked up. I'd love to see it, too, so I might be late just to screw with you, J-Mall. Peace, out, loser.”

Jamaal watched Roy bound down the street, jogging so he made it home by the time he had told his parents he would be there so that his chores would be done before they had to leave for church.

+++

“I'll just beat his ass without any questions as soon as he walks up,” Kevin said as he kneeled and re-tied his sneakers. Kevin's shoestrings matched his sneakers, and he had two different colors—purple and gold—to match his school football team colors.

The friends, by agreement, had arrived at the park fifteen minutes earlier than when Roy was expected to arrive—if he weren't purposely late to annoy Jamaal, like he had said he might be.

They crossed the outside of the basketball court, the noises of the older guys playing more intense than their own intense sounds when they played.

There were four courts, and each court had a three-on-three game going on, with multiple other teams of three spread around the courts as the groups awaited their turn.

Each group's goal was to make it to the court designated the "NBA" court. To get to the NBA court, teams had to win then play another winner, then another, then another. And once the team made it to the NBA court, the goal was to stay there, if possible, by winning against each new team that made it to the level to dethrone you.

The best teams could win three in a row on the NBA court, but most teams won only one game, stemming from the energy it took to get there, and then facing another team trying to topple them. It was tested system that ensured fast play, fast movement from level to level, and of getting run off the court and sent to the back of the line again to start the process over.

Jamaal thought he spent a lot of time fussing with his sneakers and shoestrings, but Kevin was meticulous about most things so his fixation on making certain his shoestrings were exactly aligned so that purple was on top, gold underneath was expected and one of the many reasons Jamaal and Kevin were friends: Jamaal was patient.

"Nah, don't do it. I want to talk to him first. Then I'm going to kick his butt. He should have hit me with that baseball bat instead of threatening to hit me. I learned that from you—never threaten, always hit first. He will forever regret that."

"Because he's stupid. If you don't beat his ass, I will. I'm sick of his shit for real."

"Same."

"His dumb ass believing you would set him up to buy weed is the funniest shit I ever heard. I saw y'all talking but I thought y'all were just trying to settle who is going to go hardest after Marie. I was ready to punch his ass out right then."

"I know you were. I got this."

The friends waited for Roy by the far benches beyond the basketball courts as planned, the sounds of the basketball games echoing in the park. The park lights had just blinked on and the few hours of slightly warm weather had already faded as the clouds rolled in. The fog was not far away, but it would not be enough to stop the basketball games from continuing late into the evening.

“There's ya boy,” Kevin said as he pointed to Roy who was walking across the basketball court, walking on the center divider, against all common sense and general understanding of what not to do in city parks.

“He's such an asshole,” Kevin said slightly louder than a mumble as Roy was now about twenty yards away.

Roy had a can of soda in his left hand, his gangly walk appearing almost cheery.

“What's up, losers,” Roy called out as he stopped, raised his can like it was a basketball, and tossed it near the trash bin, where it clanged off the rim before rolling to a stop in front of Kevin.

“There's still a sip in it, if you want it, Stankston.”

“I'm good.” Kevin deadpanned.

“What's up, Roy?” Jamaal moved over so that he was slightly in between Kevin and Roy.

“I ain't got time to talk; where's your joint boy, J-Mall?”

“He should be here any moment. What you gonna get?”

“I got twenty-dollars, so however many joints I can get for twenty dollars.” Roy waved a twenty-dollar bill so that the tip of the bill brushed across Jamaal's chin, before he put it back in his pocket.

Kevin remained quiet, his glare obvious to Jamaal and ignored by Roy.

"He should be here in a moment," Jamaal reassured Roy who was looking at his phone.

"Whatever. Okay. I gotta go and your joint boy isn't here. So, look. I'll just give you the money and you bring me my joints tonight at church."

Roy reached into his pocket to again retrieve his twenty-dollar bill.

The bill fell to the ground as Jamaal punched Roy square on the jaw, knocking him sideways so that Roy stumbled toward Kevin who raised both his hands like a matador as he stepped backward allowing Roy to bypass him.

Before Roy could recover, Jamaal was on top of him, again hitting him in the face and head over and over until Roy first fell to one knee, then laid prone on the asphalt.

Once Roy was on the ground Jamaal stopped punching him and began kicking him in the ribs, then hitting him, stomping him, then hitting, then stomping him over and over while Kevin watched.

Jamaal ignored Roy's screaming for him to stop hitting, feeling a surge of adrenaline-fueled anger he had been holding onto since Roy pointed the bat at his eye and head. And every ugly word Roy had said about Marie was coming back to him with every punch and every kick.

Jamaal seldom lost his temper, at least not since he had left grade school, but now he was feeling good about hurting Roy.

Out of the corner of his eye he saw Kevin standing still, unmoved since he had started punching Roy. Jamaal noticed that Kevin was smiling with his mouth closed, and the surprise of his best friend's smile knocked the anger away causing Jamaal to stop and raise up.

He was sweating, his knuckles were bloody, and his arms ached. He felt his right foot was hurting, too, but he wasn't certain, and, in the moment, he could not figure out why his foot would hurt.

He would later remember that when he kneeled to punch Roy, his right foot was folded underneath Roy's the entire time and had fallen asleep in the awkward position.

And Roy was crying while he still laid on ground.

After about a minute, Jamaal stopped and, through heavy breathing said: "If you ever threaten me again, I'm gonna really hurt you. Say another bad word about Marie and I'm gonna really hurt you."

"And if he don't, I will, my man. You got it coming one way or the other, champ," Kevin added as he picked up Roy's money and slipped it into his pocket.

"Let's go Kevin, I gotta get to church. And I've got to wrap this hand; Auntie Meredith just about faints at the sight of blood," Jamaal said as he and Kevin walked away into the fog which had finally rolled in and the early evening fog enveloped the trees that themselves surrounded Roy, who was still on the ground face down, crying into his arm.

+++

Jamaal walked into church late, the cool air following him as he closed the door behind himself. Kevin had driven him home using his mother's car, and he waited while Jamaal showered and changed, and then the two drove to church.

At the church, Jamaal walked straight into Marie at the top of the stairs.

"You look pretty tonight, Marie."

"I heard what you did, Mr. Tough Guy," Marie said, looking down at the bandages on his fingers. "I don't need you taking up for me. I'll kick his ass—(she whispered "ass")—myself the next time if he keeps talking about me and calling me out of name. And just because you had a little fight don't mean you get to be all bold telling me how pretty I am." Marie made a face as she said the word "pretty," sticking her tongue out and opening her eyes wide.

"I know. Sorry."

"Just because you're feeling yourself after getting your little cherry popped don't mean you need to be in parks fighting, you stupid boy."

"I know. I know. Okay. I gotta talk to my uncle now. You can finish yelling at me later." Jamaal walked past Marie, but not before he purposely touched her hand, and she grabbed his and said, "They're waiting for you in your uncle's office. Good luck, Jamaal," and she squeezed his hand before letting it go as Jamaal passed by her.

Marie went into church without saying another word and Jamaal became more stressed than he had been when he thought he'd only have to listen to his uncle's lecture at church and then his aunt's lecture at home.

Arriving outside the pastor's office door, Jamaal paused and exhaled. He knew what was next and what was behind the closed doors. If Marie knew, then everyone knew, and it was no doubt who had told everyone: Roy.

Jamaal sat on the sofa at the back of the office where he always sat. His uncle-pastor was in his leather chair behind his big wooden desk.

"I'm sorry," Jamaal too eagerly answered when his uncle asked him if he had anything to say.

Uncle Gerald turned his lips up which Jamaal knew meant that he was annoyed. Jamaal tried to avoid his uncle's glare by looking up, down, into his hands, and at the clock which seemed to have stopped the passage of time. Jamaal knew his uncle would tell Roy's family they had to forgive Jamaal because that is what church folk were trained to do. They wouldn't like it, but Jamaal was certain his uncle would work it out.

Church had already started; the sounds of praise permeated the office and provided a gospel soundtrack to the meeting.

"I appreciate your apology, son, but just because you apologize doesn't mean you are free to go or that I won't lecture you. You could have really hurt Roy, Jamaal."

"I know, sir." Jamaal softened his tone for his uncle, hoping it would help end the meeting early. He was ready for his uncle's lecture, and he knew what was coming next, so he kept quiet, hoping to end the session sooner rather than later.

His uncle was still talking, and Jamaal tried to listen, but he soon found himself looking at Roy, who sat near the front of the office on the opposite wall of his stepfather.

Roy's face was swollen, and he had Band-Aids just above both eyes. *He looked like he had lost a fight,* Jamaal chuckled to himself and debated if he had the guts to say it aloud.

"You are supposed to set an example. And if you can't fight my boy one-on-one, what did you prove? That you're a coward, that's what you proved," Roy's stepfather yelled across the room at Jamaal. He was a big man, an ex-con, and he wore a giant afro like it was still 1973. Roy's stepfather's voice sounded like he was a longtime smoker, or perhaps one of those overzealous fans who screamed nonstop at sporting events.

Jamaal stared at the giant man. His hair looked crazy and his suit was too small, making him look like a taller and older actor Terry Crews. His shoes looked old, too, almost a platform shoe of the type that was popular during the days of disco. Jamaal thought maybe the man was a time-traveler because he looked so out of place.

"And be a real man, not whatever you think you are now. My boy would whip you in a fair fight, and you know it, Jamaal. You better be glad I am a deacon and that I am now saved and sanctified, or I would put both your butts in the ring, and I'd bet a Sunday offering you would get your butt whipped so bad you would be crying and begging Roy to stop."

"Like he was begging me to stop, huh?" Jamaal knew he was wrong even before he finished talking but he had grown bored and annoyed with the man droning on.

"You better watch your mouth, son. I'm an adult and a grown man and deacon. You better not disrespect me." The big man took two steps toward the back of the office where Jamaal sat.

Jamaal didn't flinch. He instead wished he had a rock and a slingshot so he could launch it right at the giant's huge head and knock him to the ground.

"Deacon. Let's end this," Pastor Gerald interjected, getting the man's attention.

Jamaal knew his uncle was ready for the meeting to end, judging by the tone of his voice, and he also knew the drive home would be the particularly intense time and location where his uncle would really tell him what he felt.

"You need to apologize to Roy, Jamaal. A real apology, not that half-assed one you said earlier," Roy's stepfather again raised his voice, despite Uncle Gerald's admonition just moments ago.

Jamaal didn't like being yelled at. By anyone. But Roy's stepfather was a huge man, so Jamaal sat still and let the man rage at him. He looked tough and violent. Jamaal was terrified because the man was closer to him, and he hoped he didn't look as afraid as he felt. He looked around and figured that if needed, he could escape through the door before the big guy caught him.

None of that was needed though because soon Uncle Gerald asked Jamaal what he had to say for himself. Jamaal had learned in Sunday school the power of an earnest apology whether he meant it or not. So, he apologized though he didn't mean it. He thought he sounded earnest.

"Is that all you got?" Roy's stepfather said again, clearly, and obviously still angry.

"Yes, sir. I'm sorry Roy held a bat to my face and I kicked his ass. I won't do it again," Jamaal answered in the most smartass way he could think to answer. Jamaal knew he didn't sound earnest at all now and the smirk on his face told his uncle and Roy's stepfather the same thing.

"You sound like you want to fight some more, little boy," Roy's stepfather said in a very threatening voice that seemed like it made the floor rumble.

"No, sir. I don't want to fight anymore. I already beat his ass," Jamaal said, further infuriating Roy's stepfather who looked like he was ready to charge Jamaal and chuck him out the office window.

Uncle Gerald chuckled, further infuriating Roy's stepfather.

Roy, who had been quiet for the entire meeting, finally spoke up.

"It's fine. I accept his apology. I kept messing with him and I knew when I embarrassed him in front of Marie I probably went too far. So, we're even. But if we fight again, I promise the outcome will be different because I won't let him trick me like he did this time."

Roy's stepfather looked disgusted and after a long glaring stare at Roy, he turned to Pastor Gerald. Jamaal thought the man looked hopeless and angry with his hands outstretched like those old pictures of Jesus.

"They're teenagers, what can we say? Look, Deacon, he said he was sorry. Let it go. Tell your boy don't go around trying to pick fights if he can't back up his words with actions."

"Pastor—"

"No, it's over, Deacon. Let it go, please."

"Yes, sir. I don't like it though."

"I hear you, Deacon."

Pastor Gerald turned to Jamaal and motioned for him to approach. When Jamaal got up, Pastor Gerald turned to Roy.

"Come here, son."

Roy stood and took the two steps to stand beside Pastor Gerald, facing Jamaal.

The sound of the church music was the perfect theme music for the now less tense meeting.

The boys stood like boxers getting their instructions from the referee before a fight. Uncle-Pastor Gerald played the role of referee but instead of striped black and white colors, his bold black suit and shiny white tie presented a new-age churchified version of a referee.

"I don't want to hear any more stories secondhand," he looked at Jamaal, "about you two fighting. No revenge, no tricks, no physical confrontations at all. You both understand?" Uncle-Pastor Gerald looked at Roy then at Jamaal.

“Yes, sir,” Jamaal answered, looking at his uncle before turning his gaze to Roy who was looking down.

“Yes, Pastor Gerald,” Roy answered.

“Now, you two shake hands and this is the end of it,” he finished.

Jamaal reached over to Roy who reached back.

“Sorry, Roy.”

Jamaal felt Roy squeeze his hand. Jamaal squeezed back.

“You are sorry, Jamaal.”

“Roy!” Pastor Gerald raised his voice and shook his head.

“Boy if you don't straighten up …” Roy's stepfather grabbed Roy's shoulders and held him.

“I'm sorry, too, Jamaal.” Roy said. Then added: “That I didn't hit you with that baseball bat.”

“Lord Jesus help us!” Pastor Gerald said, pulling the boy's hands apart.

“Time for church, let's go. I want both of you in church for the full service because I am going to pray over you and ask the church to as well. I am not going make you apologize to the church—this time—but if there's any more shenanigans from either of you, I'll be locking you in church for a week and praying with you every day until God changes your hearts.”

They shook and then it was over.

Pastor Gerald and the deacon walked out first, then Jamaal offered to let Roy walk out first, but Roy motioned for Jamaal to go first, so he did. As soon as he was in front of Roy, Roy shoved him in the back, causing him to stumble. Jamaal just shook his head and continued into church.

Jamaal wondered what would happen if he didn't go up when his uncle called him up to the altar, but ultimately, he decided that tonight was not the night to test those waters.

Besides, what he saw when he entered the sanctuary shocked him.

The loudmouth evangelist was already up at the front of the church. Jamaal knew that with the pastor not in church yet, the loudmouth evangelist should not be up there talking to the congregation. No preacher should. That time before the pastor entered the church was reserved for singing, praying, and announcements. That the loudmouth evangelist was in front of the church talking was one thing, but what Jamaal and the members were watching was not talking, preaching, or singing.

Jamaal tried to make sense of what he was seeing but nothing he saw made sense.

The loudmouth evangelist was standing on a chair in front of the church. His knees were slightly bent, his face was contorted in a strange grimace, and his right hand was on his pants' zipper.

Jamaal corrected his thoughts. It wasn't a "chair" the loudmouth evangelist was standing on; it was the pastor's chair from the pulpit. Uncle Gerald's Pastor's Chair.

The loudmouth was pulling on the zipper of his pants and exposing his underwear, then zipping himself up again. And repeating this, over and over. In his left hand, he held Uncle Gerald's microphone.

"This is how you know a man from a woman," the loudmouth evangelist said into the mic, as he continued to zip and then unzip his pants.

Jamaal, like the rest of the church members, stared in shock. The music had stopped, and Dwayne was watching along with everyone else. Jamaal watched his uncle walk by the absurd and vulgar scene playing out in front of the church members.

“Men have these, and women don't. That's how you know being gay is a sin, and men sleeping with men is an abomination because you can't both have zippers,” the loudmouth said.

“What are you saying? That doesn't even make sense,” Jamaal said aloud to no one in particular. “He has completely lost his mind!” No one was paying attention to him with what was happening in front of the church, and no one seemed to hear him.

Jamaal took his seat and looked around. Even with the crazy zipper thing going on, Jamaal saw that some members were agreeing with the loudmouth, nodding their heads, and even declaring “Amen, preacher.”

Jamaal wondered why some members who he knew were extra critical of anything and everything his uncle, their pastor, said, would be nodding to the garbage coming forth from the loudmouth evangelist's mouth. He looked around for his aunt but saw that she was not in her chair which meant she was probably downstairs helping in the kitchen.

“Auntie always told me that Black preachers have an unusual hold on the spiritual and emotional lives of Black church members,” Jamaal mumbled to himself. “She wasn't lying.”

After what felt like way too long, Jamaal heard his uncle's booming voice say sternly, “Preacher, give me the microphone and take your seat.”

Jamaal knew that for his uncle to demand the microphone was not only unusual, but so rare as to be shocking, and of course insulting to the loudmouth evangelist.

"I am preaching. I am the MAN OF GOD and I have a message," the loudmouth evangelist responded sharply.

Jamaal thought back to his fight in the park and how the scene playing out in front of him wasn't too different.

"This is my church, and you will give me the microphone, or I'll ask my deacons to come get it," Uncle-Pastor Gerald said, as he motioned to the deacons, who moved closer to the pulpit. Roy's stepfather, who looked even more angry than he had in the office, was right up front.

If the deacons attack him, I'm going to try to get a punch in, too, Jamaal thought.

"You promised me ten thousand dollars. I want my money if I have to leave," the loudmouth evangelist said slowly and emphatically.

"You raised what you could. And you were probably going to do well tonight and tomorrow. But no more. Your revival is over. Leave my church now. I'm losing my patience," Uncle-Pastor Gerald said forcefully, following his words with a nod to the deacons.

The deacons moved to either side of the loudmouth evangelist and Jamaal prayed for the first time in a while: God/Goddess, if you exist, please let a deacon, any deacon, punch the loudmouth evangelist in his big fat mouth. InJesusnameIprayamen.

Jamaal's realized his prayers would go unanswered, again, when the loudmouth evangelist dropped the microphone on the floor and stormed out of the church.

The church was as silent as when it was empty.

Pastor-Uncle Gerald then started singing *I Shall Not Be Moved,* and slowly the members joined in as Dwayne started softly playing and accentuating the pastor's singing with traditional organ church music. Then Jamaal saw his uncle sense the moment, as any pastor would, and pivot to praying, in a rebuke of what had just happened with the vulgar display of the loud-mouthed preacher.

The members responded in kind and in sanctified habit, hummed and groaned along as Pastor Gerald prayed. Jamaal enjoyed the synchronicity and unity of the moment—it was what he liked most about church, when it was spontaneous, emotional, authentic.

> LORD, THE DEVIL WAS IN HERE TONIGHT AND WE CALL UPON YOU TO RESTORE OUR SOULS AND TO PROTECT US FROM THE ENEMY, AND KEEP US FREE FROM HURT, HARM, OR DANGER. WE ARE TURNING BACK TO YOU BECAUSE YOU LOVED US FIRST AND YOU ARE FAITHFUL, FORGIVING, AND FIRST IN OUR HEARTS AND MIND. WE ARE CALLING ON YOU TO TOUCH THE PREACHER WHO LOST HIS WAY AND BRING HIM BACK TO YOU FOR HEALING, AND REPRIMAND. IN YOU WE TRUST AND PRAY, AMEN AND AMEN.
>
> Amen.

Jamaal exhaled as he took his seat, content to sit through the remainder of church and hoping the day's big event would cause his uncle to forget he was planning to call him and Roy to the altar for prayer.

The choir sang for a while, and then Uncle Gerald preached a brief—for him—forty-minute sermon that remarkably included an entire portion dedicated to the loudmouth preacher as if he had studied and prepared for this exact moment all week. He quoted scripture after scripture, told two stories that connected at the end to both the events of the week and the selfishness and stories of the loudmouth preacher. Uncle-Pastor Gerald weaved through story and scripture with confidence, righteous anger, and strong supplications to God to hear him and hear His people who were humble before him, crying out to him, and praising the name of his son Jesus. In the name of Jesus, Uncle-Pastor Gerald said with the authority of an experienced and beloved preacher before a congregation that he recruited, nurtured, and oversaw as the shepherd to his flock.

Uncle-Pastor Gerald was back in control, and the church loved it.

Jamaal felt proud. He felt proud of his uncle for taking back control from the detestable loudmouth preacher and leading the church. And he knew he felt proud of the church members who responded to his uncle—their pastor—as they had learned to do and wanted to do.

After Uncle-Pastor Gerald finished preaching and while emotions were still high, instead of taking his seat and allowing the assistant pastors to raise the offering, he stayed up and called every member to the altar, one by one and asked them to bless the church with their offering, reassuring them their money was not going to the "sinful evangelist" but to the church building fund.

Jamaal watched as one by one each member came to the altar, many of them crying, and all of them placing money and checks into the special building-fund offering baskets that were shaped like a large white church without a roof, which soon overflowed with money.

Jamaal saw Sister Julie and a building-fund deacon emerge from the back room where they had taken a long time to count the offering.

Jamaal watched as the couple approached the pastor, and then Sister Julie handed him a small note that Jamaal knew had the amount of the offering written on it.

By the time the counting was finished—the building-fund committee deacons helped Sister Julie, so Jamaal did not have to—Pastor Gerald announced that the church had exceeded the whole week's offering total.

Shouts of "hallelujah" filled the church, Dwayne began playing excitedly, and the drummer banged the cymbals with precision, and for the next twenty minutes members danced, sang, clapped, stomped, and played tambourine matching the music that flowed from the organ and drums.

I bet she still got her share even though those deacons were with her. Jamaal thought, as he watched Sister Julie walking back to her seat, her face betraying no emotion. He saw her pull her coat close to her body, probably to hide the money bulging in her bra. Jamaal felt some level of admiration.

+++

Jamaal's friends were going out after church, and despite their protests, Jamaal told them, "I just want to go home and do some homework and go to bed." It had been a long week.

The drive home was quiet as Uncle Gerald drifted off. Jamaal did not have to sit through any chatter. When they parked in the garage, Jamaal said, "I'm going to do homework before I go sleep. Good night, Uncle."

"Good night, son."

Jamaal poured himself a glass of water, and a few minutes later he was lying down on his bed, the glass of water now on his dresser.

"Ahhh," Jamaal breathed out as he finally rested his head on his pillow, no homework done, but plenty of stories to think about to help him sleep.

Jamaal ran through the day's events: the fight, the office time with Uncle Gerald and Roy, and then finally the strange ending with the loudmouth evangelist. The crazy day had made Jamaal more exhausted than he had originally considered.

Jamaal was close to falling asleep when he thought about the loudmouth evangelist zipping and unzipping his pants. He turned over, annoyed to be thinking about the loudmouth evangelist.

"Marie sure was pretty tonight." Jamaal felt better thinking about Marie as he finally started to relax.

Right before fading for the night, his mind drifted to Sis Julie bending to him and kissing him on the lips.

CHAPTER 8

SUNDAY

Where then is my hope—who can see any hope for me? ~ Job 17:15

Sunday church is a weekly homecoming and a celebration and commemoration of all things—historical and current—Black. Jamaal had issues with church on any other day, but the anticipation and energy surrounding Sunday church even worked on him as he got dressed, making certain his tie was perfect, shoes were shiny, and his breath smelled good. He even decided to wear the cologne his aunt had bought for him. She had told him, "You're old enough to smell good and too old to smell bad."

Jamaal loved listening to his Aunt Meredith talk. Her words were usually serious, but always warm, and her views of church, God, and church members were more real and always brutally honest. And, unlike Uncle Gerald, Aunt Meredith did not hesitate to criticize any church member no matter how much money they gave, and that gave Jamaal great satisfaction. Aunt Meredith could even shut down Uncle Gerald when she wanted, which wasn't often, but often enough that Jamaal silently took pleasure in watching and listening to Uncle Gerald get shut down by her.

"Jamaal," Aunt Meredith had said one night as she was preparing dinner for the two of them because Uncle Gerald was visiting another church.

"Yes, ma'am?"

"I know you get tired of going to church all the time. I was like you, too, when I was young. My father was a minister, and his father, plus my uncle, and two cousins. I have no memory of ever not being in church, seven days a week, fifty-two weeks a year. It was my whole life and Lord knows there were days I wanted nothing to do with any church, preacher, or sometimes Jesus himself."

Jamaal had watched as Aunt Meredith gently placed two thin cuts of pork chops lightly coated in well-seasoned flour, into the skillet that had been warming a splash of olive oil. The meat sizzled immediately, sending a thin plume of smoke rising to the ventilation and his nose. She moved with grace and certainty, as she did most of the time.

Aunt Meredith was the only mother Jamaal had ever known, and it was at times like this that he felt closest to her.

Aunt Meredith had added more seasoned flour to the skillet then a touch of water and stirred it with the colorful cooking utensil Jamaal had given her on her birthday a couple of months earlier.

"All my friends were from the churches I had to attend, and any friend I made at school I had to invite to my father's church before they were allowed to come over for a playdate."

Aunt Meredith had tossed chopped red onions into a big bowl that already had mixed greens, sliced cherry tomatoes, and colorful sweet peppers. She had opened a small glass container of leftover cornbread croutons (a specialty of hers) and dropped a handful into the salad before finally slicing an avocado and neatly laying the slices across the top of the salad.

Seeing the avocado had made Jamaal happy because only he and Aunt Meredith liked avocado, so they only had them when Uncle Gerald wasn't home for dinner.

"Here."

Jamaal had taken the crouton from Aunt Meredith and tossed it into his mouth like he was eating popcorn.

"Thank you."

"Don't talk with your mouth full. So, as I was saying, I know you get tired of church and church folk, just the same way I did. Your mother was the same, you know? And, well, I understand, is what I am letting you know. You are not going to agree with everything, and you are going to see and meet hypocrites, liars, thieves, adulterers, and more. Some people use the behavior of church people as their excuse not to believe in God and, while I understand it, I don't agree. Where else are people who need God supposed to go?"

Aunt Meredith expertly flipped the pork cutlets, steam again rising, but less than before. Jamaal had watched as she added a tablespoon of water to her roux and stirred vigorously, scraping the pan of the cooked bits of flour that had fallen off the pork.

"There is a world out there though, Jamaal, that we want to protect you from as long as we can. I don't need to tell you how dangerous it is for young Black boys—young men, I mean—like you and your friends. And girls, too.

"The world is full of beauty, danger, hatred, fun, and opportunities to make mistakes. You will get your chance, like everyone, but we will protect you if we can and we will prepare you. Even when it makes you mad or when it doesn't make sense to you."

Aunt Meredith had placed pork cutlet, steamed broccoli, a scoop of fluffy white rice, and two servings of salad on a plate then put the plate down in front of Jamaal. She'd then drizzled gravy on the cutlet and on the rice.

"Eat. And besides, church isn't all that bad, is it? I see you clapping along with everyone else, and I know you listen closely to the sermons from your uncle and other preachers. And you're a good student in Sunday school, I'm told."

Jamaal had begun to gobble the salad, then broccoli, then a piece of pork and put it all in his mouth.

"Slow down, Jamaal," Aunt Meredith had told him then, as many times before, and since, "don't eat so fast, it's bad for your digestion."

The smell of a bacon and egg breakfast and the pleasant smile of his Aunt Meredith in the kitchen brought him back from his memory of that night, which wasn't too different from other nights, but for some reason stuck with him and made him feel warm when he remembered it. He sat down at the kitchen table and Aunt Meredith, who had almost finished her own plate of food, touched his arm and looked Jamaal right in the eyes.

"I know this past week and especially last night were… difficult… for all of us. Soon we get back on track, and I know you will enjoy church again. Sunday church, Lord have mercy, is the best organized event in this country, bar none."

Aunt Meredith began clearing her plate and cleaning her preparation areas as she continued talking.

"My mother, grandmother, and my own aunties said that Sunday at the Black church was the acknowledgment that God kept his word and protected churchgoers from 'the world,' and proved his love by allowing everyone to wake up, have shelter, have food, and not be in the hospital, jail, or dead.

"It was the culmination of a process that started hundreds of years ago, and to be respectful to your family and community meant dressing up and going to church. Not just dressing up like for a job interview, no, dressed up as if you were going to meet the Lord Jesus Christ himself.

You all in your sharp suits and shiny shoes which in any other setting, anywhere in or out of the church world, would make men and boys stand out.

"But not here and not on a Sunday.

"Today is the day the Lord had made, Jamaal, and it is for men and boys, of course, but it is the day that we women take the spotlight. You have been around it your entire life, but have you looked closely—really looked?"

Jamaal nodded, enthralled, and not wanting to interrupt Aunt Meredith.

"Our clothes are beyond colorful because we didn't always have colorful clothes. And, like the men in their shiny suits, in any other setting in or out of church, our clothes would steal all the attention. But not in church on Sunday."

Jamaal was a little confused but thought it important to hold his question, knowing that Aunt Meredith wasn't finished. Aunt Meredith took Jamaal's plate, smiled as she saw that not even a single spot of egg yolk was left on it, then continued talking.

"Sunday, Jamaal, is the day of colorful, saved and sanctified, holy-ghost inspired, and impressive to men, the Lord himself, and especially the other women in the church—hats. That's H-A-T-S with a capital H."

Jamaal smiled.

"From before I was born, to when I was your age, up until now, the hats are extra-large, or small, some have flowers, others multicolored scarves and silks, while still others have brooches, buttons, or feathers from unknown birds.

"My favorites are the ones that cover our faces, or even the ones that only cover the top of our foreheads—like the one I am wearing today.

The mothers who tilt theirs and those, like our church mother, who must turn sideways just to get through the sanctuary door! Lord have mercy, those big hats are something else!" Aunt Meredith laughed loudly as she wiped the counters, her bathrobe fluttering as she swished back and forth, cleaning the marble counters before wiping down the stove, refrigerator door and handles, and then taking out the broom to begin sweeping.

Jamaal admitted to himself that he also liked the hats, and he wondered if somehow Aunt Meredith knew that about him. He wondered if Aunt Meredith knew that the hats seemed to be more extreme the older the woman wearing it was.

"It is our weekly parade of the faithful and of the mothers and daughters of God, on our way into the church to again hear how we, in all our splendor of colorful beauty, are the cause of all the sin in the world." Aunt Meredith laughed her loudest laugh at her joke. Jamaal thought it had a ring of truth to it.

It was, it seemed to Jamaal, a celebration of the baseline what God could do for Black folk, but Jamaal wondered why God didn't do more if He was so great and loving like the church taught.

+++

Walking into church, Jamaal felt Aunt Meredith's words had come to life. The colors were everywhere, and the movement of people was reminiscent of the Hindu festival of spring Jamaal had been learning about in history class.

The hats were all shapes, sizes, and textures, matching the bodies, heads, and colors of their wearers. The energy that was generated by the hats was only matched by the people's energy—authentic and transferable. Jamaal watched as church mothers greeted one another with loud comments of laughter and compliments on each other's garb while hugging and kissing, before quickly moving on to the next person to love and compliment.

The men in their shiny suits and shoes, far fewer in sharp hats that earlier generations wore, but still dressed to the "T" and, like the women, complementing each other, but with the added teasing in joy and love.

Jamaal loved the ceremony of it all and loved seeing Aunt Meredith's words in living color. He stood in the vestibule and did what he enjoyed most: watched the flow of people.

He saw the little girls mimicking the older girls and women but adding in spinning and giggling as they showed off new dresses or shoes. Their faces smooth and shiny, their hair tied in Afro-puffs, braids, or bouncy pigtails with matching ribbons. Little boys in junior suits—some too big if they were hand-me-downs from older siblings, and shoes that were too grown-up for their ages.

The sounds brought the scene together. The kids laughed and shrieked as they ran about; their mothers and aunties yelled at them to stop running and stop screaming, while fully knowing their admonitions would be joyfully ignored—as they had also done when they were kids.

The pageantry was punctuated by the aromas coming from the kitchen downstairs in the repast gathering room.

Jamaal jumped down the stairs and poked his head inside the swinging doors, then he inhaled and filled his senses with spices that were liberally used on roasted and fried chicken, various cooked vegetables full of onion, garlic, sweet and spicy peppers, and special seasoning from whichever senior mother was in charge of bringing a particular dish.

Jamaal knew Aunt Meredith made the potato salad—she had insisted on the coveted task that only the senior most women would even dare ask to prepare. Jamaal and everyone loved Aunt Meredith's potato salad because it was traditional with a mustard base, deviled eggs on top and sides, and had just the right mix of sweet and savory. Plus, Aunt Meredith, like the other experienced potato salad preparers, didn't experiment or add disgusting ingredients like raisins, nuts, or sunflower seeds as one young woman had done once.

Jamaal chuckled thinking about how the grownups still laughed about the sunflower seed potato salad every time they got together again to cook. He had no doubt some of the laughter he had heard today when he looked in on them was about that awful potato salad.

Word of the revival breakdown the night before had gotten out and the church was crowded like it would be on Easter Sunday. Everyone wanted to see what would happen on Sunday and to talk and gossip about what had happened the previous night.

As Jamaal walked up the stairs past small groups talking, he overheard members talking about the evangelist and his zipper. There were no hushed conversations or even loud whispers, Jamaal noted, but just people talking loudly about the craziness of the night before.

Jamaal made his way to his uncle's office, quietly taking his seat behind the senior deacons and church mothers as he entered. They were all there to hear his uncle tell the regional bishop what had happened the night before.

Uncle-Pastor Gerald's voice was the only sound in the room as he regaled the visiting bishop—who had come because the word had spread to his church on the other side of town—with the story. With him were his entourage of young sharply dressed men.

The regional bishop—Ross W. L. Patton or, "W.L.," as he was called—listened intently, along with the senior deacons and church mothers who knew every detail as well as Pastor Gerald but remained respectfully quiet.

Jamaal had heard his uncle tell the story four times now and even though the story was consistent in details, he heard his uncle begin embellishing his own role in putting the previous night's disruptions to an end.

Jamaal figured it was another reason the senior staff of deacons and church mothers remained quiet while listening to his uncle.

"That is why I asked you here, Bishop. To close out the revival by actually delivering a message of revival and not a false message of 'show me and give me the money' like the evangelist did."

"Amen, Pastor," a couple of the senior staff replied in hushed voices out of deference to the pastor and bishop.

"I am glad you did," Bishop W.L. responded, his voice higher than it seemed like it would be. He was slightly older than Uncle Gerald, wore his regal purple robe with gold trimmings, and had his large Coptic-styled cross on his neck and deposited inside his robe.

"I will do my best, Pastor. I haven't preached here in a few years so maybe they'll like me," Bishop W.L. said, self-deprecatingly, knowing full well the power of his office guaranteed an energetic response from the church members.

"Maybe just a little bit, as long as you stay in the bible, and keep your zipper zipped, Bishop." Uncle-Pastor Gerald started laughing at his even as it was leaving his mouth, and as soon as it was out, the entire group was laughing.

Jamaal stared, biting back his disgust. The previous tension had completely subsided, and everyone began their standard pre-church chatting and last-minute instructions or complaints. Jamaal focused on his uncle-pastor and Bishop W.L. and tuned out the chatter to listen to their conversation, something he had learned to do from years of sitting in his uncle's office with groups holding multiple conversations.

"Remind me, Preacher, that's your son sitting in the back?" the bishop asked Uncle-Pastor Gerald.

"No, no. That's my nephew, Bishop, my wife's sister's kid, rest her soul," Uncle-Pastor Gerald answered him quickly and assertively. Even after all these years of raising Jamaal like a son, his uncle was still loathed to allow anyone to think he was anything but the orphan he took in out of the goodness of his heart. Jamaal didn't expect anything more, but it always made him feel a little rejected.

Bishop W.L. was a slight man with salt and pepper hair. He was widowed and always traveled with an entourage of well-dressed men who were much younger than him. The young men, mostly from his own church, were preachers, musicians, singers, and other hangers-on, and they were known as W. L.'s helpers because that is how he introduced them when he was asked. Jamaal had heard rumors and whispers about the young men and Bishop W.L. who were always together, though he had never heard his uncle speak about them.

"Well," W.L. started, "you had too much excitement. I will help calm the church down. I am glad you called me. Although you called too late—much too late. You interrupted my sleep." And he laughed a slightly high-pitched laugh, and his entourage of young men laughed with him.

Jamaal just watched.

"I can't stay long, so I will speak before the choir sings. How much money was the evangelist hoping to raise today, Pastor?" W.L. asked Uncle-Pastor Gerald.

"Seven or eight thousand."

"Eight thousand," W.L. repeated softly, while staring at Uncle-Pastor Gerald, who stared back with a sincere look.

"I'll take twenty-eight hundred then," W.L. said matter-of-factly.

"Yes, sir," Uncle-Pastor Gerald quickly replied.

He agreed too quickly, Jamaal thought.

They all motioned toward the door to leave, and Jamaal hung back.

W.L. moved to the door and before he did, he walked to Jamaal and held out his hand to shake.

Jamaal extended his hand.

W.L. had smaller hands that were soft. Jamaal's hands easily enveloped W. L's hands.

Jamaal felt W. L.'s middle finger scratching the palm of his hand, just like the other visiting preacher had done earlier in the week.

He looked W.L. in the eye but didn't say anything.

Then W.L. said quietly, "I have room in my church for young men with large hands like yours, son."

Jamaal pulled his hand away with force and immediately placed both his hands inside his pockets, as he watched W.L. walk through the door and into the church.

Uncle-Pastor Gerald was now standing beside Jamaal.

"Jamaal, don't let him bother you."

"Okay. Whatever. I won't," Jamaal replied, softly but angrily.

"When Sis Julie counts the money tonight, tell her to set aside five hundred for me, make sure W.L. gets all the checks—he can deal with the bad checks—and place any IOUs in his payout. And his payout will be two thousand dollars, no matter how much comes in. You understand?"

"Yes, sir," Jamaal said, and they exited the office and went into the sanctuary.

The choir was singing fantastically, as they tended to do in front of large crowds and when Dwayne was on time and neither drunk nor hungover. Marie sang lead on the fast inspirational song. Jamaal tried not to stare but she was so pretty with her thick and curly hair all over the place, bright red lipstick that the older church mothers would certainly be mad about, her skirt too short but now covered by her purple and gold choir robe that remained opened in front just enough so that when she turned, Jamaal could see her dark leg.

Jamaal hoped she would talk to him after church. Maybe they could go to the car again later, he thought, hoped, wished.

"Am I praying?" Jamaal asked himself as he smiled. He then felt a hand grab his, pulling him out of his prayer.

"It's so nice to see you smiling, Jamaal. You're always such a serious young man."

"Yes, ma'am, Mother Branch." Jamaal squeezed the older woman's hand until she released her grip.

"Isn't her singing lovely? I need to find a seat and stop talking so I can hear the rest of this beautiful song."

But at that moment, the song ended and another began. Mother Branch turned away and greeted another older lady before the two of them took seats beside one another. They both stood back up as Sister Julie hit a high note toward the end of the song.

Though she wasn't as lovely to look at as Marie, Jamaal loved when Sister Julie took her songs beyond the end of the song. She had the ability, as most of the best church singers did, of pulling the church members along with her as she praised the Lord. Her voice was powerful, her steps were loud in her thick clunky black heels landing with a hard thud each time she declared "Yes!"

Sister Julie was turning from left to right, her robe fanning behind her always a half-second slow, as she addressed the church through song and ministered through her voice, delivering salvation, forgiveness, and God's love to young and old, saved and sinner, friend, and enemy, and especially to young men just exploring their hormones like Jamaal.

Jamaal watched in admiration as Sister Julie now cried, her eyeliner smudged leaving a one-inch black streak resting on her round cheek, and her body still as she finished the song in earnest.

W.L. spoke for only a few minutes about the prior night's activities, and, because of his position, the church was fired up at his few boring and non-impactful words. He had none of the traditional verbal skills nor charisma of most Black preachers in that position, making Jamaal wonder anew about how he had gotten to that level—an area bishop who couldn't even preach as well as any random unaccomplished youth pastor?

Yeah, that's odd. Jamaal decided as he tried not to pay any more attention to the very boring W.L. Instead, Jamaal searched the choir stand for Marie but didn't immediately see her, and despite his attempts to distract himself, his thoughts returned to W.L. again. Being able to command a church's attention and impress peers were required abilities of pastors, superintendents, and bishops, and everyone knew it. But somehow, Jamaal concluded, W.L. had ascended despite having no charisma and with barely average preaching skills.

"Even the church has politics, son. More than most corporations." Jamaal recalled his uncle saying on one of their drives.

W.L. continued with a boring story that was winding around in the way teenagers tell stories. The story ended without the usual big reveal and lesson at the end that the church was used to. After some wrap up talk that was mostly about his own church and what he had planned for the remainder of the day, W.L. finished and took his seat.

Jamaal looked around the church and saw the faces of unfulfilled members who, like himself, were left wanting more. The church was quiet, with members mumbling, and others quietly—but not quietly enough, Jamaal chuckled—talking about how awful W. L.'s sermon was. Jamaal knew that members were going to criticize W. L.'s message, but he thought they would wait until after church when W.L. had left and if they did not wait, at least they would be quiet.

"Church folk have no chill." Jamaal thought the brutal and immediate feedback of church members must be where places such as the Apollo Theatre in Harlem, notorious for its audience's impatience with performers who didn't immediately grab and hold their attention, got their critique skills. Churches were even harder, Jamaal knew.

"That's crazy," Jamaal said aloud, half chuckling.

"THE DEVIL WAS HERE LAST NIGHT."

Jamaal turned his attention to his uncle-pastor, who had just taken the microphone from Sister Julie when she finished singing. She disappeared into the back, and Jamaal assumed she was preparing to count the offering.

"AND NOW WE ARE GOING TO REFOCUS OUR ATTENTION TO GOD AND HIS WILL AND AWAY FROM SATAN AND HIS WILL."

"Amen, Pastor."

"Say that."

"Yes, sir."

"Say it."

"Y'ALL NEED TO STOP. I AM JUST UP HERE TO RAISE AN OFFERING AND BLESSING FOR BISHOP W.L. I'M NOT UP HERE TO PREACH."

Jamaal recognized his uncle's solemn voice that he used when something important needed to be said or done.

"Well, sir."

"Go ahead."

"AS SAINTS, IT IS INCUMBENT ON US—YOU AND I—TO PRAY THE SIN AWAY."

"Wooooo!"

"Amen, amen, amen!"

"You already preaching!"

"Preach!"

The energy flowed through and around the church. Jamaal felt what everyone was feeling. The pent-up frustrations from the loudmouth evangelist had left the church wanting. Jamaal knew his uncle-pastor was priming everyone for this upcoming sermon, teasing them with just enough emotional energy to make them hungry for more, but not so much that they felt fully "fed" and ready to leave before he took up a second offering.

"I'M GOING TO CALL ON THE PRAYER WARRIORS LATER—YOU KNOW WHO YOU ARE—TO PRAY THAT GOD HEALS

THIS CHURCH AND TOUCHES THAT EVANGELIST AS ONLY HIS POWER CAN!"

The church erupted as the Prayer Warriors stood and offered support to the pastor.

"Let Him use you, Pastor!"

"Amen, amen, amen!"

Jamaal knew that the undefined term "Prayer Warrior" while generally assigned to older church mothers and middle-aged "missionaries," could be any woman—and they were almost always women—who felt self-important enough and believed that it was they who the scripture described in the words: "The prayers of the righteous availeth much."

> *THE DEVIL HIMSELF WAS IN THE CHURCH LAST NIGHT AND TRIED TO DRIVE OUT GOD AND TAKE AWAY EVERYONE'S TESTIMONY AND SALVATION. WE CAN'T LET THE DEVIL THINK HE CAN TAKE OVER GOD'S CHURCH, CAN WE?*

Preacher Gerald started the call and response that wasn't normally part of the offering portion of church service, but this was different, Jamaal knew, because they needed to raise a lot of money today. He knew Uncle Gerald would push and appeal for more money, and that he would get it.

Uncle Gerald raised money with skill, patience, guilt, shame, begging, crying, and passionate words about how "God's work had to go on, and we can't let the devil win now or ever."

W.L. just watched with a silly grin on his face and Jamaal knew why: W.L. thought Pastor Gerald was raising money for him; but Jamaal knew that was not true at all. *Uncle Gerald was raising money for himself—and for Sister Julie,* Jamaal thought with an out-loud laugh that, fortunately for him, was drowned out by the church music and noises of praise.

Jamaal tried not to be impressed, but he knew he was as he watched his uncle talk members out of their hard-earned money, Social Security checks, drug-sales proceeds, loans, and whatever other sources provided the money that ended up funding the church, evangelists, pastors, regional bishops, some deacons, musicians, and a few others.

GIVE TO GOD AND HE WILL RETURN TO YOU TENFOLD; YOUR CUP WILL RUN OVER WITH BLESSINGS, AND YOUR HOUSEHOLD WILL INCREASE BECAUSE GOD HAS ORDAINED IT SO. WON'T HE DO IT? WON'T HE!?

Almost all the money was paid out to men, and Jamaal wondered why that was so, when most members were women, and the female Prayer Warriors did so much work to encourage the congregation to tithe. It went right back to what Aunt Meredith said about the hustle and guilt trips.

> *YOUR LIFE WILL REMAIN EMPTY IF YOU HOLD ONTO WHAT IS GOD'S. GIVE UNTO GOD WHAT IS GOD'S AND UNTO CAESAR WHAT IS CAESAR'S—THAT MEANS GIVE GOD HIS PORTION AND PAY YOUR TAXES. TODAY ISN'T TAX DAY, SO YOU CAN GIVE GOD A LITTLE MORE, CAN'T YOU? OH, IT'S AWFULLY QUIET IN HERE!*

I'll be stuck in this church for a few more years, Jamaal thought wistfully as his attention returned to Uncle Gerald who was finally finished raising money.

"GOD HAS TRULY BLESSED US TODAY. HE TRULY HAS. LET THE CHURCH SAY AMEN."

Jamaal went with Sister Julie to count the money, and he told her how much Uncle Gerald said she could take.

"I'll agree to his amount but that doesn't mean I will always do what he says. He won't bother me much. I know him, Jamaal. You're too young to know but trust me. Your uncle hasn't always been holy. I'll just leave it at that."

"Okay," Jamaal said as he watched Sister Julie begin counting the money.

Once she was done, Sister Julie took her money, gave Jamaal one hundred dollars in twenty-dollar denominations, and wrote exactly what his uncle asked her to write on the envelope.

Then she stood up, pulled Jamaal's face to hers and kissed him on the lips. The kiss was longer and deeper than the last time, and this time Sister Julie also pressed her body against his.

Jamaal stood frozen, but his body was hot and… excited.

"That's cute." Sister Julie said, looking at where Jamaal's pants protruded.

"Oh." Jamaal bent slightly and ineffectually and tried to adjust himself without Sister Julie noticing.

"You know I am right here, right?" Sister Julie said, smiling widely. "It is nothing I haven't seen before. Calm down."

"Okay," Jamaal quickly replied, feeling anything but calm.

"Bye."

Jamaal waited for Sister Julie to close the door behind her. Once she was gone, he exhaled and thought of Marie which reminded him to take out the pocket square he had in his coat pocket and wipe Sister Julie's lipstick off his mouth.

Jamaal smiled, feeling proud that he had planned this time.

+++

Jamaal watched from the back of the office as his uncle-pastor handed the envelope to Regional Bishop Ross W.L. Patton while thanking him for visiting and helping the church get through the evangelist's meltdown.

"You are welcome, pastor and friend. I am glad I could help. Also, great job raising all that money."

Then W.L. walked to the door.

"Oh, I forgot, he said, turning around as he stood in the doorway.

The room went silent.

"Your annual tribute at our next yearly holy convocation just doubled. I know you raised all that money and kept a nice profit for yourself—you forget how long I've been in the game, friend. So, I'll see you next month. And I expect all your tribute money to be paid on day one. Day one. God bless."

Then W.L. turned toward Jamaal.

"Young man, I expect you to be at the holy convocation, too. I like how you're growing up."

"Okay," Jamaal said. He knew he would be at the convocation because he had to drive his uncle. He also knew he would try to stay far away from W.L.

+++

"You've been kissing on Sis Julie again, haven't you, Jamaal?" Marie asked when she and Jamaal were outside the church saying their goodbyes.

"She kissed me," Jamaal answered honestly, speaking too fast and not being able to think up a lie. How does she even know?

"Did you try to stop her or even tell her that you don't want her kissing on you with her old self, Jamaal? Or were you just standing there with your puckered lips sticking out?"

Marie pursed her lips and started making exaggerated kissing sounds.

"No. I didn't know what to say," Jamaal said meekly and uncomfortably.

"Do you like kissing her more than you like kissing me then?" Marie's voice had softened.

"No. I like kissing you more," Jamaal answered truthfully.

"Why?"

"I just do." Jamaal didn't know what to say; he was just trying to make sure Marie didn't stay mad at him. Or stop kissing him.

"You sure have a funny way of showing me how much you like kissing me, when you're kissing on old Sister Julie and all you do with me is say 'okay' and 'I don't know' and 'maybe.' Don't you?"

"Okay. Yes. No. I don't know what to say. Sorry."

Marie just laughed. Jamaal didn't know why. And he didn't know why he was so hot right now.

"Okay, well, I'm sure you'll figure it out soon enough. You're young. And cute. And one day you'll be a good kisser. I may help you get there. Bye."

And with that, Marie smiled, touched Jamaal's shoulder, and walked away.

Jamaal thought Marie would kiss him. That's what always happened on TV and the movies. He decided that maybe TV and movies aren't always accurate about how girls act.

+++

"The evangelist won't come back. I made sure of it." Uncle Gerald said on the ride home.

"Good," Jamaal said. The most forceful comment he could muster without using bad words.

"I heard you're getting good at kissing the ladies."

"Heh heh." Jamaal mustered a chuckle through his embarrassment. He did not want to have this conversation with his uncle-pastor. Uncle Gerald continued talking, much to Jamaal's internal disappointment, and Jamaal sped up, hoping to distract his uncle and give him something else to talk about.

"Nothing wrong with being a lady's man, son. Despite what we preach, women aren't all that bad. Don't tell your auntie I said that. Most of them anyway. Ain't nothing like sex, though. Get all you can before you get married. Use rubbers because you don't need babies and you can't support any. Plus, you never know who has a disease. Women will trap you. They are easy, so you don't have to pay for sex. Although, we all pay in the long run. Don't fall in love fast because if she spreads her legs for you, she'll spread them for somebody else. Taste the milk before you buy it to make sure it ain't spoiled. Don't be gay. Nobody likes that. The church is too hard on it, and I preach that same message; I don't believe it's all bad though. A hole is a hole. It's not for me, but I know a lot of gay folk in and out of the church. But don't YOU be gay. Stay away from all those gay singers and musicians. And preachers."

"O-kay." Jamaal was unable to process all of Uncle Jamaal's weird advice.

Speeding up had helped a lot because they were soon home, thankfully. Jamaal turned the car off and opened his door. His uncle touched his shoulder, stopping Jamaal from getting out of the car. Jamaal knew his uncle was about to say something important, so he stopped and looked at him in the eye, something he rarely did.

"Jamaal. Sister Julie kissed you because I told her to. I wanted you to experience some variety and something different than what Marie would do."

Jamaal was listening intently, pushing down his shock and unable to process what he was hearing.

"I have a special friendship with Sister Julie. It's none of your business or anyone else's. So, leave her alone. Marie is your speed, not Sister Julie. And I think you will like what Marie can do for and with you. She's very talented, too."

Jamaal felt his uncle's hand leave his shoulder and thought he was going to be sick. He got out of the car and slammed the door before walking into the house and going straight to his room. He had to pee, but he didn't want to risk seeing his uncle again, so Jamaal sat on his bed for a long few minutes, feeling confused, angry, and mad.

Very mad. His uncle's voice from the other side of his bedroom door was unwelcome.

"Get some rest, son. We get a week off and then it is the church anniversary season, and we have plenty of churches to visit for the next couple of months of Sundays. It should be glorious, and I am praying that God blesses us all. Let's each get our rest."

"Okay," Jamaal said from inside his room, refusing to open his door or to say anything more. Jamaal looked at his history, math, and English books sitting on his dresser. He needed to get caught up on all his homework for last week because there was a new batch of assignments coming tomorrow.

Before falling asleep, Jamaal's last thought was about hope, and he wondered if there was any hope for him at all.

Part Two—Church Anniversary Season

CHAPTER 9

TABERNACLE OF HOLINESS

He said to her, 'Here now, let me come in to you.' And she said, 'What will you give me, that you may come in to me?' ~ Genesis 38:16

"Jamaal! Come on Jamaal! I'm not calling you again, and I won't let you make me late again!" Uncle Gerald yelled from the car in the garage where he waited impatiently for Jamaal to climb behind the steering wheel. Uncle Gerald would later lecture Jamaal that he was, in fact, very patient and that it was Jamaal who wore his patience down every time he was slow to get to the car.

"Okay," Jamaal replied. Jamaal didn't care because, of all the church events he was forced to attend, Church Anniversary Season was the series of events he most dreaded.

Anniversary Season happened every year when most churches in the area celebrated their own pastor and wife's church leadership anniversary. At least, that was the common purpose given to the public. But Jamaal had come to learn the real purpose: raising money for the pastor and wife so they could attend the annual national convention.

And the money they needed was significant.

Jamaal knew from counting the offerings that his uncle's haul was always between ten and fifteen thousand dollars. His uncle's church was midsized compared to some of the larger churches in the area and those pastors' money haul increased with the size of their congregation.

"How much will Pastor Carter make today, do you think?" Jamaal asked as they drove to Pastor Carter's large warehouse-type church which was on a corner between two busy streets in lower East Oakland.

"Forty thousand. At least. He has close to a thousand members, and he has that local cable show he fundraises on," Uncle Gerald replied.

Jamaal thought he heard jealousy in his uncle's voice.

"Dang," Jamaal said, as they turned into the church parking lot, and followed the instructions of the big man who was directing cars as they entered the gated lot.

Jamaal followed the man's instructions, seeing his uncle wave to the man to ensure they were given a preacher's parking spot, and glided to a stop in a row of cars that were closest to the back entrance of the large church.

Tabernacle of Holiness Community Church was in a former single-story department store that had been gutted and poorly remodeled so that the inside sanctuary was wide open with black church pews, thick, dark red carpeting that looked twenty years old, and a slightly raised pulpit area where Jamaal's uncle would be seated with other guest preachers and church ministerial staff.

Or where they would sit if this church allowed people to sit at all, Jamaal, thought, standing again at the instruction of the minister who was in charge of the praise service.

> GET UP! GET UP! EVERYBODY STAND UP AND PRAISE THE LORD! GOD HAS BEEN GOOD TO YOU SO WHY YOU SITTIN' DOWN?! GET UP AND PRAISE HIM! PRAISE HIM! PRAISE HIM!

Pastor Carter's son, Jr. or "Pastor Jr.," as the congregation unironically referred to him, demanded of the full church. He had been going on for close to an hour and the church was full of energy and a few hundred members dancing, swaying, crying, shout-dancing, or standing with arms outstretched in supplication to God.

Jamaal looked around for his friends but could not see anyone through the throng of standing people blocking all his views to the back of the church, where he knew his friends were. And probably sitting. Punks, Jamaal thought.

"STAND UP! UP! UP! UPPPPPPP!!"

Jamaal begrudgingly stood up, not ready to repeat what had happened with the loudmouth preacher a few months ago.

Jamaal was ready for the praise service, which was now going on for an hour, to end. But it seemed it would only end when Pastor Carter ended it. Jamaal looked around for Pastor Carter, but he was nowhere to be seen.

"Dang," Jamaal said aloud, unconcerned that his words would be heard during the singing, screaming, crying, and general mayhem that was happening all around him. He accepted the fact that without Pastor Carter to stop the praise service, he'd better follow Pastor Jr.'s instructions, just like everyone else not hidden in the back.

"GET BACK ON YOUR FEET!" Pastor Jr. yelled into the large, round microphone, his mouth fully on top of it. Pastor Jr. looked just like his father but shorter, standing barely five feet, five inches tall. He had a booming voice that commanded attention.

"PRAISE HIM, PRAISE HIM. ISN'T HE GREAT? SAY YES. YES. YESSSS!!"

Good god he's loud! Jamaal was about to scream. No one would even notice, he knew, so that took some of the joy out of screaming. Instead,

Jamaal's attention drifted to the deacons, seven large men in black suits, who stood in front of the church, but not on the dais, almost shoulder to shoulder, and with their hands clasped behind their backs. They looked like a presidential security team. Only more deadly.

“Goons,” Jamaal mumbled to himself while he avoided eye contact with each of the huge men, wondering why they stood front and center like they did.

It had been a year since they had last visited this church and Jamaal couldn't remember if the deacons were lined up like that in the past. He decided that it didn't matter because they were now, and as much as he tried to ignore their fierceness, he was, in fact, intimidated by them.

He rejoiced in the instruction to take a seat.

“Move over, punk.”

Jamaal felt Kevin shove him as he pushed past to sit on his far side. Marie plopped down on his other side. As she sat down, Jamaal felt her squeeze his thigh, her acrylic nails digging into his leg.

“Ouch,” Jamaal whispered heavily, and Marie smiled, and Kevin elbowed him in his rib.

“I thought those deacons were going to beat me up, but you two are worse, dang.”

“We been trying to get your attention for an hour. This place is bonkers.” Kevin was now thumbing through a program that had Pastor Carter on the cover standing and pointing to the reader accusingly.

“Where's your girlfriend, Jamaal?” Marie asked him.

“Uh. What? Who?” Jamaal looked straight ahead, afraid to meet Marie's intense pretty eyes and stare.

"That old hag, Sister Julie. Boy, you know who I mean, stop playing."

"I don't know," Jamaal said quickly, hoping Marie would drop it.

"You mad you won't get to count money with her, huh? She's going to be back there with those big-ass deacons looking at her big tits and red lips."

"Marie, shhh. We in church!" Jamaal's intense whisper pushed out spittle; a small piece landed on her bare knee peeking out from her jean skirt. Jamaal was mortified. Kevin was trying to hold in a laugh but failing.

"Boy if you don't wipe that spit off my leg, I swear to God I'm going to scream."

Jamaal used his shirt to wipe Marie's leg, feeling a tinge of excitement to touch it. But he remembered he was in church and quickly thought of baseball to push his budding excitement away.

"Thank you, Sir Drool." Marie smiled as she insulted him.

"Ugh. Don't say that or it'll stick."

"Stick." Kevin started laughing.

"Here you go." Jamaal said as he wiped his shirt—the part that had wiped up his spit—on Kevin's shoulder as Kevin tried to wriggle away but realized he was too slow and pinned in.

"Imma beat yo ass after church, punk," Kevin whispered into Jamaal's ear. When he said "punk" Jamaal felt spit land in his ear and he knew Kevin had gotten his revenge.

"Oh my god, I hate both of y'all," Jamaal said under his breath to the two friends he loved the most.

The pastor's son was still going in the background but now he was leading the praise singing part of the service.

"This guy will never shut up," Jamaal said to his friends.

"I hate him and his stupid voice," Marie responded.

"He looks like a pimp, like his daddy is supposed to be. But that's none of my business."

"You always gotta have dirt on folk, Kevin."

"I just repeat the rumors, I don't make them up, son."

"How long has he been up, Jamaal? We got here after you, and he was already up. Was he up when you got here?" Jamaal again felt Marie touch his leg, and that made him realize she had moved closer to him so that their legs now touched.

"It's been... a long time. Let me think." Jamaal inventoried his memories since he and his uncle had arrived, then thought about when he saw Auntie Meredith come into church perhaps thirty minutes after they did, but then as he pondered his gut feeling he was sure: The pastor's son had been up talking since they had arrived, and it had been ninety minutes.

And now he had started raising the offering and Pastor Carter was still not even in church. Jamaal knew it was unusual to begin raising money without the pastor in the church, but that didn't stop Pastor Jr.

"NOW, WE NEED TO RAISE MONEY SO THAT WE CAN CONTINUE TO DO GOD'S WORK," Pastor Jr. was saying.

> AND WE MAKE NO EXCUSE FOR RAISING MONEY TO HELP OUR PASTOR! MY FATHER AND YOUR FATHER WORK DAY AND NIGHT FOR YOU. WE NEED

TO BLESS THIS MAN OF GOD. THE MAN OF GOD! GOD BLESS HIM, GOD BLESS HIM!

EVERYONE STAND UP AS WE PREPARE TO BLESS THE CHURCH AND BLESS THE MAN OF GOD.

Jamaal stood again but wasn't really paying attention. Pastor Jr. was raising money just like all the other preachers Jamaal had listened to, even if more forcefully. And much louder.

"NOW PUT YOUR HANDS IN YOUR POCKET. USE BOTH HANDS AND IF YOU DON'T HAVE POCKETS LADIES THEN PUT YOUR HANDS IN YOUR PURSE OR WALLET."

Jamaal put his hands in his pockets feeling the two quarters and three dollars that he had in his left pocket, and he had already decided that is where the bills would stay.

NOW I WANT EVERYONE TO COME UP HERE TO THE ALTAR. KEEP YOUR HANDS ALOFT WITH THE OFFERING HIGH IN THE AIR SO EVERYONE CAN SEE, AND WE CAN SEND A MESSAGE TO SATAN THAT HE CAN'T STOP THE MAN OF GOD FROM GETTING WHAT GOD HAS IN STORE FOR HIM. AND IF YOU DON'T HAVE ANYTHING TO GIVE, COME UP HERE ANYWAY SO WE CAN PRAY THE BROKE AWAY FOR YOU SO YOU CAN START TO SHARE IN GOD'S ABUNDANCE.

The crowd now surrounded the altar in front of the large stage that was the pulpit. Jamaal thought there were at least a hundred people that he could see on either side of where he stood. And he knew there were others he could not see. Most people had their hands in the air, bills tightly held in their grip, just as Pastor Jr. ordered them to do.

NOW WHATEVER MONEY YOU HAVE IN YOUR POCKET, PUT IT IN YOUR HANDS, THEN RAISE

YOUR HANDS HIGH ABOVE YOUR HEAD AND START PRAISING HIM. PRAISE HIM! PRAISE HIM! PRAISE HIM!

Pastor Jr. was now screaming at all the women and men standing before him, their hands aloft and almost all with bills scrunched between their fists.

"NOW CLOSE YOUR EYES AND KEEP PRAISING HIM," Pastor Jr. demanded and paced in the pulpit.

Jamaal's eyes were not fully closed, as his curiosity demanded he see what was happening around him. Jamaal had seen plenty of preachers using a wide range of gimmicks and tactics in raising money, with the most egregious being one local pastor who walked atop the pews going aisle to aisle with a common bucket while he asked members to drop their hard-earned money in.

And even that scene was nothing compared to what he was now witnessing.

The goons were simultaneously moving from person to person and grabbing each person's closed hand and literally taking the money out of their hands while each person's eyes were still closed and as Pastor Jr. continued screaming into the microphone.

> *GIVE UNTO GOD WHAT IS GOD'S AND TO MAN WHAT IS MAN'S. THE MAN THE SCRIPTURES MEAN IS THE MAN OF GOD! THE. MAN. OF GOD! SOME PREACHERS TRY TO SAY THE SCRIPTURE MEANS PAY TAXES OR GIVE UNTO CAESAR THAT WHICH IS CAESAR'S. THE DEVIL IS A LIE! HE IS THE FATHER OF ALL LIES! GOD WANTS YOU TO BLESS HIS SERVANT. THE ONE WHO SPREADS HIS GOSPEL! NOW OPEN THOSE HANDS AND GIVE YOUR BLESSINGS TO THE MAN OF GOD!*

Jamaal stood there with his mouth agape and his hands—now with one quarter in each hand—were still in the air, causing his arms to begin to sting from staying in place for so long and reminding Jamaal how much he hated Cross Fit exercise.

"At least I get to keep my fifty cents." Jamaal mumbled to Kevin, who stood next to him, a dollar in his right hand and the program he was holding earlier.

Just then Jamaal felt his arms jerked higher, surprising, and causing him to stand on his toes. His eyes widened and he tried to look over to Kevin for help, but Kevin was also being stretched tall by two other goons, one of which casually placed Kevin's program, that he had snatched from Kevin, in his pocket. The other goon had taken Kevin's dollar.

Jamaal knew his money was as good as gone. He had a fleeting thought of Marie, who hadn't come to the altar with him and Kevin. "I'm not going anywhere near those goons just so they can feel me up pretending to pray over me or lay hands on me. Deacons and preachers are the worst. Bye." And she had walked the other way as he and Kevin were swept away with the rest of the crowd headed to the altar.

The force of the pull from two of the goons shook Jamaal back to the moment just as both of his fists were taken over by bigger and stronger hands. Two goons each had one of Jamaal's closed fists in their giant hands. Each goon worked to pry open Jamaal's fingers and take his quarters. Jamaal attempted to resist but the goons were far too powerful and after a few seconds of feeble struggle, Jamaal relaxed his fingers and allowed his precious quarters to be taken away.

"Damn," Jamaal said to himself, immediately apologizing to himself, because he didn't want to freely curse in church like his friends did. It probably meant his soul was already halfway to hell.

"Shit, may as well go all the way to hell," Jamaal thought.

The long church day had started at 9 a.m. at his uncle's church, so Jamaal was happy when service was finally over. His uncle and Pastor

Jr. talked in hushed voices with each other in the church office, and Jamaal was ready to get home. It was close to eight o'clock and dark outside when they finally left the church.

Relieved they were finally going home, he thought momentarily about homework, but quickly crossed that off his list of what he would do when he got home.

"Don't get on the freeway toward home, Jamaal," Uncle-Pastor Gerald said. "Go toward downtown. We have urgent business."

Jamaal did as he was told and took the freeway entrance headed away from the sweet pillow of his bed and headed west toward the lake area. The freeway was mostly empty, and Jamaal wondered what his uncle was up to. It wasn't unusual for them to go out after late church, but they almost always went out for food, coffee (for him), or dessert. He never just ran errands and even if he did, Jamaal knew there were no errands at that time of night.

Jamaal drove on, both wanting and not wanting his uncle to tell him where they were going. He wished he had tried harder to eavesdrop when Pastor Jr. was whispering to his uncle, but after listening to his voice all night he was the last person Jamaal wanted to hear.

The fog had long ago rolled in, casting the night in a typical Bay Area evening of cool air, wispy fog, and an occasional drop of water. Jamaal chanced a glance at his uncle and saw that his eyes were closed, and his lips were moving. He was praying.

Jamaal slowed his driving to just below the speed limit in case his uncle suddenly told him to exit. They had passed six exits and there were only two more before the big interchange.

Jamaal looked at his uncle, who was still apparently praying, and decided he needed to get an answer.

"Where we going, Uncle?" Jamaal finally asked.

"Take the Grand Avenue exit," Uncle Gerald answered, his voice low, deep, and barely above a whisper.

Jamaal followed his uncle's directions, taking Grand and driving straight before slowing again waiting for directions.

"Turn right up ahead. Then pull up to the building there on the right."

They reached a four-story apartment building on a street that backed up to a small park.

"What's this place?" Jamaal quietly asked. He didn't expect an answer.

"Come with me."

Jamaal followed his uncle to the front double-glass door of the apartment building, then watched as his uncle put his finger on the top tenant's name and slowly moved his finger down, touching each name as his fingers descended. Finally, his finger stopped on apartment number six.

Jamaal looked over his uncle's shoulder at the name: K. Albertina

His uncle pressed the button. The unlocking mechanism sounded, and the door unlocked, and Jamaal followed his uncle down a hall where they stopped at the last door on the left.

Jamaal looked around, not knowing what he was looking for, as he and Uncle Gerald knocked and waited. Jamaal had no idea what was going on, which wasn't unusual ordinarily, but something seemed different this time.

The door opened and out walked a beautiful lady who Jamaal thought was probably thirty years old. She had long straight black hair and her make-up was colorful and, Jamaal thought, very thick. She smelled good, too, he noticed.

She glanced at Jamaal before her pretty eyes settled on Uncle Gerald and Jamaal saw that they looked as if they knew each other.

"Okay then. Come on in," the woman said. Jamaal thought her voice was as pretty as she appeared.

Walking into her apartment was illuminating and Jamaal thought the décor matched the pretty woman. It was so… soft. The colors, textures, lines. There were large, framed pictures of naked women on each of the large walls. The women were sexually posed while doing ordinary things. One was sitting at her laptop, another was standing in front of refrigerator looking inside, while still another was standing but bent over tying her sneakers. In each of the photos the naked men were in the room and watching the women, and between the men and the women were see-through floor to ceiling glass room dividers.

Jamaal saw that smaller framed photos showed similar pictures except in the reverse. The men were doing mundane things while fully naked while the women sat observing.

The women directed them to sit on the oversized sofa. "What will you do?" she asked his uncle.

Jamaal sank into the sofa, which was like sitting on a cloud, he thought. It smelled of a flowery perfume. The woman sat across from them in a stylish modern blue chair which somehow gave her an air of importance. And with Uncle Gerald also sitting on the plush sofa, Jamaal thought they looked like parent and child visiting his school principal.

Except his principal didn't look like the beautiful lady a few feet in front of him.

"Let me see him," his uncle said, as he stood and walked toward a hallway on the opposite side of the room.

The woman followed him.

Jamaal sat for just a moment before deciding he wanted to see as well. He had regretted not eavesdropping earlier in the evening, so he was not going to miss this opportunity.

Jamaal soon wished he had missed this opportunity.

Following the two adults, and the pretty woman's aroma, he walked down a short hall before coming to a bedroom that his uncle had already entered. Jamaal stopped at the door and saw his uncle on one side of a king-sized bed and the woman on the other side. There was an older man lying on his back sleeping. His dick was fully erect.

"He's dead alright," Jamaal heard his uncle say, catching his attention away from the old man with the erect dick that he had thought was sleeping. He knew he had been wrong about that.

"I knew it," the woman started. "We were ..." she looked at Jamaal and paused.

"He knows what's going on, Kay, keep talking, please. What happened?" Jamaal's uncle said to the woman, as they all exchanged looks.

I have no idea what's going on, Jamaal thought to himself.

"Okay, Gerald. You know him. He's a friend and wanted to fuck before church, like usual. He said the church anniversary was stressing him because he needed to raise fifty thousand dollars and he didn't know if he would. So, he wanted to come over for a quickie and I made room for him because, shit, you know I don't like last-second shit from anyone. I could tell he was stressed, too, because at first, he couldn't even get hard, despite what you see there."

Kay waved toward the dead man.

It was then that Jamaal realized he was looking—but trying not to look—at Pastor Carter. Pastor Carter, who didn't show up for church earlier, and the reason Pastor Jr. went on and on. It was now obvious Jr. had been stalling as he waited for his father to show up. And it was now obvious, Jamaal thought, that Uncle Gerald and Pastor Jr. had spoken about this very scene in front of him when they were whispering in the office after church.

"He said he wanted to keep trying because he had taken a pill before coming so he knew he could get it up, eventually. Well, he did. But just as he slipped it in, his body jerked, he straightened as his body went stiff as if he had a cramp, and then he grabbed his heart then… the next thing I knew… he fell right on top of me, just like you see him there," she said gesturing again to the body on the bed.

"I had to use all my strength to get out from under him. I didn't want his bowels to release on top of me. I turned him over and, you can't see it, but the mattress has a bedliner on it—part of the trade, you know—so I'm not worried about, but I guess I will have to throw out the blanket and maybe those thousand-count sheets."

"Kay, please." Uncle Gerald sounded sad and annoyed.

"Sorry, Gerald. I did like him. You know that. His cheap ass was actually very kind. Good in bed too, most of the time. Well, some of the time. It's too bad."

"What did you do after that?" his uncle asked.

"What the hell do you think I did? I screamed and then worked like hell to get him out of me and off me. Took me a few minutes. It was terrible. He was heavy and stiff and… then I went through his wallet and found his son's business card. I knew you were at his church, but I didn't want to call you because, Mered—"

"Yes. I know. Go on."

Jamaal listened and watched with all his attention and each of his senses attuned to what was happening. He certainly didn't miss that this lady Kay knew about Aunt Meredith and that she and Uncle Gerald knew one another, too. He was certain Aunt Meredith did not know they were at this apartment and that she would never know it from Uncle Gerald.

"So that is why I called Jr., to ask him to get the message to you. I don't need the police coming here. So I am hoping you can help in some way."

"Wow." Jamaal didn't mean to talk but he had gotten wrapped up in the woman's words and voice and he just forgot himself for a moment.

Uncle Gerald and Kay looked at Jamaal.

"It's okay, cute young man. I'm not embarrassed so you shouldn't be, either. But he and his family will be if they find out he died here in my apartment," she said softly to Jamaal. She then winked at Jamaal.

"And his church," Uncle Gerald grumbled.

"What can you do?" Jamaal asked his uncle. He didn't think he would answer, mistakenly believing there were still secrets in this room of three adults—two still alive—and a teenager.

Uncle Gerald didn't answer. He left the room and walked to the living area where he picked up the landline phone, punched in numbers, and began speaking quietly.

"Grand Avenue, end of block, press button for apartment six. I'll still be here."

“How old are you?” Kay asked Jamaal, taking his attention away from trying to hear what his uncle was talking about.

“Seventeen, ma'am.”

“You have a girlfriend?”

“No, yes. Well, sorta. I don't know. I think so.”

“That is a perfect answer. Don't be embarrassed. Girls are far more advanced than boys at your age so just go with the flow. Though you will never catch up because women are more advanced than men. She knows what she's doing so if you like her, let her know in no uncertain terms.”

“Oh. Okay. I will. Thank you.”

“How many?”

“How many what, ma'am?” Jamaal was genuinely perplexed and curious. He felt comfortable talking with Kay and he didn't know why.

“How many girlfriends have you had? You are very handsome, and I can't see only one church girl being attracted to you.”

Jamaal was quiet. He thought about Sister Julie kissing him and leaning over in front of him.

“Or, women? I think there are probably a few older ones who may have their eyes on you. That's it, then, young man?”

Jamaal's eyes widened, shocked that she seemed to know his exact situation.

“Yes, ma'am. There is… uh… a… one more. Older, I mean.” Jamaal felt as if he were in a confessional like the Catholics went through.

"With the older one, just... be yourself. It'll take care of itself. She's looking for comfort and a safe space and your youth and good looks take her to that space. But she won't be in that space for long. Don't have sex with her, because you will be hurt—and it's illegal at your age—and it will have lasting effects. But if you kiss or hug or something, don't let it go further. She probably won't anyway unless she's more desperate than I even imagine. In any case, guard your heart, Jamaal, you only get one and if gets hurt or wounded, it can take years to heal."

Kay exuded caring and concern, like Auntie Meredith, but wasn't motherly in the way Auntie Meredith was. Jamaal wondered about his own mother and if she was like Auntie, which he always assumed since they were sisters, or if it was possible, she had been more like Kay. He knew he felt comfortable talking with Kay. She was easy to listen to and hard not to look at. And she was sharp and perceptive in that way Jamaal was realizing older women seemed to be. He couldn't hold her gaze, so he looked around the room, but his eyes went straight to the naked pictures of her on the walls.

"It is okay, Jamaal. Nakedness is natural and should not bother you, but I understand being uncomfortable at your age; it is natural. It took me a long time to accept my body-beauty. And I still have a few issues now and then, but I love myself, so I love my body. And it is okay if you stare at the photos. I won't be offended or flattered. It is art and everyone has their own type of art they love or hate."

"I think you're pretty. Uh, your pictures are pretty, I mean." Jamaal felt himself stammering.

"Have you ever seen a naked woman?"

Jamaal thought about the Playboy magazine he once found in one of the high up kitchen cabinets. He had taken it down, certain that his uncle had hidden it where Aunt Meredith would not look—high up in the cabinets that were rarely investigated because they held old dishes. Jamaal recalled thumbing through it to see the centerfold before he got embarrassed and quickly put it back. But on occasion he found himself taking the magazine out of the cabinet and retreating to his room to masturbate. He was careful not to damage it or put it back incorrectly, lest his uncle find out. Or his aunt.

At the thought of Aunt Meredith finding out, Jamaal closed his eyes and absently shook his head.

“There's a lot going on in that head of yours, isn't there?”

Jamaal chuckled and closed his thoughts, irrationally fearing Kay could see inside his mind.

“Are you a… prostitute?” Jamaal didn't know where the question came from or why he even blurted out like he did. He felt the blood rush to his head and sweat form on his hands. For some reason he thought of how sweaty his hands were with Marie and that made him even more nervous, pushing his emotions in a vicious cycle.

“Settle down. You look like you're about to faint, Jamaal. I am a sex worker, yes.”

“Oh… okay. I'm sorry for how I asked.” Jamaal was genuinely sorry.

“I accept your apology, but it isn't necessary. I am also a photographer—all these …” Kay waved her hands above her head, “are my own work. I do boudoir, erotic, weddings and anniversaries, proms, and of course church events. Some of my best customers are church folk.”

Kay winked with her last statement and Jamaal thought he knew what she meant by the wink but there was no way he was going to say anything.

“Church members use all my services, is what I mean, in case you aren't certain what I meant, Jamaal,” Kay said, again stunning Jamaal with her ability to know what he was thinking.

The sound of the door buzzer caused Jamaal to jump. He had been intently listening to his hostess speak to him with respect and not as if he were just some dopey kid staring at her pretty face or her naked pictures on the wall. The buzzer sounded again, and she stood, winked at him, and went to the door where Uncle Gerald stood by waiting for her to open it.

Uncle Gerald stepped aside, and Kay moved past and opened the door. A man entered, shook Uncle Gerald's hand, and followed him and Kay to the bedroom. The man was tall and wore a long black trench coat, and an old-style fedora hat that rested on his head at a tilt. He walked over to the body and placed his hand on the body's neck, lower back, and bottom of the dead man's left foot.

“Dead as all get out. Damn, Ms. Albertina, what you do to him and how much you charge?”

The man, who Jamaal later found out was the city coroner's assistant, George, laughed along with Uncle Gerald and Kay.

Jamaal thought they laughed as old friends laughed and he decided that they were, in fact, all old friends.

“How is Carter's church doing, sir?” George asked Uncle Gerald.

“Pastor Carter,” Jamaal said out loud. Everyone in the room looked at him then turned to one another again. Jamaal wasn't certain why he spoke up but something about them laughing over the dead man's body made him uneasy.

“They will be in good hands. We were there tonight, and Pastor Jr. really stepped up. Raised over twenty-thousand dollars and the church didn't miss a beat with this fella,” he pointed to Pastor Carter lying dead on the bed, “out here screwing his way to heaven. And when I say heaven, I mean that area between Ms. Albertina's legs.”

Uncle Gerald had started laughing before he'd even finished his joke, Jamaal noticed. Kay and George started laughing while Pastor Carter just lay there unable to join in.

“Help me move him to the edge of the bed,” George said to Uncle Gerald.

“What about that boner, George?”

Pastor Carter's penis was pointed upward still erect.

“Let me,” George said. He then grabbed Pastor Carter's dick and snapped it so that it laid flat again.

“Ouch,” Jamaal heard Uncle Gerald say.

“I told him I was going to break him off, but I guess you broke him off, George. At least he went out in style,” Kay said with a sly smile.

George said, “I'll call a couple of my friends and we will get him out of here and over to the morgue. Sir, please call his wife.”

Jamaal watched as his uncle made the call and quietly explained to Pastor Carter's wife that Paster Carter had gone to pray for a lady who was sick before church, and on the way out to his car, he had a heart attack and died. It took a while for someone to call 911 about an old Black man laying down on the street in the neighborhood. The hospital had called her son, and the deceased was at the morgue. Junior would be home any minute.

Jamaal watched his uncle lie without any hesitation, express sorrow without a hint of actual grief but with enough gravity to his voice even Jamaal believed him—despite what he knew.

Jamaal admitted to himself that it was probably a good plan. At least better than telling his wife the truth, he figured. He also thought Auntie

Meredith would almost certainly have a different opinion about... everything he had just witnessed.

Uncle Gerald then called Pastor Jr., expressed his condolences, and told him to head home with this story. He hung up the phone, nodded to George, and said, "Thanks, man. Obliged to you."

They all said their goodbyes, and Jamaal watched Kay hug Uncle Gerald, and then turn to him, pulling him in close and squeezed him tightly. Jamaal inhaled her body and hair aroma and then pulled away, feeling warm. And ashamed. And aroused.

+++

Jamaal pulled into the garage and as his uncle always did when he wanted to tell him something important, he pressed his finger against Jamaal's neck and told him to turn the car off. Which Jamaal always hated because they were in the garage. Why wouldn't he turn off the car? Jamaal knew he was tired, and it had been a long day.

"Listen, not a word, okay?" Uncle Gerald's fingers pressed harder into Jamaal's lower neck.

"Okay."

"Pastor Carter is respected, his church is respected, and his family deserves to have a proper homegoing for him. Nobody needs to know what happened there and what you saw tonight. And certainly, nobody needs to know about Kay, you understand?"

"Yes, sir, I do. Okay."

"Good, because I am certain I can talk Kay into... teaching you... when you're ready."

"Okay," Jamaal said. It was all he could think to say at that moment. Later he practiced better responses but the best he could come up with was screaming "HELL NO!" to his uncle.

When his uncle's finger left his neck, it signaled that he was free finally to go into the house. Jamaal felt relief and headed straight to the bathroom where he undressed, brushed his teeth, and walked quickly to his bedroom in his underwear. He glanced briefly at his backpack which held all his schoolbooks and homework assignments, and he was proud that for a moment he contemplated doing his English assignment.

The moment passed.

Jamaal laid his head on his pillow and stared up in the dark with his last thoughts shifting between Kay's aroma and the sound of Pastor Carter's penis being snapped.

He tried thinking of Marie's soft kisses, Sister Julie's tight dresses, or even the Playboy that was in the kitchen and out of reach for the night.

"Church anniversary month is going to be crazy again," Jamaal thought as he drifted off to sleep.

CHAPTER 10

SPIRITUAL CHURCH OF COUSIN JEAN

The woman said, 'I see a spirit coming up out of the ground; an old man wearing a robe is coming up.' ~ 1 Samuel 28:14-16

"I'm going over to Cousin Jean's house, okay?" Jamaal asked Auntie Meredith and Uncle Gerald over pancakes, bacon, fried eggs, and a bowl of blueberries.

"Drink your juice, Jamaal. I'm not pouring it back in the container, so don't waste it."

"Yes, ma'am." Jamaal took one long drink and finished the glass of orange juice, ignoring the bitterness that conflicted with the real maple syrup that Auntie Meredith insisted was the only syrup she would allow in her house.

It was Saturday and Jamaal wanted to visit Cousin Jean because her home was like another world.

"Imma spend the night. She said it's been too long since I stayed with her, and she said she's making burgers and apple pie."

"Close your mouth when you're chewing, son," Auntie Meredith admonished him.

“Okay,” Jamaal answered, his mouth full of a new forkful of pancakes. Auntie Meredith rolled her eyes and sipped her coffee, but Jamaal could see her smiling behind her large cup.

Jamaal loved his older cousin Jean. He thought she was strange, eccentric, and sometimes odd. But she'd always been extra kind and giving to him and so he'd taken a liking to her.

“Your weird cousin needs to bring her big butt to church sometimes,” Uncle Gerald piped in.

Jamaal knew this was his uncle's way of giving his permission.

“She's coming to church tomorrow. She said she likes the church we are visiting. Imma spend the night, okay?”

“Just be on time to Sunday school. We have a big day and our visit to the Center of Love will be Holy Ghost-filled. They like to start and end on time so I will not be late, you hear me, Jamaal?”

“Yes, sir. Okay, I will. I mean, I won't. Will,” Jamaal said, stuffing two pieces of bacon in his mouth.

“Stop talking. I will drop you off. After you wash the dishes.” Auntie Meredith, whose plate only had eggs and bacon, took one last bite, and cleared her plate, putting it and her coffee cup neatly into the sink.

“Okay, I'll be done in ten minutes, Auntie.”

They left thirty minutes later after Auntie Meredith inspected the kitchen and made Jamaal clean the table, wipe the counters, and wash and put away her good pans and skillet.

The drive to Cousin Jean's was only a few miles and her house was in a neighborhood that was past its prime with older unkept homes, and inoperable cars on the street, on lawns, and lined up in driveways. Some were on cement blocks, and others were covered with tarps.

It was just past ten in the morning when he arrived at Cousin Jean's home, a bungalow-style house that was about fifty years old. Cousin Jean didn't work, she was on disability for something Jamaal wasn't aware of and never asked. He just thought it was because she was strange.

Jamaal exited the car and walked up the driveway, where he stopped and waved to Auntie Meredith.

"Thank you. See you tomorrow, Auntie!"

"Say hi to Jean for me. And tell her to dress up tomorrow. No pants, please!"

It was a cool morning, and the day was expected to be like every other day—cool in the morning, warming in the afternoon, then cooling again when the fog and clouds returned.

Jean treated Jamaal like a son, though he was a bit too old to be her son. She felt more like his Auntie, but Meredith had that role locked up so, she would just be Cousin Jean to him. Part big sister, part Auntie, part older female friend, and always in his corner.

Jean was Aunt Meredith's youngest cousin, and the age difference meant that Meredith was often left in charge of Jean, like a babysitting situation, when they were growing up. Jamaal's mother, Deborah, was a bit closer in age, and attitude, to her cousin, and the two of them made it hard on Meredith during those babysitting days. Jamaal could tell that his Auntie Meredith still thought of Cousin Jean as a bratty kid, and maybe even resented her a little bit for the close relationship Jean had had with his mom.

Jean had told Jamaal that Deborah taught her about boys, sex, and drinking, and that Jean developed "titties" when she was only ten and fully developed by the time she was fifteen, so Deborah helped her figure out how to fight off those lecherous men who forced their attention on her.

Jean rebelled from all the attention by being open about her sexuality which caused the women of the church to constantly chastise her, shame her, humiliate her, and blame her for the attention the men forced upon her wherever she was in the church.

A famous family story about Cousin Jean was when she went braless to church, and it caused such a ruckus and commotion the choir was asked to not sing because she stood in front—she was a soprano—and refused to wear a choir robe, preferring to wear her white Lauren Hill t-shirt. Like every shirt she wore, it too was tight, but by that time Jean had worn out her welcome with the church, and the church had restricted her for the last time.

When the choir was walking out, Jean waited for everyone to leave and then she faced the church, stood as tall as her five-foot-three frame could stand, stuck her chest out and yelled to the church, "Mary had titties just like these and your Lord and savior sucked her milk all day and all night right from her nipples." She had placed her hands under her breasts and then when she said nipples, she was pinching her nipples through her t-shirt so they protruded even further than normal.

The church mothers were aghast, with most praying louder than when they were praying over a sinner who had decided to repent. The ministers on staff watched and did nothing.

The teenagers were apoplectic, laughing hysterically as they watched Jean finally walk out of the choir stand and down the aisle all the while pushing her chest out like a proud strutting peacock in full plumage.

Cousin Jean had once suggested that that rebellious display might have been partly his mom's idea, or at least Deborah was there and didn't dissuade it. Jamaal got the clearest vision of his mother from his Cousin Jean, and that's one of the reasons he enjoyed her company so much.

And she was always there when something big was happening with him. Whether it was a birthday, school recognition, or the sad anniversary of his mother's passing. Occasionally, she would go back to the church that had shunned her. She rarely said anything, but always was there to hug or arm rub with a kind word that was usually something simple as, "I miss her and love her, too. And I know she would be proud of you."

Jamaal hugged her tighter each time she said that to him, and one time last year he full-on cried in her arms, prompting Auntie Meredith to mention she had never seen him cry.

The stairs on the porch squeaked and there was a bench swing, two old wooden chairs that were probably painted red at one point, and pet crates and beds stacked in one corner of the porch. Cousin Jean didn't have kids of her own, but she fostered animals from the shelter and did pet-sitting for folks from her neighborhood. It was her main source of income.

Jamaal pressed the ringer but couldn't hear the doorbell, so he pressed it again. Jamaal bent down outside the door to talk to one of the outside cats. The dogs were barking inside the house.

"I love it here," Jamaal said to the cat.

A moment before he knocked again, he heard Cousin Jean move the piece of metal that covered the peep hole, and she opened the door. Jamaal was happy to see her, but as he leaned forward to hug her, he abruptly stopped mid-hug, and stood straight up and looked Jean solidly in the face. Jean smiled her biggest smile.

Cousin Jean was in her underwear. Except only on the bottoms. She was naked from the waist up. Her breasts were large and full and hung down her wide stomach to her navel.

Cousin Jean was short and overweight. Some called her fat, but Jamaal thought she was solid and proportional—up to this moment. He still didn't think *she* was fat, but he now thought her breasts were fat since they seemed to be the entire middle part of her body. And they were wide. Her nipples were thick and long and the round area the nipples came out of—Jamaal had no idea what that area was called—were also large, as large and the same color as a toasted hamburger bun, Jamaal thought, trying to imagine a different way to think of Cousin Jean's breasts.

"I just started preparing the food for later. The burgers and whatnot. We won't eat until much later. Come on in." Cousin Jean's voice sounded far away but the word "burger" jolted Jamaal to attention just in time to see Cousin Jean turn and walk away. Her turn caused her breasts to swing so that when her back was to Jamaal, he could still see them for just a moment.

Jamaal stood there unable to move or talk.

"Boy, you gon' see a lot of titties in your life, if you haven't already and if you're even into titties. And if you haven't seen titties until now, well, now you have. Come on in and close the door behind you," Cousin Jean said. She walked into her house, unbothered by Jamaal's mouth hanging open.

"I guess I have seen breasts now," Jamaal said, as he entered the home, causing her to laugh.

"Take the broom and sweep up the living room, sweetie. It's a mess and too dusty. I want it cleaned up for next week."

"Okay, cousin."

Jamaal dutifully swept the living room, then the dining room, both bedrooms, and finally the back porch. Every time he thought he was finished, she sent him off to another room. Maybe she would send him out to sweep the garage next.

By the time he had finished, he was good and hungry. Jamaal had heard Auntie Meredith on the phone tell her how much he had been eating recently.

"Put the broom away, honey, and let's eat. Thank you for doing all the sweeping. The sooner we finish cleaning the sooner we can get to enjoy our day and night. I'm grateful you helped. You've gotten tall since I've seen you. You'll also start filling out soon, as teenagers tend to do. I made you a milkshake. That's your payment for all the work. Deal?"

"Deal." Jamaal smiled as Cousin Jean handed him a tall glass containing lumpy vanilla ice cream, a few peanuts, and a cherry on top.

"Stir it good to mix it all up. My blender doesn't work, so there's milk, but you're the shake."

Jamaal got a spoon out of the creaky drawer that was full of every kitchen utensil Cousin Jean had and began happily mixing his unmixed milkshake.

After lunch, while looking at his empty plate and using a spoon to get the last of his milkshake, Jamaal said, "Cousin, you make the best burgers ever."

Cousin Jean cooked and ate while still topless but had put on sweatpants. Her breasts fell below the table so all Jamaal could see was her chest.

"I really do. You have always liked them. You'll never have burgers, shakes, and titties at the same time again. But then again, maybe you will. You're young and handsome and I heard you and… Marie, is that her name? I heard you and Marie been getting wet with each other."

"Cousin!" Jamaal laughed hard and shook his head.

Of course, she knew. It didn't matter that she wasn't at church every Sunday, nobody gossiped like church folk.

"Letis clean the mess because we're going to have a séance later tonight."

"A what?"

"Séance. We're going to call a spirit back from the dead and talk to them."

Cousin Jean said this all matter-of-factly like she was talking about her delicious burgers. She went about clearing the table, her boobs freely flowing, and she remained unbothered.

"Okay," Jamaal said, in equal parts frightened and intrigued. He never quite knew what was going on in Cousin Jean's head and so he just went with the flow with her because he had to and because her element of excitement was why he loved visiting her.

"Once you finish with the dishes, come to the dining room. I'll be in there setting up the séance."

"Okay," Jamaal answered as he started washing their lunch dishes… and dishes from Cousin Jean's breakfast and dinner from the night before.

"And I hope you didn't bring any homework with you. Do that at your aunt and uncle's house, not here. But if you did bring some, I will be glad to help you after the séance and after our movie night."

"Thank you, Cousin. I have some in my backpack," Jamaal answered, giving about one minute's thought to the Spanish quiz he was supposed to prepare for, as he wiped the counters, the table, and the stove, then neatly folded the dish towel and placed it across the sink divider.

Jamaal readied himself for what was coming next. The great unknown of Cousin Jean's séance.

"I got the table ready for us. You go turn off all the lights and I'll light the candles," Cousin Jean instructed.

"Okay," Jamaal said as he walked around the home turning off all lights. When he was done, the only light in the house was from two candles at the table where they had eaten dinner.

It was now dark outside and in, and Cousin Jean, who was still topless, directed Jamaal to the far end of the table. He had a long day, and was feeling exhausted, a bit scared, and, he had to admit, a bit tired of titty drama.

"Clear your mind, Jamaal. Spirits need clarity in order to enter a home. Close your eyes and think of nothing."

The three small candles in the center of the six-foot dark wood table flickered in a small discordant dance projecting their movements around the room, dancing off walls, ceilings, and Jean and Jamaal's faces.

"Okay," Jamaal said, realizing he had inadvertently been staring at her breasts, resting on the table, when she pulled them off and out of Jamaal's view.

Jamaal instantly relaxed.

"We are ready, spirit. We are honest and we are respectful. Let our presence guide your presence to us. Please come to us."

Nothing happened for about four minutes. The candles flickered their dancing in unison before again separating, their light telling different stories across the faces of Jean and Jamaal, the walls, and curtains.

"Jamaal!" Cousin Jean screamed loudly and stood up, hands on the table, and breasts again resting on top of the table. Jamaal jumped up startled, hands on the table, then looked at Cousin Jean's eyes, then breasts, and back to her eyes again.

"Don't let these big ass titties make you not see the spirit that has come back. Look!"

Cousin Jean pointed to the window that was to the left of where they sat and that looked out to the side of the house. Jamaal turned his head to look at the window, the window that was open.

"Wasn't that window closed, Cousin?" Jamaal asked, his voice quiet. "Did you open it when I was in the kitchen?"

Jean looked to the curtain which was drawn and moving slightly.

"Is that the wind, Cousin?"

"Jamaal, the spirit is in the house now. Look at the shadow! Look! Look!"

Cousin Jean was pointing slightly to the right of the window and curtain where Jamaal was also now looking, concentrating hard and opening his eyes as wide as he could.

"Is that a shadow you see, Jamaal?" Cousin Jean asked, matching her question to what Jamaal seemed to be looking at.

"It's just the candles, Cousin."

Jamaal didn't believe the words as they left his mouth because just as he said them, he saw the shadow Cousin Jean saw and it was moving through the curtains.

"That—" Jamaal didn't finish his thoughts as Cousin Jean screamed.

"It's in the house, Jamaal! Let's go find it!"

Jamaal's feet were frozen, and his senses couldn't settle into normalcy with the big breasts, candles, wind, and now, apparently, a spirit in the house.

"GO!" Cousin Jean yelled as she raced through the house screaming for the spirit to show itself, her breasts dancing as wildly as the candle fire.

Jamaal finally started moving. He walked to the hall, past the bathroom and stared into Cousin Jean's bedroom.

"Jamaal, look in the hall closet. Spirits like to hide in closets and mess things up," Cousin Jean yelled from the living room.

Jamaal looked to his right. There was the hall closet. It was a full-sized coat or linen closet, and it had an old-style glass door handle. Jamaal twisted the glass door handle, feeling his sweaty hands tighten to ensure the old knob turned. He slowly twisted the handle, hearing the screech that during the daylight would be annoying, but in the middle a séance and looking for a loose spirit, sounded foreboding. The door opened to blackness and a void of light, sound, depth, energy.

The shove was hard and violent, and Jamaal fell forward hard into the closet, hearing the slam of the closet door over and through the noise of his falling.

Then he heard something that sounded like a scream or a laugh or both.

Jamaal screamed, his budding deep voice fully retreating and clearing space for his youthful high-pitched voice and scream.

As he gathered himself to stand inside the closet that was full of musty clothes and unknown things on the floor, Jamaal felt a presence that moved, placing pressure on his upper back.

Jamaal screamed again after realizing the inside door handle was missing. He banged on the door, hitting it with the side of his fist repeatedly and until the door quickly opened and light instantly blinded him causing him to raise his arm to shield his eyes, while still trying to see who, or what, had opened the door.

“Boy, what are you doing in there?!” Cousin Jean said curtly as she grabbed Jamaal's shoulder and yanked him toward her. She yanked so hard, Jamaal stumbled forward into her and her large, wide dangling breasts.

“Uh. Okay. Uh. Sorry.” Jamaal stuttered, sweating from head and hands, and breathing rapidly.

“Child you really need to get over these titties. They ain't going nowhere. Shit, they too big even for me but it's worse when I wear those stupid bras. Look, I don't know why you closed the door behind you when you went into the closet, but that was dumb. You were scared, too, so I don't know why you even did that, Jamaal?”

Cousin Jean laughed and laughed as she moved away from Jamaal and back into her dining room where she turned on the lights, closed the window, and blew out the candles.

“Why you push me into the closet?” Jamaal asked directly, his voice quivering.

“That must have been the spirit. We brought his whoring ass back and I guess he was mad at you.”

“Who was it, Cousin?” Jamaal was genuinely perplexed.

“Pastor Carter. He died screwing that whore and think nobody knew. We all knew he was a whore. Your uncle knew, too. I wanted to call him back so I could tell him good riddance.” Cousin Jean had gotten a container of ice cream and had started scooping it into coffee cups for each of them.

"How much ice cream do you want?" Cousin Jean asked, already having scooped two large spoonfuls into both cups.

"How do you know how he died?' Jamaal asked, genuinely perplexed because no one was supposed to know.

"Ha ha ha. Child, you think something like that—dying with your penis inside a whore—stays a secret? What will stay a secret is how he tried it with me, too. Got all handsy one night. His stupid ass showed up on my porch uninvited like a damn vampire. Except he wasn't looking for blood, he was a nookie vampire. And unlike you, the sight of these big ass titties was too much for him to handle so he grabbed this one with both hands." Cousin Jean grabbed her left breast to show Jamaal.

"What did you do?" Jamaal suddenly felt bad for Cousin Jean.

"Since his hands were tied up holding my tit, I kicked him in his holy nuts. That was the first and last time he tried grabbing my titties. Come on, let's have our ice cream and watch scary movies."

Cousin Jean carried her coffee cup full of ice cream to the sofa, where she picked up her remote control and turned the TV to the horror movie channel and started the movie before Jamaal had even moved.

Jamaal stood there incredulous, confused, hurt for Cousin Jean, mad at Cousin Jean, and fully enthralled with Cousin Jean.

"Come on, Jamaal, Night of the Living Dead is starting. The original."

Jamaal picked up his coffee cup full of ice cream and sat at the other end of the sofa from where Cousin Jean sat. He looked at Cousin Jean enjoying her ice cream, giant breasts lounging on her stomach, nipples still protruding, and the toasted hamburger area now as dark as the closet he was shoved into by her, no doubt.

"I have to get up early and you have to take me to Sunday school, Cousin." Jamaal said as he tasted his ice cream.

"I'll get you there when we get there. Now shut it and let's enjoy some fake horror."

"You crazy, Cousin, but I love you."

"And I you, Cousin. You're a bit braver than your mom. She would have still been screaming, and would have kicked my ass, too. She was a tough broad. Tougher than… most people.

"That girlfriend of yours better be ready for me, Cousin. Because I will make certain she's tough enough for you and me. I ain't gonna have your momma mad at me and paying me a visit because your girlfriend is a wimp, you hear me?"

"Yes, ma'am, I do. She's not a wimp. Marie is tough. But she's not my girlfriend, Cousin."

"Boy, you can lie to yourself, but you can't lie to me. Your mother couldn't either."

Cousin Jean made Jamaal watch two full length horror movies and he didn't get to bed until well after three in the morning.

"There's nothing that'll top this night for crazy," Jamaal said, as he finally went to sleep across from naked Cousin Jean in her bed, drifting off to the sounds of her steady breathing.

CHAPTER 11

CENTER OF LOVE CHURCH

I sent Moses to lead you, but also Aaron and Miriam ~ Micah 6:4

The choir was singing so loudly the church seemed to be a concert hall, with women and men dancing and shouting all over the church in unison, as if they personally knew and were having a conversation with the beat that the two drummers pounded into the drums and cymbals.

Jamaal was standing and clapping to the beat and watching all the colorfully dressed men and women praise the Lord. The dancing and tribal thumping music had been going on for thirty minutes and there didn't seem to be an end.

This was one of those times, Jamaal knew, that things would not settle down until the pastor shouted himself and stopped, which would have the effect of calming things down. Most of the time, that is.

Today was different. The entire feel of the church was different from what Jamaal knew and understood of the order of things.

The church was modern, having been built only ten years ago in the middle of one of the most violent neighborhoods in the city. And who was brave enough to build a brand-new church in that area? Pastor Augustina C. Meers. After years of male pastors talking about new outreach in the area, she went further and built her new church in the very center of the toughest most dangerous area in the city, and Jamaal admired her for that. The Pastor of Center of Love Church, Augustina C. Meers, was an anomaly in the area. Auntie Meredith had explained it to him one afternoon while they were shopping.

"Look, Jamaal, the national church does not allow women preachers, ministers, evangelists, and certainly not pastors. But Augustina, she did not care what they said or that they said no. She ignored their nonsense, built her church, and they are full every Sunday. And you best believe the money she is sending to the national church helped all those men accept her church faster than they accepted Jesus as their Lord and Savior-if they have, that is."

They had both laughed as Auntie Meredith had retreated to the dressing room to try on five new dresses she had picked out. Jamaal grabbed a seat outside the dressing room.

"Her church is at least three times the size of Gerald's—and growing. So, if you hear your uncle complaining, tell him maybe if he was as open and inviting as Augustina is, maybe his church would start growing again," she continued from behind the curtain.

Jamaal was looking around, hoping no one was listening to Auntie Meredith, who was almost yelling from the dressing room. But none of the other women seemed to care, he saw. In fact, many of them were loudly talking across the department store and they were as loud as Auntie Meredith, so no one paid her, or him, any concern.

"But Auntie, how come she can be a pastor, but no other woman can?" Jamaal spoke as loud as Auntie Meredith had. He looked around and just like when Auntie Meredith was speaking, no one was interested in what Jamaal had to say.

"Her father was a big shot with the national church and folk loved him. She is his oldest daughter and when he was dying but still attending church, the old man told folk she would be his successor and if they had problems with it, to take it up with him before he died. So Augustina became acting pastor when her father was unable to stand or even come to church more than once every couple of months. By the time he died she had established herself as pastor and their church members accepted her, having known her since she was a young girl growing up in the church."

Auntie Meredith returned from the dressing room, dresses draped across her arm, and still talking.

"Most folk, anyway. Some rebelled and after constant fights, she left to start her own church. She used her inheritance and her father's connections to get loans and before anyone knew what was happening, she'd built the church and within a couple of years she grew her membership to close to ten thousand."

"Wow," Jamaal had said. All his life he had heard so much hatred directed at women in his uncle's church that he struggled to understand how she could be in her position. "I'm glad she showed them."

When the music at her church finally died down, Jamaal watched as Pastor Meers got up to talk. Her movements were deliberately paced, like he had seen his uncle do countless times in that preacher way of bringing seriousness to the moment prior to raising money.

She was tall and thin, and her robe hung on her like there wasn't much underneath it. She was very dark with sharp angular features that gave her a royal appearance, her skin was shiny and smooth. When she spoke, her voice was husky, Jamaal thought, husky and thoughtful with a slight tilt-up at the end of each word.

She looked tired, but her warm smile and wide-open eyes gave her the appearance that was familiar: that of an auntie, like Auntie Meredith, Jamaal thought. She looked, as Auntie Meredith did, warm and loving, and not one to allow nonsense.

As she spoke, Jamaal finally took the time to take in the membership, choir, ushers, and others. It dawned on him that there were a lot of women in the church who seemed to be in pairs. And the men who were there Jamaal believed but did not know for certain, were also in pairs.

Couples, Jamaal thought.

Pastor Meers turned her fundraising talk into a mini-sermon and the church membership was back on their feet doing their part of the classic call and response.

Jamaal used the opportunity to slip out of the sanctuary and into the kitchen where dinner would be served after church. The kitchen smells at any Black church were the smells of heaven, and because Uncle Gerald was determined not to be late, they hadn't stopped to eat. Jamaal knew he wouldn't have dinner for another couple of hours. But the smells coming from the kitchen, which was in a separate building adjacent to the main church sanctuary, were strong and Jamaal knew there was fresh hot church food.

Entering the kitchen was like drifting on clouds. The aromas were wonderfully overwhelming and inviting in all the best ways. Jamaal breathed it in, walked over to the counter and asked for a plate. That was all that was needed in the church: Just ask for a plate and you'd usually be served fried chicken, greens, potato salad, macaroni and cheese, string beans, maybe red beans and rice, a piece of lettuce, and one or two pieces of cake, one of which was certainly red velvet. Your drink was something beyond sweet and full of red dye number twelve, or super-sweetened iced tea.

Jamaal didn't pay, and the women working the kitchen were fine with it because they knew Uncle Gerald, so they said they'd also save him a big plate for later and he could pay then. Taking his plate to a table that he could have to himself, Jamaal sat down and dug into his heavenly meal.

Not more than a few minutes later, a young man sat down next to Jamaal, his plate also full, so much that Jamaal was jealous of his full plate.

"Mind if I sit here?" He was a bit older than Jamaal, very handsome, and his suit was tight and fitted.

"Yeah. That's fine." Jamaal answered, absently scooting his chair over a bit, then moving his drink closer to his plate, which was quickly emptying.

He also dove into his plate just like Jamaal had a few moments earlier. They ate and at first didn't speak much beyond a few grunts to indicate how good the food was. But soon the young man started asking Jamaal questions about himself.

"You a preacher's son? I'm Craig. What church do you go to? You like it here?" Craig asked the questions without looking up and while continuing to eat.

"Uhm, well—" Jamaal tried answering but Craig kept talking.

"This is a nice church. I just started going here. You been here before? You like Pastor Meers? I like her. She gets things. Gets me. And my friends. What do you think about women preachers? You ever hear a choir like that? My… friend was the lead singer of the second song. Julian is his name. The cute one up there, you couldn't miss him."

"Oh. Okay. I'll look next time. The songs were good, yeah." Jamaal spoke quickly, before Craig began talking again.

"I'm queer if you can't tell. Gay. Homosexual. Fag. Whatever. I still love God and God loves me. Don't let church folks put you in hell for who you love or who loves you. God don't like ugly and most of those folks who are putting us in hell are sinners, too. I ain't got time for their B.S. Excuse my Black-French."

"You're funny." Jamaal finally got another word in.

"And you're cute. The girls and boys will like you. What's your name? Who do you like, girls or boys?"

"Girls," Jamaal answered.

"I thought so. But don't knock it until you try it, sweetie."

"Okay," Jamaal answered but wasn't sure that was the right answer.

"Now you're funny. What's your name even? I'm just running my mouth and I don't even know who I'm talking to."

"Jamaal."

"Cute. Jamaal. I like it."

"Me, too. How long have you been with your... partner?" Jamaal asked, genuinely interested because he had, up to this point, never had a long conversation, to his awareness, with a gay person who was just a little older than himself.

"Three years. I love him and he loves me. Our families support us—it was rough for a while but now they do. It's a blessing that many of our friends don't have. I got kicked out of my church, though. Kicked out and told I was 'damned to hell.' Oh well. If this church is hell, then I'm staying!" Craig said and they both laughed.

"Can I ask you a personal question, Craig? About being gay, I mean. I've never talked to a person my age who is gay."

"I'm older than you, honey, but thank you for the compliment. You probably have and just didn't know, but that is neither here nor there. Yes, ask away."

"Sorry if I sound stupid."

"Ask. You don't sound stupid at all. Most people our age assume and all they know are homophobic tropes, so I don't mind you asking at all."

"How long have you been gay?" Jamaal wasn't certain he asked his question correctly, but he thought Craig would let him know if he got it wrong. Then he would apologize and try again.

"I was born me. And I'm gay. I have always been gay is what I am saying. I was born me, born gay, day one, minute one. So, God made me this way and I accept it."

"Okay. Sorry. When did you know you were gay?" Jamaal hoped his new question was better phrased.

"I think I've always known but I didn't always know the words and language, sorta how you are struggling now with your words. I knew the hateful language of my church—St. Anthony's Church. Catholics, ugh."

"When did you tell your parents? Was it like TV and the movies with the big reveal and coming out moment?"

"Ha! You're funny. Too cute for your own good. Are you going to eat that drumstick?" Craig said all at once before drinking his red drink.

"You know what you see on TV and the movies? You see white boy stories. You don't see our stories. So, forget that stuff, okay? That ain't it for us. It just ain't. Good for them white boys and their afterschool special versions of coming out." Craig was opening a moist toilette, once he did, he began wiping his hands.

"How did you do it? Sorry I am asking so many questions." Jamaal genuinely was curious and hoped he wasn't offending Craig.

"I came out to my priest when I was ten years old. That's what I had been taught to do; talk to my priest. So, that's what I did."

"Oh, okay. Did the priest tell your parents then or help you tell your parents?"

"Yes and no."

"So, he did tell them, or he didn't tell them?" Jamaal tried to clarify.

"Why you want to know so much about the gays? You curious, Mr. Cutie?"

"I don't know. I just want to know, and you seem nice and so..." Jamaal's voice trailed off before he caught himself. "It's just that in church the preachers are always talking about gay people going to hell and... my uncle is a pastor."

"Pastor Gerald, right?" Craig interjected.

"Yeah. That's him. So, I get to hear what preachers say when they are not in church and... I just, uh, uhm."

"Those preachers can be just as gay as anyone else, huh? They are no different than the preachers who whore around while preaching against pre-marital sex, adultery, and all that. They do it too. We all know. Gay is just easy for all the preachers to rally around and hate. It really is a problem in all communities, but especially ours because we are all we have and what sense does it make to ostracize our own?"

"Yeah, that is what I mean, was trying to say, I guess."

"I know you were. Eat your cake, or those church mothers over there staring at us will have a few words." Craig placed a chunk of yellow cake in his mouth.

Jamaal watched Craig eat before finishing his own red cake.

"Your priest was kind, then?" Jamaal asked, getting back to his earlier question.

"I told my priest and my priest told me he'd show me how awful and sinful being a homosexual was, so he began having sex with me at church whenever I came to confess. He said he'd fuck the gay out of me. I was ashamed and scared to tell my parents because the priest told me they would disown me, and the church would condemn me to hell. I was so young I believed his gaslighting and didn't see what he was doing at wrong—it was rape, in case I am not clear."

"Oh. I… I am sorry. And… sorry for asking, Craig." Jamaal didn't know what else to say and just apologizing seemed… too little.

"Thank you. But don't be sorry, it's not you. It was that priest who took advantage of a young me. He's still there, too. I told my parents and they brought it to the church but... whatever they did, they did a whole lot of nothing. Father Wilford, the rapist. Bastard."

Jamaal could think of no more questions.

Craig was quiet, too.

"I'm sorry, Craig. I shouldn't have asked so many questions."

"Cutie, it's fine. When I told my parents the priest molested and raped me—because that is what that fucker did—he told them I came on to him because I was gay and he was trying to counsel the gay away and that I was now making up stories because I didn't want my parents to know and so, even though I confessed to him, he told my parents. I hate him to this day, the old fucking drunk."

"Gosh."

"Right. Well, the joke was on him because my parents knew or at least suspected, so they weren't surprised at all. Well, maybe my dad was.

More so than my mother. I can't say they were happy-happy"—Craig made air quotes with his hands—"they didn't beat me or throw me out or send me to conversion therapy or any of that shit so, here I am. I left his church and eventually found—this!" Craig waved his hands around pointing to the kitchen.

"I like this church, too, it's different."

"Oh, so you noticed, huh Sherlock? What gave it away, the lesbian pastor, the gay choir, the gay couples? You're so smart, cutie!"

"I noticed but I… I don't know. I guess I didn't know for certain. But, yeah, this place has a nice feel to it. A little lighter and not as heavy as a lot of churches we visit and even my uncle's church."

"You should join. I'll introduce you around and make people jealous. There are some straight girls here that will like you, too."

"I have to go to my uncle's church."

"Well, if you ever want to change churches, you know where to find us. We are very welcoming, as you can see, and we stick to the actual bible and promote loving God, loving each other, and believing in forgiveness."

"Thanks, Craig. I have to go back into church. Good talking with you."

Jamaal went back into church, thinking about Craig's experience in his church and how even after what he had gone through, he had not turned against God.

+++

"How much money did she raise?" Jamaal asked his uncle as they pulled into the garage. It was past midnight and Jamaal's homework would have to wait until the bus ride to school again.

"For the week she raised over fifty thousand. Tonight, she raised twenty-two thousand alone."

"Wow."

"Wow is right. She's not even supposed to be a pastor and she's out-raising us all and she has one of the largest memberships in the area. And she's homosexual."

"Oh, she is?" Jamaal responded, playing dumb because he wanted no part of this conversation.

"She is, and her church is full of 'em. It's why I am the highest-ranking preacher that will even visit her. Her father was a great man. I never thought she'd make a pastor, much less a good pastor but, she is, and I respect that."

Jamaal was surprised by his uncle's apparent openness.

"She and her gay members need to get saved, sanctified, and filled with the holy ghost or they're all going to bust hell wide open," Uncle Gerald added as he got out of the car.

Jamaal sat still for a few seconds before he followed him into the house.

Later as he was in bed staring at the ceiling waiting for sleep to come, he thought about something Craig had said: "I was born me."

I was born me, too, Craig, Jamaal thought just before sleep took him.

CHAPTER 12

ECUMENICAL BREAKFAST

He makes wine that gladdens the human heart ~ Psalm: 104:15

"How did you did you manage to both approve and not approve the liquor store?" Gerald asked Pastor F. "Virgie" Virgil.

"Political skills, my friend. Nothing but skill. I worked both sides and found a way to give the city the backing it needed, show my congregation that I listened to them, and got an all-expenses paid Caribbean vacation for me and the wife," Pastor Virgie said, sipping his coffee and feeling satisfied with himself.

"I followed this story and I gotta admit I never thought you'd pull it off, Virg. They had you cornered there for a minute, didn't they?" Gerald replied and asked.

"Yep, they did. Look, I didn't care for the liquor store at all. And especially a few blocks from here. We've been working for years to clean up this street and I just didn't see how a liquor store would help. And it was going to be owned by folk from Iran and I've got nothing against them, but if a store was going up, why couldn't our people own it? So, I approached it from that perspective."

"Smart," Gerald replied, cutting up the fried eggs and mixing them with his hash browns.

"So that was the first point the city conceded, and I found an investor who now owns twenty-five percent of the store. Now that investor happens to be my son, but he ain't saved anyway. And he likes to drink a little bit... for the stomach's sake, like Apostle Paul said."

Gerald and the other preachers in the room for the monthly ecumenical spiritual leader's breakfast laughed. It was attended by Evangelical, Catholic, Methodist, Baptist, African-Methodist, and Pentecostal, among others. The men were friendly with one another, putting down their religious differences for the sake of unity and common causes that usually centered on jobs, police violence, gangs, drugs, and neighborhood clean ups. They also had been pushing more often into politics and though they could find themselves on the opposite end of mostly democratic positions, they almost always came together to support the eventual Democrats except the Catholics who almost always sided with Republicans. Their dealbreaker was always abortion, though Jamaal had learned from listening to the meetings that priests also paid for abortions—their own babies, and the babies of their kids and parishioners.

Jamaal sat in the back of the kitchen—it was more like a small restaurant, Jamaal noted—listening to all the ministers talk and ignore the music coming from the church above. Most were finished eating and waiting for Pastor Virgie to finish out of respect for it being his church. He noticed Father Wilford was there and wondered if any of the other preachers knew that Father Wilford did things to boys like Craig.

They were at one of the largest, oldest, and established churches in the city, Booker Temple, named after its founder Curtis Booker, who opened the church over eighty years ago.

Now Pastor Virgie led the church and under his leadership the church jumped into city politics. Through his efforts, the church opened its own credit union, three apartment complexes, and owned a city block worth of buildings, offices, and homes. The church wasn't officially part of the ecumenical group, but because Pastor Virgie's church was so prominent in the city, the group included him in their events, and he invited the group to his anniversary services. He was so important that his was the only anniversary the group attended.

"The city knew they needed my agreement to get the liquor store built but my congregation didn't want it there. They pressured our city council person, our boy Fred, to vote no and if he voted no his peers—a voting block'—would as well. They also expected me to lead a protest at the council on the night of the vote. I was stuck. But being stuck is temporary when you have money, and me and my church got a lot of that."

"You paid off Fred?" Jamaal heard Uncle Gerald ask.

"Yes and no. I told him I wouldn't support his re-election if he voted no and he knows he can't win this district without my support, so that took care of him."

"Makes sense. Good move, preacher." Gerald was standing now, as were a few of the other ministers.

"Then I had a meeting downtown with the liquor store owners."

"You did some arm-twisting, didn't you, you gangster-preacher?" Gerald asked again as if he already knew the answer.

"Not really. I merely told them to move all their banking to our bank, to hire a few of my church members, and to sell twenty-five percent of their business to an associate of mine—my son."

"Boss move, Rev." Gerald and a few of the ministers were patting each other on the back while they laughed.

"Oh, that's not it. I needed to secure a bag for the church, too, so they generously pledged to donate three percent of their gross sales to the church. That should be about seventy-five thousand a year for me, uh, the church, if you know what I mean."

"How did you come up with three percent?" another of the preachers asked.

Now Pastor Virgie stood, fixed his tie, pulled up his pants, and looked at his peers.

"Three percent—one percent for the Father, one percent for the son, and one percent for the Holy Ghost."

The religious leaders erupted in laughter and began filing out of the kitchen area.

"Oh, the last thing is—the Iranian paid for me and the wife to go on a Caribbean vacation so that I was gone when the final vote at the city council took place. With me out of town, and my church occupied with meetings and planning that I left them with, there was little to no opposition and certainly no protest during the vote."

When Pastor Virgie and the ministers began filing out of the kitchen area, Jamaal followed the last of them, and Pastor Virgie stopped just outside the door of the kitchen and turned to continue his story.

"That store has been raking in the bucks ever since it opened a few months ago. Hasn't it, Father Wilford?"

The preachers again laughed, and Father Wilford, now red in the face, laughed as well.

"I'm just teasing you, Father. That's how we show our love to one another. You stay away from that store and that liquor, good sir. You are doing fine in your recovery, I hear."

"You and especially Pastor Gerald have uplifted and blessed me, and I am grateful. God is indeed looking over me," Father Wilford responded, the redness highlighting his thin cheeks.

The men smiled approvingly to a person. Jamaal was fixated on Uncle Gerald's reaction which was no different than the other men during Pastor Virgie's speech of wheeling and dealing, nor of Father Wilford's alcohol confession.

Jamaal had watched the men celebrate the jokes on what they called "securing the bag" and realized he had again listened to plots and plans he'd rather not know about. Jamaal followed the preachers, deep in thought about what he had heard. His thoughts settled on thinking about his upbringing that generously described these men as a group of holy men chosen by God to preach His word and lead His flock.

Jamaal sat down in the back of the church so he could do homework, along with Marie, Kevin, other friends, and kids from Pastor Virgie's church. He was surrounded by other young folk also doing homework, but unlike at Uncle Gerald's church, Pastor Virgie spoke up about the large group of kids—there were now about twenty as best Jamaal could determine, doing homework, a few in small groups, older siblings helping younger ones, and a few older ones like Jamaal and his friends in their own worlds and books.

The service was loud and lively and the choir, one of the best in the entire area, were so good Jamaal and the other kids momentarily stopped homework to listen and join in when they sang one of their more popular songs. Once they started raising money though, Jamaal and the other teenagers tuned out and refocused on their homework.

Jamaal was deep into his algebra assignment when out of the corner of his eye he saw an usher walking fast toward the pulpit, brushing past the money counters and other ushers.

The white glove-wearing usher walked straight to Pastor Virgie who was sitting in his pastor's chair watching and listening to the organ music that was now playing as the choir took their seats.

The usher, an older steely-eyed woman in a black dress, sensible shoes, and her hair pulled back into a tight ball, looked intense as she whispered into the pastor's ear. Slowly most of the eyes of the congregation shifted so that, by the time the usher had finished whispering, most of the congregation was looking at the pastor wanting to know what had been so important for usher to spend extended time talking in the pastor's ear during service.

Jamaal watched as well, switching his attention from Pastor Virgie to Uncle Gerald and then back again.

Pastor Virgie was still with his hand on his forehead like he was worrying and in distress. Jamaal saw him lean over to Uncle Gerald and whisper something to him. Jamaal, like everyone else, watched both men and tried to read the moment.

Something happened.

Jamaal then saw Uncle Gerald place his hand on Pastor Virgie's leg and squeeze it just as Pastor Virgie stood up and politely took the podium and microphone away from the minister who was still asking for money.

The music stopped and all eyes were on Pastor Virgie as the congregation waited for what must have been important news to interrupt anniversary fundraising.

"Family," Pastor Virgie started. "I have news. Sad news to share."

The church was eerily quiet. The organ had stopped and there was no movement. The kids in back were at attention, indicating that everyone was listening to the pastor.

"God is good. God is always good, and we don't always know His ways or His reasons." Pastor Virgie started with sober tones and a quiet voice.

"Uh-oh," Jamaal said a little too loudly, causing a few of his peers to angrily look at him. Jamaal knew that when preachers invoked God in the way Pastor Virgie just did, the news was going to be bad.

"I just got word we lost one of our own early this morning."

Many members gasped, and some began looking around for clues and indications of who had died.

"Mother Charles's son, Paul, was shot dead this morning."

The congregation gasped louder and there were sounds of whispered prayers and folk started hugging one another looking around for Mother Charles, who had lost her husband not even a year ago to diabetes.

"Jamaal, look at your uncle, he looks sick," Kevin said, tapping Jamaal on the arm with his English book.

Jamaal looked at his uncle.

"Paul was a good man who struggled. We all know it. Paul was a son of this church and we saw him struggle with drinking and he just couldn't beat it, God bless him."

"God bless him," the congregation responded in unison.

"Kev, the preachers were just talking about this before church," Jamaal said with heightened interest, hoping to convey the same to Kevin.

"Talking about Paul?" Kev asked, confused.

"No, talking about drinking and that new liquor store." Jamaal tried to get Kev to understand in a few words what he had learned over a long breakfast and a lot of words, but he knew he was failing.

"Oh, well there are liquor stores all over, big deal." Kevin said, still not grasping what Jamaal was attempting to get across to him.

"Paul was shot outside that new liquor store we all opposed. They say he tried to rob the store to steal alcohol." Pastor Virgie spoke somberly.

Jamaal shook his head at Pastor Virgie's intentional omissions.

"See. That's the store, Kev. Pastor Virgie was supposed to help stop it from being built but he faked it." Jamaal had to quiet his voice after seeing some heads turn to shush him. He was certain though that Kev would finally understand what he was trying to get across.

"Ooohhh. Oh, okay, I think I get it, Jamaal. Damn." Kev said, causing the little kids to begin laughing, which then caused the older kids to shush them, and that caused the older church member to shush them.

"Are you going to ask your uncle, Jamaal? You should," Kev said, answering his own question.

Pastor Virgie went on talking.

"We told them devils not to put the Satan's store in our community!" Pastor Virgie's voice was rising, and the congregation's responses were rising in response, righteous indignation growing.

> *THE DEVIL MADE THE CITY PUT THAT DEN OF INIQUITY RIGHT DOWN THE STREET FROM GOD'S HOLY HOUSE! WE FOUGHT THEM—YOU FOUGHT THEM—BUT THE COUNCIL IS GODLESS! NO, WAIT, THEY'RE NOT GODLESS, THEIR GOD IS MONEY! THEY'VE TAKEN MONEY AND THE DEVIL HAS TAKEN OUR SON! WE WON'T STAND FOR IT, WE WILL MARCH ON THAT LIQUOR STORE, WE WILL MARCH ON THE CITY COUNCIL, AND WE WON'T*

STOP UNTIL OUR NEIGHBORHOODS ARE WIPED CLEAN WITH THE BLOOD OF JESUS!

The congregation was now on its feet yelling in unison and support of the pastor's own righteous anger directed at the evil liquor store and city council.

Pastor Virgil ended his announcement by telling the church that he would personally talk to the owners of the liquor store, the police, and the corrupt city council and see what type of redress the family could expect and what kind of redress the church, Paul's home church, could expect.

Jamaal watched as the pastor then told his congregation that tonight was going to be the largest offering of the year, so they could help Paul's family and his mother.

+++

Jamaal looked to Uncle Gerald who was quieter than usual on the drive home. A lot was running through Jamaal's mind, but he stayed quiet, as he usually did. He kept expecting Uncle Gerald to speak up, but he remained quiet with his face stoic betraying nothing.

He thought about what Kev had said, that he should ask his uncle.

Jamaal was replaying the strange day, from the breakfast with the preachers, seeing Father Wilford who had abused Craig, and then the whole liquor store and Pastor Virgie incident and the death of Mother Charles's son, Paul. It was a strange day in a strange anniversary season.

"Will he really lead a march on the store and city council?" Jamaal asked, finally breaking the silence as he turned into their home's driveway.

"I doubt it." Uncle Gerald responded somberly and with a flat voice that Jamaal realized he rarely heard from his uncle-pastor.

"But he will speak even more at the funeral, which is going to be big, sad, emotional, and great for reminding the crowd about his building fund. He should get a nice bump in members and weekly offerings."

Jamaal was quiet, uncertain how to process what his uncle was sharing, and wishing his uncle had not shared anything at all.

"Funerals can be big business if you know how to capitalize on them. It is a delicate road though because nobody wants to be accused of exploitation.

"Do you feel guilty, Uncle Gerald?" Jamaal felt his bottom lip quiver. He seldom directly questioned his uncle on matters that involved his uncle's words, actions, and his siding with and laughing at the lies Pastor Virgie told his congregation. He could feel sweat forming on his back, but he didn't open the car door. He felt this was an important moment in his relationship with his uncle.

"I do not, son. Pastor Virgie did what he thought was best for his church, community, and his family. That is really all anyone can expect of anyone else."

"Okay," Jamaal responded, completely unsurprised but nonetheless disappointed in his uncle's easy acceptance of all the lies and casual dismissal of Jamaal's concern.

He felt something had changed in how he looked at and respected his uncle, but he pushed down his desire to ask more questions and instead got out of the car and went to his room, tired, confused, angry, and disappointed. It was past midnight, and Jamaal knew he would fall asleep as soon as his head landed on his pillows.

Within minutes, Jamaal started to drift off to sleep, but before he did, he decided he would not be a drinker and would always try to tell the truth.

CHAPTER 13

REVELATIONS

Wound for wound, bruise for bruise ~ Exodus 21:25

"Jamaal. Jamaal. Wake up, honey, wake up. It's your uncle. Wake UP, Jamaal, I need you."

Jamaal had been sleeping for less than an hour, in that deep stage of sleep where outside noises integrate with the dreams you are having.

"Jamaal, please. It is your uncle. I think he's having a stroke. Please wake up, Jamaal!"

When Auntie Meredith began shaking Jamaal, like she did when he was young and she wanted him to get up and get his chores done nice and early so that he would have plenty of time to play or watch cartoons, he woke up from a dream in which he was dissecting a frog next to a Bunsen burner. Auntie Meredith's voice was frantic but distant. Jamaal incorporated her urgency into his dream which was now full of stress causing his body to stiffen.

After an unknown amount of dream-time, Jamaal's dream began to fade.

"Auntie?" He heard his own groggy voice as he sat up, eyes blinking.

“Oh, thank God. Jamaal, get up, we're going to have to go to the hospital with Gerald, your uncle.” Meredith did not know why she was identifying Gerald like that, but her mind was so muddled she could have been saying anything.

“Get dressed, honey. We have to go. You are driving. Put your clothes on and come to our room to help me get your uncle covered up.”

Jamaal sat up, confused but also understanding that Auntie Meredith was in distress. Jamaal searched for his pants and t-shirt while trying to shake off the strange dream and wake up. The grogginess would not let go of Jamaal as he searched for socks, now his shoes, and now his jacket. Inexplicably, his mind turned to Marie. He wanted to talk to her, kiss her, and have her there in the house.

Jamaal shook his head and pushed the thoughts about Marie out of his mind.

“Jamaal! Come on, son. Come on. He's not going to die on me tonight!”

Jamaal jumped hearing Auntie Meredith both stressed and determined. Angry even, and certainly rushed.

“Yes, ma'am. Here I come, Auntie!” Jamaal yelled back, maintaining his respectful tone despite speaking as loudly as he could.

When he turned the corner and entered his Auntie's and Uncle's bedroom, he felt sick to his stomach.

Uncle Gerald was on the floor writhing back and forth, his eyes rolled to the back of his eye socket, and he was naked. Though Jamaal understood that Auntie Meredith stood so she blocked Jamaal from seeing his uncle's groin area.

Jamaal exhaled, then opened his mouth to talk, but he was interrupted by loud knocking at the door.

"Go and open the door, Jamaal. Bring them back here. I will finish covering up your uncle."

Jamaal ran to the door, pulling his pants up as he did so and regretting that he didn't put a belt on. He made a mental note to put a belt on before they left.

"Come in. It's my uncle. He's on the floor and…" Jamaal stammered, unable to find his words.

"Show us where he is." The first responder was a heavy-set man who wore a blue shirt and a Raiders baseball cap. There was woman behind him, then another man behind her. They filled the small hallway.

"Oh, okay. Come on…" Jamaal turned to lead the responders to his Auntie who was yelling for them to hurry.

"Stand back." The woman said, emerging from behind the big man who Jamaal had thought was in charge.

"How long has he been like this, ma'am?" The woman asked Auntie Meredith who had stood and backed away and now stood behind the other two men.

"Fifteen minutes now. Twenty. I don't know. Please just help him."

Jamaal wanted to stand next to Auntie Meredith but there wasn't enough room.

Jamaal watched the woman check Uncle Gerald's pulse, check his eyes, and listen to his heart by placing her head on his bare chest. Jamaal was grateful Auntie Meredith had covered Uncle Gerald.

"Ma'am, what insurance do you have? Do you have a preferred hospital?"

"We've got the church insurance. I'll get the info, you just bring him to the nearest hospital," Meredith said.

"Okay guys, let's get him up. He seems to have had a seizure, but I can't tell what caused it. It could also be a mild stroke. Let's get him up and take him in."

"Jamaal, get the car ready. We are going to follow. Go." Auntie Meredith pointed toward the door to emphasize which way to go, which Jamaal did not mind at all.

"Stay in the fast lane, Jamaal. There's not a lot of traffic, but we don't need to get behind anyone other than that ambulance."

"Okay, Auntie." Jamaal kept up with the ambulance at a safe distance. He seldom drove Auntie Meredith as she preferred to be in charge of her own car, but tonight she wanted them to drive Gerald's car and Jamaal was pleased since he was used to his uncle's car.

"They are getting off at the next exit, Jamaal. Start to move over."

"Yes, ma'am." Jamaal said as he switched lanes a bit too fast for his aunt's liking.

"I don't want to be in the hospital with your uncle, Jamaal. Be careful."

"Yes, ma'am. I was trying to keep up and—"

"Stop talking and pay attention to the road and the ambulance in front of us. Your uncle says your driving is getting better. Don't make him out to be a liar. Do better, please," Auntie Meredith said matter-of-factly.

He wished the closest hospital wasn't in such a bad neighborhood. He knew that the care in places like this wasn't as good as in some of the better areas, and they sat in the lobby with Uncle Gerald on a stretcher for too long before the triage nurse finally brought him back and he was seen by a doctor and wheeled up to an emergency surgery.

Sitting just outside the emergency entrance and intake areas, Jamaal watched Auntie Meredith pray to herself. Over the last two hours, she had refused water, coffee, snacks, and candy. She was quiet and it was unnerving to Jamaal who wanted to help, but no matter what he offered she said no.

"Auntie?"

"Yes, love?"

"He's going to be alright. Don't you worry."

"Okay, Jamaal. I think so, too."

The lobby was not sparkling clean, and the chairs were uncomfortable and old. It was a busy ER, with ambulances arriving every few minutes, and mostly dark-skinned patients sitting around in wheelchairs and on gurneys waiting to be triaged and seen for the emergency that brought them in there. There were several faded colored lines on the floor and Jamaal guessed if you followed those lines that they'd take you to different departments. He began to consider picking one and having a walk when he heard someone call his aunt's name.

"Meredith Ferguson?"

Jamaal looked up to see a tall striking woman in a long white coat standing in front of him and Auntie Meredith.

"Mrs. Ferguson, I am Dr. Del Rosario," the woman said as Auntie Meredith stood up.

"What is it? What is wrong with Gerald, with my husband?"

Jamaal remained seated, but noticed his aunt was suddenly even more upset than before.

"His appendix burst—apparently a couple of days ago—and the poison that has been leaking into his body almost killed him. He had to have been sick these past few days. Did you or anyone notice anything?"

"Nothing. I mean, he's been in church almost every day and every night these past few weeks but… other than being tired, he seemed… the same. Jamaal, did you notice anything strange with your uncle?"

"Doctor, this is our nephew—Gerald and mine—his name is Jamaal. He was born in this hospital. A preemie."

"How old are you now, Jamaal?" Dr. Del Rosario asked.

"Seventeen," he replied, looking between the doctor and his aunt, who was staring intently at the woman in the white coat. "But what about Uncle Gerald? He seemed fine in church, just tired, like Auntie said."

"He is resting in post-op and under observation. He's developed peritonitis, an infection in the abdominal cavity. He was probably feeling sick for a few days. Had he not passed out tonight, the outcome could have been much worse. He might have developed septicemia; however, this has been avoided."

Jamaal was relieved to hear Uncle Gerald avoided the worst and turned the medical terms around in his head. He watched Auntie Meredith and as she turned to him, he could see that there was something bothering her still. He couldn't figure it out, but he knew it was there because when their eyes met there was—something.

"He is out of the woods, as they say, but there will be work to do. Go home and get some sleep, and when you come tomorrow, he should be awake, and you can spend time with him. We will get him fixed up and then turn him over to you to finish his care at home."

Aunt Meredith, who had been surprisingly quiet, spoke up with a question that seemed, to Jamaal, to be abrupt. "Dr. Del Rosario, did you work here seventeen years ago?"

Dr. Del Rosario turned. "I have been here for a long time."

"I believe you were Jamaal's birth doctor."

"This is a very good possibility, Mrs. Ferguson. I have delivered many babies here over the years."

"His mother, my sister, died here under your care. Her name was Deborah Andrews."

Dr. Del Rosario looked at the ceiling when Aunt Meredith first brought up that she might have assisted in Jamaal's birth. Then she looked at the ground when she heard that my mother had died here. "Deborah Andrews." She looked as though she were rolling the name around in her head. "Of course. I haven't forgotten her. My condolences, again." Dr. Del Rosario spoke, breaking up what was, to Jamaal, an awkward moment.

"Regarding your husband, and your . . . uncle," Dr. Del Rosario looked at Jamaal again before settling her eyes on Meredith, "His healing might take a while. We will send you home with instructions once they are ready to discharge him."

"Thank you, Doctor."

"Good night, Jamaal, it was good to re-meet you. Good night."

Jamaal watched the doctor walking away until she turned a corner.

"Why did you say that to her, Auntie?" Jamaal felt his lip again shiver, as it did earlier in the evening when he asked his uncle about Pastor Virgie's lie.

“Not tonight, Jamaal. Let's get your uncle healed and headed home. We need to talk, but not tonight, okay?”

“Talk about what?”

“Never mind, Jamaal. Never mind.”

“If it's about my mother, I want to know, Auntie.” Jamaal held in his breathing, which was choppy, causing his voice to also be choppy.

Aunt Meredith was quiet all the way home.

+++

Neither had slept much after going home. And Auntie Meredith woke Jamaal at six, telling him to get showered and dressed because she wanted to be at the hospital when Uncle Gerald woke up.

Jamaal did what she said and then before they left, he phoned both Marie and Kev, telling them what had happened despite Auntie Meredith admonishing him not to tell anyone because, “Once one church person know, everyone will know.”

“Yes, ma'am,” Jamaal had said knowing full well he would tell his two best friends.

“I told Pastor Virgie since that is one of his best friends,” she continued. “I asked him to keep it quiet, too, so I am hoping he does but the way preachers talk, there's no guarantee, so we will just have to see, I suppose.”

Jamaal thought Auntie Meredith sounded unlike herself, and, if he did not know her better, angry.

At the hospital, Jamaal and Auntie Meredith found Uncle Gerald just waking up. “Hello, sleepyhead,” she said, gently holding Gerald's hand, having just wiped tears away from her round cheeks.

Jamaal watched, standing off to the side and behind Auntie Meredith. She had been quiet on the drive to the hospital and as they walked into the lobby where Jamaal hoped to see Dr. Del Rosario again. Hearing her say she was there at his birth had made him want to get to know her more than just as a random doctor passing by in the hospital.

Auntie Meredith seldom talked of his mother, her sister, unless prompted. And it was usually an older church member or a visitor who was Deborah's age who did the prompting. But those conversations were brief and seldom. And Uncle Gerald rarely if ever spoke about Jamaal's mother. Only occasionally would he say something about her, and it was always with a quiet voice and kind words.

"She was a kind young lady who died too young, God bless her."

All these years later, Jamaal knew only what Cousin Jean had told him about his mother, and knew nothing about his father. Despite being raised by his mother's sister, he had very few pictures, and really did not even know much about her childhood other than the few stories Auntie Meredith shared, which always, naturally, turned more toward her own childhood rather than his mother's childhood stories.

Jamaal had long grown accustomed to just being left to think about them without much help from his family or church family. He never thought of Uncle Gerald as his father or Auntie Meredith as his mother, even though they raised him and filled the role in most ways, and he was grateful to them and loved them. But he knew he held something back, just like he knew they held something back. He just figured his aunt held back because of the pain of losing her sister and having to raise her nephew who probably reminded her of her sister every time she looked at him.

Jamaal didn't know anything for certain, so he just tended not to initiate talks about it. And their family unit just sort of carried on. Sometimes his life felt like one of those TV shows he watched, and he could just be there and not really do much to affect any outcome or cause anything to happen.

Jamaal didn't hear the initial request from the nurse as she started explaining the at-home treatment of Uncle Gerald's significant surgical wound.

"What do you mean?" Auntie Meredith asked the nurse in a tone Jamaal recognized from having listened to her question his uncle or other church members. "Why wouldn't he stay here—in the hospital—until he is healed? This plan makes no sense." Aunt Meredith's arms were folded across her body and her stance was tense, causing the small area in the room to feel crowded, hot, and filled with anxiety.

When she asked a question in that particular way, Jamaal recognized, it meant Aunt Meredith knew the answer, but she wanted to make certain the person asking the question also knew the answer.

"I mean what I said. Your insurance covers one night in the hospital for this procedure. We will be releasing him to your care. You will need to create as sterile a field as possible. Can you do that?"

"I can clean a house, young lady, yes."

"After setting up a clean zone, you'll need to scrub your hands, nails, and arms and then take a new pair of plastic gloves from the box that you'll need to buy at the pharmacy when you pick up the pain meds. At home you will need to take the gauze out of his abdomen, clean the wound with saline, then re-pack the wound with clean gauze, which you also must buy at the store. Do not let the gloves come in contact with anything before you reach into his wound to take out the gauze that is in there now. Give the pain meds an hour or so before so they have time to take effect before treating the wound."

Jamaal thought about his aunt's problems with the sight of blood and how she couldn't even really deal with a bloody set of knuckles, much less an open abdominal cavity. He thought too about the day he got to slice open a frog in biology class, and how he hadn't read the biology chapter until after class and that was when he learned why there wasn't any blood squirting out of the frog. The strange scene played out in front of him like a TV show as the nurse tried to explain the situation to Aunt Meredith.

"The poison is in his body and needs to be flushed. And because his appendix exploded, the poison is all over, what the doctors call peritonitis—that is why he was so ill and almost lost his life. Now, the way to do that, flush the poison, is to give plenty of fluids and flush the toxins. The wound needs to heal from the inside out, and the way to do that is to leave the wound open and packed so it can drain. The gauze that will be packed inside will collect it and help with healing. After a week or so it should be mostly drained, and then the surgeon will see him again."

Jamaal watched Aunt Meredith shift from foot to foot, swallow hard, and wrinkle her nose, wondering how she was going to get out of this. He knew she usually got her way at home and at church, but this was different, Jamaal felt, because she wasn't just fighting with Uncle Gerald—she almost always won those arguments—or with church members when she could use her clout as First Lady, to settle things like this. But here in the hospital, Jamaal thought, she is just another family member with no power over doctors or staff.

"You all are talking about me as if I am not here," Uncle Gerald said, speaking up for the first time, and Jamaal moved so that he could see Uncle Gerald's face.

Auntie Meredith reached for Gerald's hand, her face showing sympathy and care, unlike a moment ago when it reflected stress and anxiety.

"Mr. Ferguson—"

"I prefer Pastor."

"Pastor, your wife and son—"

"Nephew," Uncle Gerald interrupted, his voice hoarse but loud enough to be forceful even in his weakened condition.

Jamaal had heard his uncle correct people who assumed they were father and son all his life. It didn't always to bother him, but he always noticed how quick Uncle Gerald corrected anyone who made the mistake, and more and more often now, after all this time, his feelings got hurt.

"Nephew, then. Yes. Your wife and nephew—"

"My nephew," Auntie Meredith said, looking at and away from Jamaal as quickly as she could.

Jamaal thought he understood what his aunt was saying: She was his aunt by blood because his mother was her sister, but he wasn't clear why she was saying it. Especially right now.

Why was it important for her to clarify that he was her nephew? She made it seem as if he were not Gerald's nephew and that made no sense. Jamaal decided both his aunt and uncle were stressed and not themselves.

"I am sorry, Jamaal. You know that I cannot, can NOT, clean Gerald's wound. I can't even stand to see my own blood if I prick my finger; I know I can't dress his wound. I just… can't."

"She's telling the truth. I've seen her faint a few times. Once I accidentally tore my fingernail halfway off. I showed it to her and before I could tell her how, I was catching her as she fainted forward into my arms."

Jamaal looked back and forth between his aunt-by-blood and his uncle lying in the hospital bed and then over to the nurse who had apparently seen this kind of reaction before.

"Ma'am, there aren't many partners who look forward to doing a job like this for their spouses. Alternatives are… cost-prohibitive."

"My nephew," Aunt Meredith repeated, looking over to Jamaal.

What she was saying became clear to Jamaal and even the nurse seemed to understand then. It took a moment before it registered with Jamaal what had passed as understanding between his auntie and the nurse.

"Jamaal. I need you to do this, okay? Can you, honey? Auntie doesn't have the stomach for it."

"I… guess so. I think I... I… don't know but…" Jamaal stammered, trying to figure out how to please his auntie but also stating his hesitancy.

"We can talk about it later, okay? I will learn it with you, I just need you to actually do it. But I will be there with you, I promise."

"Meredith, Jamaal can step up. I know he can," Gerald's deep voice interjected, adding confidence that Jamaal didn't have.

Jamaal watched as Auntie Meredith touched Uncle Gerald's arm after he spoke. He then looked at the nurse who was now smiling back at him.

"I know he can, Gerald. I trust him. I just also think we are—both of us—asking too much of Jamaal. He's just a kid and I should be able to do this. I feel terrible. Just awful."

"Don't, Meredith. We have raised him right. Like our own."

"He is our own, Gerald," Meredith said sternly as she looked to the nurse then to Jamaal, then quickly back to her husband. Her face was now strained in a way Jamaal hadn't noticed before.

Jamaal thought they all looked relieved and satisfied that a solution was determined but he also sensed there was more to his auntie and uncle's conversation. He figured there was probably some type of prior medical issue between them that was causing their weird behavior.

He was the solution and it had all happened so fast, he thought. Adults had settled the matter and he had barely gotten a word in. He looked again at his auntie and now she had a half-smile on her face, the kind teachers have when they are half-happy with a student's half-finished project.

"Young man, looks like you're it," Nurse Jazmin chimed in, pulling Jamaal's attention back to the task they all decided he would do.

"The procedure is straightforward, but it requires you to do exactly as I will show you, okay? You are cleaning a deep infection that requires care and delicate movements because of the pain your uncle may experience. I have never taught this to a teenager, but your family believes in you so I will as well."

Nurse Jazmin turned to Meredith. "Health insurance should cover this," she said. She waved her hands over Gerald's prone body as if she were blessing him as part of some ancient healing process.

"But the most his insurance will cover is one home visit which is… clearly not enough. So, we have what we have."

Nurse Jazmin looked at Jamaal before she went on.

"Care is expensive, of course, and many insurance companies cover this procedure, but we checked your insurance, and it is not covered. We encounter this all the time," she said that part directly to Meredith, her face expressive with empathy. "Drains are expensive, pain meds expensive, hospital care expensive, Black folks don't get the same level of care. Insurance? Well, insurance is insurance, right? But the types of policies that I see sold to churches tend to be high in premiums and limited in coverage."

Meredith looked to Gerald who closed his eyes in that way Jamaal recognized as him trying to look prayerful when in fact he was avoiding telling Meredith she was right about something.

"You will be cleaning the wound," Nurse Jazmin continued, ignoring the unspoken communication between Meredith and Gerald. "Come over here and I will demonstrate how to do it. We will clean it before discharge to demonstrate how to properly clean and dress the wound. Usually we ask the spouse, but whoever is willing. Let's get those hands and nails scrubbed and find a pair of gloves for you Jamaal," Jazmin said.

Jamaal did as he was asked, until he was standing beside his uncle and slightly behind Jazmin. He noticed Aunt Meredith had inched toward the door, finding an escape for her eyes and body when and if she needed either. He knew then that she would be no help once Uncle Gerald was back home, despite what she had said just minutes ago.

Turning back to face Nurse Jazmin and his uncle, Jamaal saw that she was rather aggressively removing the bandages that covered Uncle Gerald's wound.

"You okay, Unc?" Jamaal instinctively asked upon seeing his uncle wince.

"Yes. Let her work, Jamaal."

"Okay, Jamaal. Watch closely." Jazmin motioned for Jamaal to get closer. "Closer."

To Jamaal, it looked like the wound in his uncle's side was about five inches wide and four inches long. It was ugly, almost like the edges had been through a meat grinder. The insides were bloody and beige in sharp contrast to his darker outer skin. Jamaal thought the open wound looked like it was sweating. Different than the frog from his class.

"What you are seeing is the poison draining."

Jamaal heard the nurse, but did not react, instead he focused on the fact he was looking deep into his uncle's gut.

"Watch, Jamaal. Gerald, this will feel uncomfortable."

"Go ahead, nurse. I'm ready."

Jamaal held his breath as he watched Nurse Jazmin slowly move her gloved hand into the wound, her fingers slowly disappearing inside Uncle Gerald's side.

Jamaal saw Uncle Gerald's face tighten, his brow furrow, and his eyes close signifying he was praying. When Jamaal looked back to Nurse Jazmin, he saw that her entire hand was now inside his uncle's gut, and all he could see was her dark arm. A short moment later, she started removing her hand and as she did, she began pulling out the gauze that had already been packed inside the wound.

Once the gauze was exposed to air, the smell hit Jamaal's nose with such a force he instinctively turned away, grabbed his nose, and began coughing.

"You will get used to it, and it will get better as the wound continues to heal. Right now, you are smelling the infection. Now, watch as I clean it and re-pack it. We are almost finished." Nurse Jazmin began working again.

Jamaal watched as the nurse first cleaned out the wound with a spray solution.

"It's just saline to clean and sterilize the wound," Nurse Jazmin said. "Once you have used the full bottle of saline solution, use the gauze to gently pat it dry on the inside. You won't be able to get all the water, but just get as much as you can. The gauze will get the rest. Now, when you reach inside, you'll need to remember to pack it as tightly as possible because we do not want air getting in because with the moisture, he would risk more infection and the wound would not heal. So, it will feel uncomfortable to him—and maybe you—but it is important that you pack it as tightly as you can, so that will mean the gauze—and your hand—will touch his insides. That is why you will need to ensure he has his pain medication at least forty-five minutes before you start the process. And, why you must be certain to have very clean hands and gloves."

"Don't worry about the pain meds, Jamaal. I will do that part, honey," Auntie Meredith said, standing in the doorway, her body still poised to walk out of the room.

"Yes. Well, then, you two will both have your jobs."

"Okay." Jamaal didn't have anything else to say, as his mind was still processing that his hand would have to go deep inside his uncle's open wound.

"Then, you pack it tightly—and you should use the full roll of the gauze you will have. Each time you clean and dress the wound, you will use a full roll of gauze, you understand?"

"Yes. Yes, ma'am. A full roll of gauze," Jamaal said, feeling overwhelmed and unsure of himself, despite the nurse and Auntie Meredith having confidence in him.

"The wound is now packed tightly—see? And now I'll cover the wound like this." Nurse Jazmin placed a large bandage over one side of the wound opening, then placed another to fully enclose the wound. Then she placed an even larger bandage over top the other bandages and secured it to them.

"There. Now, that's not hard, is it, Jamaal?"

Jamaal looked at Nurse Jazmin and realized she had placed her hand on his shoulder.

"Yes. How many times do I have to do this changing thing?" Jamaal thought he could do it a couple of times at most. Maybe.

"Every three hours for a week," Nurse Jazmin said, her face telling Jamaal that she fully understood his question and the fear he was expressing.

"Every ..."

"I will be right there with you, Jamaal. I am so sorry to ask you to do this. I should be able to protect you from... a procedure like this, and I feel terrible that I cannot."

Jamaal started to say something to Auntie Meredith, but his uncle spoke up first. "Don't you feel bad, Meredith? Jamaal can handle it."

Jamaal suddenly felt very angry hearing Uncle Gerald so easily count on him to care for him. Jamaal didn't know exactly why it upset him so much, but it did. Jamaal faced Auntie Meredith now. She had stepped further into the room now that the gruesome work was done, and Jamaal pushed down negative comments toward Auntie Meredith that would certainly end badly for him if he dared to utter them in this moment.

"Yes, ma'am. I can do it," Jamaal bluffed, dreading the moment he would soon face.

CHAPTER 14

HOPE CATHEDRAL

Blow on my garden... and let my lover come into his garden and taste its choice fruits ~ Song of Solomon 4:16

"Jamaal! Jamaal! Hey you, come here!" Marie happily yelled at Jamaal from across the street. They were both on their way into church for choir rehearsal ahead of their visit to the next and final church for church anniversary month—the regional bishop's church—Hope Cathedral—and their choir was scheduled to sing two songs. They had been visiting so many churches that choir practice had been canceled all month. So now that the next church visit had been postponed to give the pastor time to heal, Dwayne had announced that attendance at choir practice was mandatory.

"Why are you rushing to go inside? We're early. Let's hang out," Marie said outside the church, taking Jamaal's arm as she often did and squeezing her body to his.

As always, Jamaal felt something when Marie held him like she was doing now.

The couple sat on the stairs of the church talking about a lot of nothing and Jamaal felt good listening to Marie talk. Her singing voice was pretty because her speaking voice was pretty. Jamaal enjoyed listening to Marie talk about her grades, her divorced parents, and how she planned to attend a historically Black college in the South.

"That's a long way away," Jamaal responded when Marie paused.

"And that's why I'm going. I know this city and this city knows me. I want to get to know another city, state, place, and people. I want to explore." Marie looked distant like she was imagining herself traveling the world.

"That would be really, cool, Marie. You should get out of here. I will one day, too. It won't be college though, that's not my thing."

"College is everybody's thing if they want it to be."

"Not really, but I do agree that college can be good. You will be good at college, that's for sure. I'll be at your graduation, that is also for sure." Jamaal was looking right in Marie's brown eyes, and she looked back.

"Come to my house after choir practice," Marie suggested, changing the topic so quickly that Jamaal paused to consider what she was asking.

Jamaal had driven his uncle's car to practice, after promising Auntie Meredith he would only go to the church and then come straight home.

"Come on, Jamaal. You never have a car. We can go anywhere! But I see how nervous you already seem, so just take me home." Marie stood up again, pulling Jamaal with her.

"My Auntie Meredith will—"

"Be mad. Yes, of course. So what? Have a little fun for once, Jamaal. Fun with me. We never get time away from this church and these people. I got one more year before I go away. Just come over, gosh."

Jamaal felt Marie's words and felt she made a lot of sense, and even talking about Auntie Meredith made him think back to the hospital when she said she couldn't change Uncle Gerald's wound and just assumed he would. She really didn't even ask, just assumed he would do it even though he was still a teenager.

Jamaal's mind was reeling as he looked at Marie standing before him, as pretty as ever and with expectation in her eyes. At least he thought that was what he was seeing.

Why should I do her job? If I gotta do her job, I should at least enjoy myself when I get a break. And with Uncle Gerald sick and me having to change him, I get to be outside and free from driving him around to church every night. I really do deserve a break. I hate that Uncle Gerald is sick, but he is recovering, after all, and I will be in charge of him getting better. I deserve a break. With Marie. She sure is pretty. But I really want to do the right thing and maybe going with Marie isn't the right thing right now. But if I am home before ten, it should be fine since I won't have to change him until eleven. Really, if I go it will be no different than if I were sitting at home talking to Marie on the phone. Auntie Meredith didn't mind me talking on the phone with Marie late into the night, so she shouldn't be mad I go with Marie to talk with her tonight.

"Okay let's go," Jamaal said it loud. He felt proud he had logically thought it through, mindfully considered the rights and wrongs of his actions, and thought about how others would be impacted by his decision—all things his aunt and uncle had taught him at home and at church.

"I knew you had balls, Jamaal. Others may think you're a wimp and churchified, and honestly you are and that's why I like you, but also, I always knew you had some dash and dare in. Let's go!"

Marie jogged across the street and Jamaal followed her.

Jamaal felt light and excited. He felt his feet were barely touching the asphalt that suddenly felt like a field of grass and wildflowers. The drive to Marie's home was a blur for Jamaal except for when she placed her hand on his neck and gently rubbed it. Jamaal thought about how annoying it was when Uncle Gerald continuously pressed his neck and shoulders when he drove. He much preferred Marie's hands.

"Jamaal, park there," Marie said, pointing to the house next to her mom's house.

Once inside, Marie told him to sit on the sofa and Jamaal quickly sat down on the sofa that was much lower to the floor than he expected, causing him to sit harder than he had intended and causing the sofa to loudly slide backwards, its legs scraping the hardwood floors.

"Slow down, Hulk," Marie said as she closed the door to the bathroom.

Looking around the small home had Jamaal feeling nervous. He had been in the home once or twice before, but it had been with a few of their other friends during the breaks between morning and evening church when Marie's mother, Magdalena, invited them over for snacks. Jamaal looked across the small living room and looked right into the eyes of Magdalena's large portrait that hung on the opposite wall from where he sat.

In the photo she wore a light blue dress and stood alone in a room, giving her the look of a prime minister. She had a slight smile and her eyes had literal sparkles in them, of the type one might see in a cartoon or anime indicating exaggerated love. Jamaal thought the artist was probably a relative. He continued glancing around the room and noticing things he had not noticed when he visited with his church friends.

The coffee table was older and full of bibles in English and Spanish, and there were family pictures on all the walls—most of Marie, but also of her brother and other men who Jamaal thought could be uncles or grandparents. There were a couple of crosses hanging on the wall, pictures of Michelle Obama, Oprah, and Shirley Chisholm in a row behind the dining room table, and, in a small alcove, a kind of Virgin Mary shrine full of small votive candles and rose petals. Jamaal knew Marie's family used to be Catholic, so he wasn't surprised by the Catholic items in the house, but he was surprised he hadn't noticed them before.

Jamaal thought the house smelled good. It could have been the candles or the rose petals, but he thought it smelled like… Marie. Or she smelled like the house. The house also smelled of food, like a big meal was cooked earlier in the day and the smell lingered.

"Jamaal! Gosh, how many times do I have to call you!?"

"Oh. Yep. What you …" Jamaal never finished because Marie had walked out of the bathroom and now stood in the hallway in front of her bedroom, where she was using her finger to motion to Jamaal.

"Is your mom gonna come home, Marie? I don't want to be in your room if she comes home." The last thing he wanted was Marie's mother yelling at him and then telling Auntie Meredith she had caught him in Marie's bedroom.

"No, she's working. She won't be home until after midnight. She closes tonight and the restaurant doesn't close until eleven, and after she gets everyone to clean up and she feels good they'll finish properly, she will leave. And most of the time she is home after midnight."

"Okay, here I come."

For some reason, Jamaal's legs felt heavier, the floor felt like quicksand, and Marie's room was now a mile away as he trudged across the dining room to the hall, passing the bathroom before he stopped at the doorway of her room.

"Come on, silly. Let's kiss. We can kiss all night, and nobody is going to see us or interrupt us."

"Okay. Yeah. No interruption is hard to imagine."

"You don't have to imagine it. Now come kiss me."

Jamaal took a couple of steps before he stopped at the side of Marie's bed. He looked around her room and, like the remainder of the home, he just barely had memories of it. It was still decorated like she was much younger, though he saw makeup, lip gloss, and multiple pairs of sneakers under the desk upon which sat a laptop, her cell phone, and a small fan that was oscillating, causing a faint hum and a breeze to swish through the bedroom.

"Sit."

Jamaal sat and, using all his bravery, immediately leaned in to kiss Marie, just like she asked.

"Whoa, speedy. What are you doing?" Marie asked, her voice lilting.

"I thought you wanted to kiss?" Jamaal asked, genuinely confused.

"I do, silly. But I want you to kiss me slowly and romantically. Don't just drop your face on mine and stick your tongue in my mouth. That's not at all romantic, Jamaal. Haven't I taught you anything?"

"Ah, okay. Yep. You have. How about this?" Jamaal said as he slowly bent toward Marie, his hand lightly touching her shoulder, and his other hand slipping into hers. He sightly turned his head—remembering what she had told him to do when they kissed in the car—and gently placed his lips on her, smiling as he did so, before closing his mouth and lightly kissing her on the lips. Jamaal's lips were bigger than Marie's so he felt that they covered hers and he hoped that she would like it.

"Mmmmmm," Jamaal heard and felt Marie's soft hum.

"Now, that was much better. You are almost a Jedi, Jamaal. Jamaal the Jedi, may the force be with you as you kiss me again." Marie laughed at her own silly joke.

Jamaal laughed a silly laugh that was too full-throated, too quick, and his voice was too high-pitched, but he couldn't help himself, and hearing it made his blood boil from embarrassment.

"It's hot in here."

"Are you saying that I am making you hot, Jamaal? Are you complimenting me? How sweet."

"Uh, I am. Uh, not sweet, well, I am sweet. But I am also complimenting you, but I am also hot. Well… I just…" Jamaal stammered.

"Shut it. Come on. We've got time to have fun. Let's kiss some more."

Jamaal's mind was all over the place as he repeatedly kissed Marie. She reclined on her back, or side, and occasionally sat up, while he felt it was best to remain sitting on the side of her bed—just in case. And Marie didn't seem to mind either, so he stayed firmly planted exactly where he had first sat down over ninety minutes ago.

They kissed, talked, and kissed some more until Marie pulled away.

"What's wrong?" Jamaal asked, expecting more instructions from Marie.

"Your hand got really close to my breast, Jamaal."

"Oh, sorry. I didn't mean to, I don't think. I was just trying to adjust how I was sitting because my shoulder is burning."

"Why didn't you just say that, instead of creeping up on my boob?"

"I, uh, I think that …"

"It's fine, silly. It felt good. I wasn't expecting it, but I did like it. Come on, let's kiss some more."

"You've never done it, have you, Jamaal?" Marie asked.

He could smell her minty breath, vanilla in her hair, and maybe lavender lotion that was on her hands and arms. "No. You?"

"Not really. That time that jerk tried to feel me up doesn't count." Marie pulled her panties down.

"Oh." Jamaal felt mad but didn't quite know what to say. They had been kissing now for two hours, and at some point his hand had moved to her breast and she didn't reprimand him, and he knew he didn't want it to end but he thought he needed soon to go home. The thought of Auntie Meredith being angry was giving him anxiety.

"You want to kiss some more, or… do more?"

Jamaal froze and felt his excitement go up and the blood that had been residing in his penis suddenly retract from the fear of the words he had just heard. Of all the reactions he had imagined to just such a scenario with Marie, this wasn't the one he expected. Suddenly, everything in the small bedroom became uniquely interesting and in need of his attention.

"Your curtains are nice and I also like how you have that little cloth-thingie on your dresser underneath all your lip gloss and that jewelry box I bet it plays a nice tune and that little dolphin spins probably, huh, how do you fit all those clothes in that little closet, well I guess you really don't because the door doesn't even close all the way, ha that's funny, where is your phone so we can check our messages and the time, it is getting late, Auntie Meredith… what did you say?" Jamaal paused to ask after realizing Marie had in fact been trying to interrupt him.

Jamaal had never seen what he was now looking at which was just a few inches from his hands.

"Touch it softly and then kiss it just like you were kissing me," Marie instructed him.

Jamaal tended to be a good listener because he was always listening to adult conversations, preacher conversations, and even in school he listened to teachers intensely even though he often ignored their instructions.

But right now, Jamaal celebrated internally that he heard every word, and every instruction Marie gave him over the next fifteen minutes. He did exactly what she told him and when she finally gently put her hands on either side of his head and gently pulled him up, he didn't resist.

Marie kissed him on his cheeks as she held his head.

"That was good, Jamaal."

"Thank you," Jamaal said goofily.

Marie buttoned her pants, kissed Jamaal one more time on the lips, grabbed his crotch and said, "You liked that too, I see."

"Um, yes," Jamaal started, but Marie put her hand over his lips.

"Oh, Jamaal! My mother is here! She must have gotten off early. You need to go, Jamaal! Don't just sit there—go!" Marie shouted as she extended her arm and pointed toward her bedroom door.

"Okay. Dang. Okay. Bye," Jamaal whispered, feeling it necessary so her mother wouldn't hear him. He looked back to Marie and saw that her face looked concerned but also looked like she was holding in a smile which made him smile.

"Why are you smiling at me, get out before she catches us and kills us both!" Marie said again, her hands waving above her head in exasperation.

Marie's voice caused Jamaal to again jump realizing he had misread Marie's face.

"Go out the back door, slowpoke!"

Jamaal heard Marie and turned right after exiting her room and ran down the hallway before he heard the front door open. Jamaal panicked and instead of next turning left to where the back door was, he turned right and found himself in another bedroom.

Just as the front door slammed closed and voices drifted through the house, Jamaal saw another door and quickly hid inside. It was a closet and he tried to measure his breathing so that he could hear Magdalena's walking direction so he could know when to get out of the closet he was in.

Closing his eyes, Jamaal concentrated trying to hear through the doors and walls. He could hear muffled talking and assumed Marie and her mother were talking. It came to Jamaal that Marie didn't know where he was, but she knew he was in the house. She was probably trying to distract her mother so he could leave.

Pushing the door slightly open, Jamaal peeked out and looked into the room he had run into. The clothes on the chair in the corner, the books on the nightstand, the large, oversized pillows on the bed, and then finally, the nightgown laid out neatly at the foot of the bed told Jamaal he was in Marie's mother's bedroom. The place he least needed to be on the entire planet was exactly where he was.

Before Jamaal could think to back fully into the closet and re-close the door, she was in the room. And her boyfriend was with her. Initially Jamaal thought she was talking to Marie and though she probably was, she had also been talking to her longtime boyfriend, but Jamaal had been so focused on listening for Marie, that he had overlooked hearing any other voices.

"I'm tired and I'm going right to sleep," the man said.

"No, you're not. Sex. Remember that? It's been three weeks," Magdalena said, causing Jamaal to recognize for the first time how much Marie sounded like her mother.

"You know what? I'm tired but… yeah, okay, let me use the bathroom. Take off those old jeans old lady," the man said, his voice drifting away, indicating that he was now close to or in the bathroom that was a small doorway on the opposite side of the room from where Jamaal hid.

Jamaal listened as Magdalena hummed a tune to herself as she busied about the bedroom presumably getting ready for bed.

Sex. She's getting ready for sex, Jamaal forced himself to admit. And at that moment he noticed the smell of Marie was all around his face.

"Come on, I'm ready. And you know what I mean by ready," Magdalena shouted.

Jamaal heard the toilet flush and water begin running before, a moment later, the creaking sound of the door opening indicated the man had reentered the bedroom.

"Oh, baby, you look sexy tonight," Jamaal heard the man say. Now it was the bed that was creaking.

Jamaal held his breath, hearing the sex sounds that were only a few feet beyond where he stood. Eyes closed, breathing slowed, and the door of the closet gently touching the tip of his nose, he held as still as he could, not wanting to either open or close the door for fear of it creaking like the bathroom door he had just heard.

"Uh-uh-uh-uh-uh."

Magdalena and the man grunted in unison, the bed creaking beneath them, and Jamaal felt embarrassed, hopeless, and scared while his mind raced to think of Auntie Meredith growing angrier by the second.

"Ugh-ugh-ugh-ugh-ughughughughugh-ahhhhhhhh-ugh-ugh," the man grunted one more long continuous sound before he stopped.

"Okay, you got yours. My turn."

Jamaal wondered what Magdalena meant but he also knew there was no clear way to ask her or anyone sexual education questions at the moment.

"Just three times a week. That is all I ask. I used to want seven, then five, but I know you won't do that, but I need at least three times," she said to the man who had remained silent since he stopped grunting.

"I can do that, babe. I work too much to do more than that. Hell, I get tired, too."

"I just want someone to love and want me as much as I love and want them. You."

"Well, we just did it, so can we relax in this moment at least?" the man asked.

"Come here, baby. Relax on these breasts while you finish me, then you can sleep," she said.

His curiosity piqued, Jamaal tried his best to hear the moans and instructions Magdalena gave the man, figuring he could learn something for his next time with Marie, since he had made it to third base and had little idea of what came next.

It was better than asking a teacher or anyone at church, he told himself as he held his breath and imagined his ears growing.

Each time he responded, she said something else, to do something else, before her moans led to one long continuous sound.

Jamaal decided her last sound wasn't so much a moan, as it was an exclamation of a moan, but one that was passing by and decreasing in depth and volume, like the Doppler effect his science teacher had taught about.

In what seemed like another world of sounds, Jamaal finally heard what he had waited for: the sounds of sleep. He had no idea what time it was, all he knew was he had to get out of this closet and house and get home to Auntie Meredith and Uncle Gerald to change and dress his uncle's wound.

His own breathing had slowed and because he had remained still with his legs locked in place, he felt his legs cramping, his neck was still, and his hands were sweaty. But there was no movement from inside the room and none from the bed, which Jamaal took to mean they were both now sound asleep. As best he could determine, it had been about five minutes since they'd finished having sex.

He knew it was time.

Using his left hand, he gently touched the door to steady it as he then grabbed the door handle with his right hand, being careful not to accidentally twist it and thereby making the old knob squeak.

The door opened and just had the slightest noise that to Jamaal's ears were as loud as an ambulance if one was in the room. He slowed its opening just enough to ensure it did not swing into the tall dresser that was on the other side. Jamaal told himself not to look but his head ignored his protests and turned eighty degrees to his left before stopping just as his eyes focused on the two naked, partially covered bodies of his girlfriend's mother and her boyfriend. He tried not to look at Magdalena's exposed breasts, but it was too late because he was staring directly at them.

After feeling up Marie's breasts, which were small but not too small, and round, and soft as silk, he now found himself staring at her mother's breasts in an absurd continuation of an evening he would never forget, if he could just get out of there to live to think about it.

Jamaal closed his eyes to get Magdalena's breasts out of his sight, and then turned toward the door. The closet door swung back just enough to squeak but it was so low in volume that Jamaal didn't even flinch. He took two steps, and he was at the doorway, then he turned to his left and he finally exhaled, having cleared the bedroom. Looking down the hall he had a lapse in judgement and thought he should go to Marie's room and say goodbye, and kiss her, but he thought better of it and instead pointed his body toward the kitchen and the exit that was just on the other side.

Once out in the night air, Jamaal took in the cool air, then felt his body tighten as it indicated to him his burning need to urinate. Suddenly, he couldn't hold it in. Racing to a big bush that was just a few feet away from the stairs landing, Jamaal fumbled with his zipper as his fingers clumsily struggled to gain a handle on the zipper. Jamaal was certain he was going to spill his entire bladder—he hadn't used the bathroom in more than five hours he was at Marie's house.

The stream of urine sent up warm steam as it hit the cool night air, its familiar smell filling Jamaal's senses.

After wiping his hands on his pants, Jamaal checked the time and saw that it was eleven-fifty. Auntie Meredith would lose her religion when he walked through the door more than an hour late.

+++

Jamaal leaned against the door, exhaled, then turned to lock the bottom lock and then the top chain lock. He pulled the chain with extra emphasis as he if could lock out any memory of the strange and crazy evening he just had.

Slowly walking down the hall, he could hear Auntie Meredith talking so he stopped to listen before letting her and Uncle Gerald know he was home. He knew it was wrong to snoop but he also felt he didn't want to walk into their conversation blindly.

"He should be here any minute, Gerald. Just let your pain medication work and don't worry. Even if he were here, you would still need to wait for the medicine to kick in."

"You should never have let him drive my car, Meredith."

"I don't need to hear you giving me orders right now, Gerald. He is a good boy and I trust him. You trust him. And he is as stressed as I am, and he needed some time alone."

"If you think he's out this late and alone, Meredith …"

Uncle Gerald's voice was raspy and strained. He was exerting himself and talking as much as he was now certainly pushing his stamina while straining his sides.

"I know he has eyes on Marie. Everyone knows. She's a smart girl and he's a smart boy. I am not worried about either of them, and neither should you."

"I'm not worried about him, Meredith, but I do want to make certain he knows the consequences of having sex. The boy needs to be careful because these young girls trap boys like him all the time."

"Then you should have taught him about sex because if you don't, he will learn it on the streets, and you will be a grandfather sooner rather than later. And I don't need to remind you that boys are responsible for themselves, Gerald. Just like girls are."

"That's enough, Meredith."

"Is it? Is it Gerald? Because if Jamaal is old enough to for us to talk to him about safe sex and birth control, then he's old enough to know about his own background."

"Now is not the time, Meredith. I'm sick, we have the anniversary going on, our trip to national church is coming up and—"

"Just say you have no interest in Jamaal ever learning what you and I both know he needs to know, Gerald."

"Not now, Meredith. Not now," Gerald said, exhaling heavily.

"He's going to be caring for you, Gerald, why not now?"

"Not now, Meredith. That's all I will say."

Jamaal hoped Auntie Meredith wouldn't stop. What does he need to know? Is there some mystery? Also, he was enjoying listening to his aunt refusing to give Uncle Gerald the last word. He was surprised to hear his auntie calmly talk about his relationship with Marie, but it was good to confirm his suspicions that she did in fact know about Marie. That meant everyone in the church knew and not just Sister Julie.

"I love Jamaal, Gerald. And I know you do, too. He is my sister's son and I never stop thinking about that. Although I feel with all my heart that I am his mother, I would never suggest he call me that. It is just not right but I feel he misses something just by not uttering the word 'mother'."

Jamaal remembered trying the words "Mommy" and "Daddy" when he was quite young, and his auntie always kindly reminded him that his mommy had passed and he should call her Auntie. Uncle Gerald, however, wasn't so kind, and had yelled at young Jamaal the moment he dared utter "Daddy."

"Auntie?" Jamaal announced himself as he walked in the bedroom door.

Meredith jumped at the sound of Jamaal's voice.

"Sorry I'm late. I was with Marie."

"Sorry didn't do this, you did, Jamaal, and I am very disappointed. I trusted you to come home on time and to keep your word. But you decided tonight of all nights you wanted to be away with that girl. She got her smell all in your nose and caused you to forget your uncle nearly died and needs your help?"

"I'm sorry, Auntie. I can do it now."

"I don't want your apology, Jamaal. I want you to know this is serious and that Gerald needs you. I need you. And before you start, I think we need to talk." Meredith stood up from where she had been sitting to talk directly to Jamaal.

"Follow me," she said as she passed by Jamaal in the doorway and led him to the other end of the long hallway.

Jamaal followed his aunt down the hallway toward the other bedrooms.

"I know what to do, Auntie."

"I know you do, love. But I want to talk to you before you do the cleaning and dressing. You are helping to save Gerald's life. I know I am being a bit dramatic, but I think you know I mean your role is important to Gerald's recovery and healing."

"Yes, Auntie."

"And I would not want anyone else to do what you are about to do. And it is the task, but also the person. The person who is doing this is and should be the closest family relative. And you are that relative, Jamaal. Do you understand me?"

"I think… I do, Auntie?"

"I am confusing you. I have thought about how to say this for so many years and now I can't find my words." Meredith held her hands tightly, she stood straight and certain, even though her words were hesitant. The small hall was crowded, and the warmth of the heater had seemed to gather in the tight space where she and Jamaal stood.

"Should I do Uncle Gerald's dressing now, Auntie?" Jamaal asked earnestly.

Aunt Meredith pulled Jamaal into his own bedroom and shut the door behind them. "He's your father, not your uncle, Jamaal."

Jamaal felt a smile come across his face. Finally, those adults who raised him were deciding to embrace their roles as parents. He nodded and sat down on the edge of his bed.

"We have all hidden this from you. I think you should know that before you start cleaning and dressing his wound. And, before you get Marie pregnant or something."

Jamaal began to process what she had just said. Jamaal had always been quiet and introspective, slow to anger, and inquisitive. The way she mentioned Marie caught him off guard. What were they hiding?

"Jamaal, there is so much to say, but I can't possibly cover it all right now. I loved my sister, your mom, and I know… Gerald had feelings for her, too, and she for him. There's so much for you to learn and I am… sorry… Jamaal, to be sharing this with you now. You had the right to know when you were younger, but… I was afraid to talk for fear you would hate us. We are a family, and you are... like my own son. I love you so much."

"I know, Auntie. I love you, too."

Meredith began to cry.

"I am going to correct an error we have repeatedly made during your entire life, Jamaal. I will forever be sorry because you deserve better. You deserved—deserve, your Auntie and Uncle to always tell you the truth."

"You do, Auntie."

"No, I do not. But I am fixing that right now, love. Uncle Gerald is not your uncle, Jamaal."

"Huh? Who is my uncle then?"

Meredith's broken heart shattered at the innocence and honesty of her nephew's question.

"No, Jamaal. That's not the right question. What I am trying to say, and what Gerald... and I... should have said to you years ago, is that Gerald is not your uncle, Jamaal, Gerald is your father."

"Is Marie my cousin?" Jamaal was still trying to make sense of what Aunt Meredith was saying. Why is she worried about me getting Marie pregnant? What's going on?

"Marie is not your cousin. Listen to me, Jamaal. He is your father, Jamaal. Not your uncle. Gerald is your father." Meredith bent down and put her hands on his shoulders and lined her face up with his.

"Gerald and I were newly married when he and my sister, your mother, had an affair that resulted in her becoming pregnant. Pregnant with you."

"Uncle Gerald is my real father? But he always told me he wasn't my father. He tells everyone that, Auntie."

"Meredith," Gerald's weak but loud voice called from the bedroom.

"It has always been a lie, sweetie. And I told it, too. We both lied to you—for different reasons—but that's no excuse, because the lie we both told was equally harmful to you. I should never have gone along with it, and I am sorry I did. Jamaal, I want you to decide on what you will and will not forgive, though I desperately ask your forgiveness and pray that Gerald will too. Whether you forgive him or not is up to you, baby."

"Okay," Jamaal said. He was too stunned to come up with anything other than his standard response.

"We will talk later, hon, your uncle—sorry, father—needs you to clean and dress his wound. I am sorry, it will take some getting used to, but I promise to work on referring to Gerald as your father. Meredith turned, taking a step toward Gerald's room before turning back to Jamaal.

"Come here." Meredith pulled Jamaal to her. He stiffened but didn't pull away. Then he let her gather him in and hold him. Meredith held him fast. She had betrayed his trust and love and the moment she let him go, their relationship would forever be changed. She never could make it up to him.

When his aunt finally released him, Jamaal tried not to meet her eyes but couldn't help himself. His aunt and uncle had trained him to always look them and all adults in the eye when speaking and he had long stopped looking down and away when talking to adults. Aunt Meredith's eyes were sad but hopeful, and Jamaal was drawn in and didn't want to look away, feeling his aunt had more to say.

But she said nothing, and Jamaal didn't either. The moment passed and Jamaal went to Uncle Gerald's bedside.

"Uncle Gerald?" Jamaal whispered, sensing more than seeing his uncle in the dim lighting that delayed his eyes adjusting after he looked back at his aunt who trailed him by a few steps.

"Thank God you are here, son."

"Yes sir," Jamaal replied, hearing the word "son" differently than he ever had before and suspected ever would again.

"Did you take your pain pill, Uncle?"

"I gave it to him about an hour ago, yes. That is why I was so agitated when you came home. Jamaal. I wanted to make sure we—you—changed his dressing while his pain medicine was still working."

"Yes, ma'am. Auntie. I understand," Jamaal replied, moving over to the dresser where the dressing materials were.

Jamaal tried to forget what his Auntie had just told him and focus on getting through the first time cleaning, sterilizing, and dressing his uncle's wound.

But he couldn't get it out of his mind. All the times Gerald had corrected those who'd assume Jamaal was his son. All the public denial. The more he tried to put it out of his mind the angrier he became. He tried to sort out his feelings about his auntie and uncle-father, but his mind was afire with anger, hurt, shame, and sadness.

Jamaal put on the gloves like the nurse showed him, slipping his hand inside one, then using that gloved hand to being certain not to touch the outside of either one, then deftly slipping on the other glove. Jamaal felt that he had done this part better than he even expected.

The two adults who raised him and who he trusted more than any adults in his life, had also lied to him for his entire life.

Jamaal slowly pulled the current bandage from his uncle's side, noticing the dried fluids and blood that stained the inside of the bandage. Then he ripped the final piece off, before tearing open a small alcohol wipe.

Even though they lied to him, they had cared for him and taken care of him his entire life. Auntie and Uncle had taken him on vacations, taught him to play sports and video games, and allowed him to play on sports teams and try to learn art, computer programming, how to play the piano, and even indulged him every time he decided he wanted to learn to cook.

Jamaal squeezed the bottle of saline solution into the wound, placing a small towel on the bed just below the side of his uncle's stomach. A moment later the excess saline began dribbling from the open wound. Jamaal squeezed more saline solution into the wound until the bottle was empty, and the dribble was a steady, if tiny, flow.

He felt himself getting angry thinking about every time his uncle corrected someone who had referred to him as Gerald's son. The corrections were always immediate and then forgotten. Jamaal had long been used to hearing but not hearing his uncle deny paternity but now it seemed like he remembered every time his uncle denied him. And Auntie, too, Jamaal reminded himself, increasing his anger to the point he now wanted to tell each of them how angry he was.

Jamaal quietly inhaled and, while his left hand was on his uncle's belly, inserted his gloved right hand that now held gauze into the wound.

“Ugh. Ehh. Owww… ehhh… that is uncomfortable!”

Jamaal ignored the sounds of pain. He also tried not to feel good about hearing the sounds. He thought: *Uncle-Father Gerald didn't feel my pain every time questions about my mother or my birth father were dismissed. They didn't feel my pain when I was teased at church by the other kids who made fun of the fact that I had "No mother and no father just like the Old Testament's Melchizedek."*

Jamaal's hand was deep inside the side of his uncle's belly, and he used his fingers to press the gauze into the back and sides of the wound as the nurse had instructed. Once he had placed all the gauze, he began retracting his hand, careful not to bump the inside flesh. But bump it he did, causing his uncle to let out a short intense scream.

When Jamaal was eight years old, Uncle Gerald had given him his first significant whupping. He was having a meltdown over his uncle's order to re-write the multiplication table because he had skipped over the number seven. Jamaal didn't want to do it, but Uncle Gerald told him he would, and in the back and forth, Jamaal had finally lost his temper and yelled, "I WON'T DO IT NO MATTER WHAT YOU SAY, SO JUST STOP TALKING FOR ONCE IN YOUR LIFE!"

Jamaal had screamed in pain when Uncle Gerald grabbed him first by his shoulders, squeezing them tightly, and then again as the man violently shoved and kicked Jamaal into his bedroom, slamming the door behind him. In anger and frustration, Jamaal had kicked, banged, and kicked some more at the door until Uncle Gerald returned, pushing open the door so fast and hard that the doorknob dented the wall behind it. Uncle Gerald had grabbed him again by the shoulders, and launched him through the air, where he landed safely on the bed. But before Jamaal had even completed a full bounce, his uncle had slammed his fist into his stomach with what seemed like his full strength. Jamaal had been unable to breathe and was terrified.

"You damage my shit again, and I will damage you, Jamaal. Don't you try me like that again, boy. Don't do it."

As he remembered this first, of many, whuppings, and thought of the lie he had been told, Jamaal let his hand briefly linger in the wound and then pushed with his middle finger knuckle before allowing the back of his hand to hit the inner walls of his uncle's stomach, his anger streaming from his heart to his hand. He was fully aware of the pain he was causing and he didn't care.

His uncle deserved to feel pain and be uncomfortable, since that's what he has given me all my life, Jamaal told himself as he finally pulled his hand from the wound. He heard his uncle groan and let out a long exhale.

"That was a tough one, Jamaal. I am glad it was you, son, and not your Auntie there. She's heavy handed."

"Gerald. Be quiet. Jamaal is trying to concentrate."

"Yes, sir. I am trying my best." Jamaal ignored his Auntie and briefly thought about hurting his uncle again before deciding to just finish dressing the wound and go to bed.

After fully packing the wound with gauze, Jamaal placed two of the larger bandages on the wound, taped them so they wouldn't move, and then finally removed his gloves.

"Finished. I'm going to bed." Jamaal walked out without waiting for his uncle to speak and he walked past his auntie without looking at her.

The night was long enough with what happened at Marie's mother's house, and now he had to try to sleep with the crazy secret that was no longer a secret that his auntie shared with him.

Laying on his bed on top of his covers and in nothing but his underwear, Jamaal stared at the ceiling seeing nothing and feeling nothing except confusion. He waited for sleep to take him and when it finally did, his body jerked, causing him to wake up anew. Jamaal laid awake just a few minutes before again dozing off. He jerked awake mere minutes later.

"Going to be a long night," Jamaal said aloud. The cycle of sleep and jerking awake continued long into the night.

CHAPTER 15

RESPITE

For we all partake of the one bread ~ 1 Corinthians 10:17

Several days and nights went by in a blur. Jamaal cared for Uncle-Father-Pastor Gerald with minimal words. As the doctors promised, the putrid smells lessened, and the wound began to close. At least, the wound in Gerald's belly did. Other wounds were just as gaping as ever.

"It is time we talked," Aunt Meredith said. "Or rather, time I listened to you. I realize I have done enough talking."

Jamaal ignored Auntie Meredith as she fussed in the kitchen, preparing dinner while he sat in the adjacent room watching college football. He was quiet, as always, hoping she would feel that his quiet now was different. Jamaal knew how to cover his emotions on his face despite his mind being in turmoil. He wanted to hide his feelings from everyone and act as if nothing in his life had changed.

Truth was, he didn't want anything to change. At least now with his relationship with Auntie Meredith.

"How many tacos do you want, nephew?" Meredith was standing in the doorway between the kitchen and family room where Jamaal sat on the sofa on the other side of the room. Jamaal had noticed his aunt was being even nicer to him than she always had been since she had told him about who Uncle Gerald really was. She must feel guilty, he thought, because she lied to him all those times. Maybe she feels guilty for the way she told him the truth. Maybe she feels guilty for when she told him. In a way, he hoped she did.

Jamaal was in jeans, a light green Oakland A's t-shirt, and mid-calf white athletic socks. He had gotten a haircut earlier in the day and had come back home, missing choir rehearsal, and refusing to talk to the choir director Dwayne when he called. It had been a few weeks, and he was not getting any less mad as time passed and his desire to talk about Uncle Gerald was lower than it had ever been.

"Three," Jamaal finally answered.

"Three what?" Meredith answered, playing the game she had always played with Jamaal when he didn't include "please" with his response. She knew he always ate three tacos. She just wanted to get him to talk, and Jamaal wasn't biting.

Jamaal wondered if his auntie regretted finally telling him the truth about his uncle-pastor-father, but he wasn't certain how to ask her and wasn't even certain he wanted to ask.

"Three, please," Jamaal added.

"Three it is. It'll be just a moment, Sweetie."

She was trying to be normal. For him, but also for her own self and for his uncle and the church, Jamaal told himself, and immediately felt bad for telling himself that he was only the third most important thing in his auntie's life.

Jamaal wished he could just start talking to her and not be stuck in his thoughts hoping she would talk to him about all that had happened. He knew they would be able to work through whatever he was feeling—she always made sure of it. He was prepared to yell, blame, accuse, and assign all the guilt to her that he felt she deserved. He wanted her to apologize unreservedly and make her husband do the same.

She brought the plate of tacos to him on the couch and went back into the kitchen to sit down to her own dish.

"The tacos must be good, you're so quiet."

"Mmhmm. They good, Auntie."

Truthfully, Jamaal, thought, he wanted things to return to how they were and just be the same as it always was, with his uncle being rude and dismissive, and his auntie being …

Jamaal never finished his thought as he looked into the kitchen where Auntie Meredith was looking at her phone and drinking water. She seldom ate much, even when she made tacos, eating one at most even though she would prod Uncle Gerald and him to eat as many as they could.

Jamaal bit into his second taco just as on television the A's were scoring another run. He watched the batter hit a long ball that bounced off the wall.

"Jamaal?"

Jamaal turned away from the A's game to see his auntie standing in the space between the kitchen and family room, her arms folded in front of her, head tilted, and her face showing the type of concern Jamaal recognized from her when she was about to say parental things to him.

Jamaal welcomed the familiarity of moments like this.

"Yes, ma'am?" Jamaal picked up his third and final taco, realizing the moment he did that it would appear he didn't want to talk to her.

"You're holding that taco as if you think I want to take it from you." Auntie Meredith moved closer to Jamaal, then sat on the arm of the sofa where Jamaal sat.

Jamaal bit into his taco as the television blared a car commercial during a pitching change in the A's game.

"That commercial is so loud. Can you turn it down a bit? I won't interrupt your game or your eating—you don't have much left, do you? I just want to say something to you, okay?"

"The tacos are good, Auntie," Jamaal blurted out in a way that he knew made it obvious he was nervous.

"Good. I'm glad you like them. Now, before I make you any more uncomfortable, I just want you to know that I love you and I am sorry for when and how I chose to tell you about… Gerald. I am truly sorry, Jamaal. And I want you to know that when you choose to talk about it with me—whether now, or next week, or next year—it will be fine. Or never. It is entirely up to you."

"Okay." Jamaal wanted to say more but he didn't know what to say. He felt his heart begin to race.

"We will work through this like a family and like we always have. I am still your Auntie Meredith, and I always will be. I hope you know that. I'll let you finish that last taco you've been holding onto like it is a piece of gold."

"Okay, Auntie. Thank you. I mean, I will, I uh, the taco, I mean, thank you." Jamaal wished he could just stop talking!

"I understand," Auntie Meredith said as she got up from the sofa and walked into and then through the kitchen.

"Maybe we should go to family counseling because you are dealing with far too much on your own and your sense of family, trust, and certainly love, were all damaged by our actions and words. But what is damaged can be repaired, healed, made better from the experience," Auntie Meredith said from the kitchen sink where she had started rinsing dishes.

"Yes, ma'am," Jamaal said, joining her in the kitchen and sliding his plate into the sink and watching as Auntie Meredith turned on the water and then rinsed it and the drinking glass he handed her before gently placing both in the dishwasher.

"Now, let's go bring dinner to Gerald," Aunt Meredith said.

Jamaal helped her set up the tray with a bowl of rice and meat and a cup of hot tea, as he wasn't quite up for tacos yet.

When they got to the bedroom, Aunt Meredith sat next to Gerald and handed him the tray, and Jamaal hovered by the door.

"Meredith, I am blessed to be home. I want to thank you both for tending to me during this time. Son, take a seat. I have a story to tell you and your aunt. A man of God deserves respect. The respect for religious leaders isn't the same as when I was young. Black folk still know how to act, but white people—uh, uh, uh."

This was the most Jamaal had heard his uncle-father say since they had been home from the hospital.

"Something happened when I was in the hospital for my short stay. You and your aunt were taking a well-earned break from my side, and I was hoping for some fellowship and prayer with the religious leader on duty. Turned out, that was Father Wilfred."

Jamaal cringed at the mention of the pedophile's name. Hearing it here in the context of his uncle-father's story couldn't be good. He hoped he wouldn't be asked for his opinion of the man or asked to confirm or deny rumors he may have heard.

"The Father came by to see me and I had just woken up from a catnap. 'Rev,' he said, 'You look tired, but good. I'm glad to see our Lord has decided to leave you with us a while longer. There's still work to do.' Then, he pulled up a chair to my bed.

"'Father, it is good to see a godly representative,' I said to him. 'I am well taken care of, and I go home later, God willing, and I am truly looking forward to being back at church and being able to fellowship there and with our ecumenical alliance.'

"'As am I, dear friend,' he replied. 'May I pray a healing blessing from the Virgin?'

"'Yes,' I said, 'Of course. We respect the Virgin as well, though we pray straight to Jesus and the Father. I welcome and honor your prayer, Father. I wonder also, if I might, if you can administer communion to me? We do it at my church every fifth Sunday, today, and I missed it for the first time in my adult life.'

"'I will pray, of course,' he told me, 'But I cannot serve you the communion, as you know.'

"Father Wilford was refusing me communion! So, I went on, 'Father, I know you have your rules. We're both ministers of the gospel and followers of Jesus, surely we can share in the communion.'

"'I am sorry you misunderstand,' he said to me, 'but I cannot administer the Holy Communion to non-Catholics. It is against the Church's teachings. However, if you convert to Catholicism I certainly can, but I recognize that you cannot convert here and now. But perhaps it can be a long-term consideration.'

"I was confused! What was I hearing? Why would my friend deny me communion? The communion I had never in my adult life missed except for this day?"

"Oh, Gerald, this is just terrible!" Auntie Meredith exclaimed.

And even Jamaal felt a moment of insult and pity for the man he had known all his life as his uncle, but now knew as uncle-father.

Gerald motioned for Auntie Meredith to pass him the teacup and he took a few thoughtful sips. Jamaal hoped the story was done and that he could get away to his room instead of sitting here with this secret—no longer a secret—still lingering between them. But Uncle-Father Gerald continued.

"'Father, we have been religious friends for close to twenty years,' I said. 'Our group sets the example for our different denominations on how to get along. You and I are personal friends.'

"'Our friendship does not supersede my order's instructions. We do not give communion to those outside of God's grace.'

"'What? I am a man of God, just like you. Saved, sanctified, and filled with the same Holy Ghost as you.' I didn't have the strength to argue with him, but I did remind him of the favors I have done for him, and which I will tell you both now: He is a drinker. And he has been accused of truly heinous sins against God and man. But when I reminded him of this, he merely said, "'My sins are no bigger or smaller than anyone else's, including yours. God's grace covers us all and the Virgin hears our supplications. And I listen to my Holy See. I will pray the Virgin's prayer for your strength and healing. I will not serve you the communion.'

"I never thought twice about supporting him. And now, now I regret it."

Uncle Gerald's eyes were watery as he finished relating this experience to his wife and Jamaal, and the food on his tray was cold.

Jamaal looked at his uncle-father's teary eyes and didn't speak. How stupid of him to think Gerald would have been laying here with thoughts of his own sins? What did any of this have to do with the lie he had been living for the last seventeen years?

“I'm going to bed. Goodnight,” Jamaal said abruptly, leaving the room, but only retreating so far as he could eavesdrop on his aunt and uncle as he had many times before.

“Those days of him hugging and kissing us goodnight are long gone, Gerald. Though Lord knows I wish the better part of those days would return but I guess at his age much of the distancing he's doing is to be expected.”

“If he did it right now, he would be faking it, don't you think?” Uncle Gerald asked, his voice low and rumbling.

Jamaal could barely hear him and only because he had long grown accustomed to his uncle's deep voice.

“I do, Gerald. Those days are long gone, as I said. It makes me sad and, yes, I do not want him to fake it just so we can return to formalities bereft of true meaning, and which only serve the purpose of reinforcing the distance we put in place between us and Jamaal.”

“Oh, okay. Wow. You said that with your whole chest, Meredith. Go ahead then,” Gerald responded.

Jamaal realized he had been holding his breath as Auntie Meredith spoke. He slowly and quietly exhaled, being careful not to move as he did so.

“I know you're feeling better, Gerald, and there is something I need to talk with you about.

“Jamaal is nursing and caring for you. He's doing really good, Gerald, and you should tell him so. I was repulsed and frightened while he just dove right in. We—I—should not have put that on him.”

"Let's not talk about it again."

Jamaal frowned hearing his uncle's words dismissing Auntie Meredith's words.

"You cannot control the narrative of his life forever, Gerald. You know that and that is why you are so angry—"

"I'm not angry, Mere. Stop it." Gerald interrupted.

"Just because you say it doesn't mean it is true. You are angry. And afraid, and feeling like you've lost control, and when you feel that way your words become sharp and hurtful.

"Jamaal is old enough and mature enough to know the truth–his truth."

"Can I just heal, Meredith? We can talk about this later. You're rushing me trying to force me to do what you want me to do, when you want me to do it. You know I don't like being pushed or backed into a corner."

"Seventeen years isn't being rushed. And I told him because I knew you would do exactly what you're doing."

"Why in the world would you do that, Meredith? That wasn't for you to tell and you know it!"

Jamaal noticed Gerald's voice sounded strong again, if only for that one statement.

"It was for both of us to tell, Gerald, but only one of us had the nerve and empathy to do it. Finally. Jamaal deserved to know long ago and we should have sat him down and told him. We are both wrong and it is time we started making it right with him and repairing as much damage as we can and he allows."

Jamaal knew more than anyone how disturbed Uncle Gerald was that his seventeen-year-old secret was out and that he now had no control over where the story went or how and what details would inevitably, exaggeratedly, be added on.

The one thing Gerald hated, Jamaal knew from years of watching and listening to family disagreements, and observations at church, was not having control of whatever narrative he was spinning. And now, there was nothing more important or dangerous to his ministry than his congregation and the other area-wide churchgoers finding out that he had fathered a child out of wedlock and then went on to raise the child as a nephew following the death of the child's mother.

Uncle Gerald's carefully nurtured reputation, his leadership, and his solemn dignity would be gone forever, Jamaal knew. And with his losses, Auntie Meredith would also lose. No one would believe she did not know—and they would be right, of course. Her condemnation would be different but as harsh and it would stick to her, Jamaal knew, no matter what she or Gerald said because that is how church worked—sins were never forgotten.

Auntie Meredith would forever be tainted just like her husband and pastor, even though she was also a victim. Jamaal knew that she would forever be a co-conspirator befitting her partnership and marriage. The pastor and first lady were always a package deal. If he fell, she fell. They could both lose so much, and perhaps that was the driving force—one of them—that kept her quiet for all the years.

Uncle Gerald needed to heal for the final anniversary event that was the biggest church event his church would host, rivaling Easter for attendance, but raising far more money. Jamaal knew that while Gerald was surely thinking and stressed about the need to deliver a dynamic message, he would also be clearly unnerved and stressed by the idea of confronting Jamaal. And true to who he knew Uncle Gerald to be, tough at church and in public but non-confrontational in his personal life, he would find all the reasons to avoid Jamaal.

"You still make the best tacos, Meredith," Uncle Gerald said as he took a bite of his cold meat and rice.

"You need to talk to Jamaal, Gerald. And I do. And then we do, together."

"I know, Mere."

"I know you do. But you haven't done it, have you?"

"The boy doesn't want to hear from me, and you know that."

Jamaal winced at being referred to as "the boy" and became immediately angry.

"Yes. However, you need to hear from him. This is not about you talking, Preacher, it is about you listening."

"He needs to deal with it in his own time, Mere. You can't force it. He is old enough to deal with the truth on his own terms. And in fact, this is why I—we—didn't tell him. Although I am glad he now knows, it wasn't the best timing. I got a big message to preach at the anniversary, and I gotta raise a lot of money."

"What are you even talking about, Gerald?! This isn't about you or your church or money, for goodness sakes. Stop changing the subject to be about you. Stop it! It isn't about you."

"Look, Mere—"

"Do not 'look Mere' me, Gerald. You need to call Jamaal in here and let him say what he needs to say to you uninterrupted. Give him the space to let out whatever he needs to. It is not about you—I don't know how many times I have to say it—it is about him."

Jamaal's heart raced as he thought Uncle Gerald would listen and do exactly what Auntie Meredith told him to do. Jamaal reminded himself that his uncle-pastor-father rarely took orders from anyone. Jamaal felt his anger rise even higher.

"It ain't about you, either, Mere. I guess you conveniently forgot that didn't you?"

Right on cue, Jamaal told himself, feeling nothing but anger, his nervous energy drifting away.

"You feel better, old man? Taking shots at me is still your go-to defensive move, isn't it? You know what? I'm not even here for your… bullshit… Gerald, just stop it."

"If you had kept your mouth shut, we wouldn't be here, and everything would be fine, just like it always was."

Jamaal detected real anger coming from his uncle. He wondered who was angrier.

"It wasn't ever fine."

Something about Auntie Meredith's voice, tone, body language—he knew she'd be marching out of the bedroom any second, and Jamaal snuck fast into his bedroom and shut the door.

CHAPTER 16

THE UNIFIED CATHEDRAL

Oil and perfume make the heart glad, and the sweetness of a friend comes from their earnest counsel ~ Proverbs 27:9

Church was banging. It was hopping. It was the place to be tonight. Better than all the clubs, bars, and gatherings. The Black church at its best, most festive display of humans praising God. Perhaps only surpassed by older traditional churches in some African countries that melded traditional celebrations with Christian and, mostly, Black American celebrations.

But in the States, this was the pinnacle and Jamaal took it all in. It was a relief in a way to be back in church. There was comfort in the common and relief in the familiarity.

After purposely hurting Uncle Gerald the first time he dressed his wound, Jamaal was able to bring himself to dress the wound other times without hurting him. Jamaal felt guilty because he wanted to hurt him and the opportunity was there. Jamaal didn't do it though, the guilt from the first night tore him apart as he had tried to sleep, and into the next day at school. He could not escape his thoughts until the next night when he dressed the wound without incident and without Auntie Meredith standing over his shoulder.

She had been quiet since telling him about his uncle. Jamaal had told himself he never would refer to Uncle Gerald as "father."

After delaying anniversary visits while Uncle Gerald recovered, the services were back on and everyone was feeling the joy that comes with a church leader recovering because it was a big reason to credit God for the sickness and the healing, as proof of God being in charge and able to heal when He wants.

This was the penultimate service of the revival season, and all the area church members were in attendance. It was a happening place to be, and even though the Unified Cathedral held thousands, it wasn't big enough to hold the crowd. There were discussions about renting one of the local sports venues but those were ultimately shot down because "the main night needs to be in God's house, not in the 'world.'" In this case, "world" was a euphemism for sin, sinners, and sinful places that were patently ungodly.

Even though they had ridden in the car to the service, neither of them was ready to dare try to talk to the other. Jamaal thought that Uncle Gerald should have talked first, but he knew he was content to let the moment pass and blame it on Jamaal not wanting to talk.

Jamaal was glad a parking space was reserved for his uncle since parking was impossible to find around the neighborhood, parking lots, and on the streets up to a mile away. He sat alone in the car after having dropped off his uncle, following the long, quiet drive to church.

Jamaal turned the car off and just sat silent. He needed a moment. It had been a long day and it would be a long service tonight, he knew, so before going in he just wanted to do nothing for a spell. It had been a long morning and longer day. At breakfast he rushed eating to avoid being trapped and talking about "The Big Story." And again, he had brushed past Auntie Meredith on his way to the car and she had made no effort to move or to stop him.

Jamaal watched cars drive past him as they searched for parking spaces that were long full. Time passed slowly as he watched churchgoers enter the church, many after walking from blocks away. The older folk moved slowly but determinedly. A steady stream of women and men, dressed to the nines, joyful noises trailing them is an extreme slow-motion Doppler effect.

Jamaal turned away from watching the churchgoers.

Thinking back to breakfast again, he hadn't wanted his aunt to say anything but now that he reflected, he kinda wished she had.

"I don't even know what I wanted her to say," Jamaal said aloud, safe in the car and safe from responses he didn't want to hear.

There was a loud knock on the window of the car, its force causing Jamaal to jump and his memories of breakfast to fade away. Jamaal looked toward the knock where he saw but barely heard the words being spoken

"Are you going to sit in the car all night or come inside and get saved?"

Marie smiled through the window. Jamaal saw her arm moving then realized she was tugging at the door handle. He started to roll the window down, then realized he was going to get out of the car so he stopped, took the keys out of the ignition, and opened the door.

"Just because you can sit in the car all night, doesn't mean you should, cutie pie. Come on, let's go, Jamaal. It's been long enough since I've seen you!"

"Okay." Jamaal was now out of the car with Marie pulling his arm, laughing as they moved in unison now away from the car and out of the parking lot.

"Let's sit on the side tonight, okay?" Jamaal asked as the duo passed through the sanctuary doors, each quickly dropping the other's hand.

“Sounds good. Let's go.”

When they did go inside, Jamaal led them to an auxiliary space off to the side of the main church area. He liked being out of the main sanctuary and near the kitchen and restrooms of the large church where he could see things from a distance that kept him out of the line of sight of the pulpit where his uncle-pastor-father was sitting. And tonight, he liked Marie sitting with him. Being with her helped him to not think about his family and allowed him to be out of sight and away from most of the church folk from his home church.

And away from all the young men who found time to shake his hand with their not-so-secret handshake, and the few who propositioned him. Jamaal was prepared for the attention because this church more than any other was called a gay hub. The area bishop, the same one who had visited his uncle's church and who had repeatedly commented on Jamal's big hands, oversaw the large congregation that on appearances did seem to have an unusually large number of fit and single young men. And the bishop exclusively traveled with young men.

No one in the church seemed to care or pay much attention to the young men or the fact the area bishop's attendants were young and fit men. Even the preachers who routinely preached about “praying the gay away” and the sin of homosexuality remained mute on the subject while in this one church.

Being area bishop had its benefits, Jamaal thought as the music got louder.

The area-wide combined choir was singing now and the sounds, the music, the voices were out of this world. Americans who love Black singers and entertainers are seeing a small fragment of Black talent. Most of the talent remains within the walls of Black churches and tonight, Jamaal knew, was one of those nights that Black Americans were familiar with, but all other Americans simply had no idea of the talent and power that were a routine part of church.

The beauty, colors, hats, sharp suits, and stylish dresses, jewelry, and makeup put most red carpets to shame. And then there was the hair of the women. Every style, length, color of the rainbow, wigs, braids, twists, Afros, perms, and styles that there were so new they weren't even named yet. From this scene of Black women and gay men much of American culture flowed.

It would be a year or two or even three, but the styles, slang, mannerisms, and so forth started in these scenes before making their way to the general Black population, then to white people, then to TV and movies and social platforms. By then, Black women and gay black men had long moved on to new soon-to-be cultural shifts.

Jamaal was enjoying the service and thinking of Marie and how she smelled and how her hair smelled as he listened to another world-class singer belt out another song.

Jamaal was watching the choir when he saw that Uncle Gerald was looking back at him. His uncle motioned for Jamaal to go to him, so Jamaal patted Marie's knee and pointed toward the pulpit where his uncle sat. He walked to the back of the church, went through the kitchen and a stairwell behind the dining area which led to a long hallway that ended with a door. Jamaal opened the door, and he was now behind the pulpit where all the preachers were sitting. He had used the preachers' entrance, and he waited at the stairs that led up to the pulpit. The stairs were guarded by one of the big goons from Pastor Carter's church, and Jamaal wanted nothing to do with those strong goons. His uncle saw him and indicated that he come to him. Jamaal asked one of the goons, motioning to Gerald on the other side of the pulpit.

"Go 'head," the goon said in a voice that Jamaal thought was too high-pitched for such a large man.

Gerald leaned over and spoke to Jamaal, "Jamaal, I need you to go pick up Sis Julie; her car broke down and she needs a ride. I need her to be one of the money counters tonight, so take the car and pick her up. Hurry because we'll start raising money within the hour."

Jamaal walked quickly out of the pulpit, down the long hallway, through the kitchen, and out a side door to the parking lot where the car was parked.

A short drive later and he was at Sister Julie's apartment.

"Come in, the door is open." Jamaal heard Sister Julie yell through the door. He entered the apartment and closed the door behind him.

Her apartment was small and neat, and smelled of lavender, Jamaal thought to himself.

"Jamaal, is that you?" Sister Julie's voice came from the hall to the right of the kitchen.

"Yeah. It's me."

"Okay, good. Come here, please. I'm in the bathroom getting ready. Come talk to me while I do."

"Okay." Jamaal walked slowly toward the hallway, turned left, and walked down the hall until he saw the bathroom on the right side. He did not see Sister Julie initially and for an instant he thought she had gone to her bedroom which looked to be the next door to the right of where he now stood.

Jamaal was relieved until he stepped into the bathroom and saw Sister Julie sitting in a bathtub full of bubbles.

"Don't just stand there, get in," she ordered.

"I'm dressed for church!" Jamaal felt his voice crack.

"I can see that. Don't you want to get in my tub? The water is hot." Sister Julie was slowly moving her arms around the bubbles, the aroma moving around with the bubbles. "That's cute. You're nervous. I heard you like baseball."

"Huh? Oh, yeah, I do. I like most sports," Jamaal answered, not certain what they were talking about.

"I guess so, seeing as how you made it deep into third base with your little girlfriend."

Jamaal froze.

"Oh, I know it all, Mr. Man. Come over here and wash my back."

"Okay," Jamaal said. He didn't know why, but he was embarrassed about Sister Julie knowing what had happened between him and Marie.

He walked toward the tub and sat on the edge. She handed him a big sponge. Jamaal made circles with her sponge, and he tried to not smell how good the bubble bath smelled. It smelled good though, and he liked the lavender aroma.

"Wash it all. There you go. How does it feel? I know it doesn't feel like third base with Marie but, it's a nice back, don't you think?" Sister Julie was leaning forward exposing her entire back to Jamaal.

Just then, she leaned backwards, exposing her breasts to Jamaal. Her wet breasts had bubble bath sliding off the side where they rested and where they were most plump.

"Wash my front too young man. I need to be clean and fresh for church."

Jamaal looked at her breasts and froze. The steam from the bath and heat from their bodies caused his forehead to begin to shine just like her breasts.

"You like them, huh? They seem to like you, too. You didn't see your girlfriend's, did you?"

"No."

"How you like mine? Do you want to touch them?"

"They're nice. We have to go to church," Jamaal said as he stood up and backed away from the bathtub.

"Looks like you really enjoyed that," Sister Julie said teasingly as she motioned to Jamaal's crotch, where the outline of his erection pressed against his pants.

"We have to go, Sis Julie." Jamaal's voice cracked but he had turned his back to Sister Julie so he thought perhaps she hadn't heard it and wouldn't further comment on it.

"I thought I'd get you ready for your girlfriend, but I guess not. When you grow up and your voice stops cracking every two sentences, you're going to look back on this moment and regret it. Trust me. You will." Sister Julie stood up and stepped out of the bathtub, grabbing a towel that was hanging next to her sink as she did so.

Jamaal watched her dry herself. She was pretty, and she still had a few bubbles on her legs and behind, which Jamaal could see since her towel was loosely draped around her waist, keeping her breasts exposed.

"I know you've never had full sex before—home run sex—so, if you want to learn from an experienced woman, not a girl, then you come back to me. I'll show you what you need to know."

"Okay." Jamaal thought he must look afraid because he felt so afraid.

"Boy, you gotta learn to talk with game. You look and sound scared. 'Okay okay okay' won't get you girls and it sure won't get you women," Sister Julie said half-laughing while she put on her panties and then her bra.

"Okay. Uh, yeah, I do. I will be in the car. Uncle wants you there to help count today's offering." Jamaal walked down the hall and out the front door.

Jamaal drove to the reserved parking and parked again in his uncle's space. Sister Julie was mostly quiet on the drive and Jamaal was grateful because he had no idea what to say to her after seeing her naked, saying no to sex, and her seeing and commenting on his erection.

Jamaal turned the car off and looked at Sister Julie, who was looking back at him.

"Sis Julie, you're nice to me. Even when you yell at me when we're counting money. I think you're pretty, too. And when I saw you naked tonight, I was intimidated but I was also… Uhm. I was… I guess… I like you. I just think that even though you're young, you're a little older than me and I don't think ... I don't know ... I just… well, I guess I'm trying to say I like you, but I think that is all we should do. If that is okay with you." Jamaal knew his hands were a sweaty mess, but he had said what he really felt, and he hoped his honestly would be returned in kind.

Sister Julie placed her hand on Jamaal's face and smiled.

"Jamaal. Jamaal, Jamaal, Jamaal. You're sweet. I know what you mean, and I respect it. Marie and you can be good together. You're both sweet and honest. And you both want to have sex, so, when you do it, get and use protection. She plans to go to college, and she won't do that if you're dropping babies in her belly. She may be on contraception or may not; it doesn't matter because if you are using that thing—she poked Jamaal's pants in the crotch—then it is up to you to use condoms and stop your sperm. All these men running around with babies and blaming the girls are wrong. You won't hear this in church or hell, even in school or television, where they all blame the girls. It's your sperm, keep it to yourself. Catch and release, I call it. Now, you've received sex education; go forth and live your life."

Sister Julie leaned over and kissed Jamaal on the mouth and lingered there.

Jamaal kissed her back and when she pulled away, he started the years' long thoughts of how she had been right earlier in the evening: He would regret turning her down.

Jamaal would always consider these few minutes as the best sex education he'd ever received. In fact, it was the only sex education he'd ever received.

Jamaal took his seat again in the auxiliary area and watched the services for the rest of the night alternately thinking about Marie, sitting next to him, and Sister Julie and how they were so different but similar. And both smelled good enough for Jamaal to have internalized their scents.

The pastors were now in locked arms celebrating the end of anniversary season and the money raised tonight for the regional church—over fifty thousand dollars.

Once the amount was announced, the assembled congregation's celebration went up to an even higher level than it had reached with the choir singing and the preachers preaching. The congregation was shouting and dancing, while the preachers, still arm in arm, paraded around the pulpit celebrating the tremendous amount of money raised tonight and over the past month.

Jamaal knew that most of the money raised was going straight to the pastors, with much smaller amounts going to the pastor's top lieutenants, a few choir directors and organists, and a still smaller amount to a few local politicians. Almost all the money though, Jamaal thought, went to men while most of the money was given by women.

Jamaal pushed those thoughts away and tried to focus on Marie's soft front and Sister Julie's soft back. And not think about his uncle-pastor-father who had taken the dais and began a long speech that would lead to him collecting the offering. This was the final anniversary church service of the season, and Jamaal admitted to himself he was looking forward to getting back to his own church—his uncle's church. His father's church.

"Ugh." Jamaal pushed the thoughts of his uncle-father's lie out of his mind and tried to focus on the quiet song the choir was singing as the parade of team captains passed by the front of the church to shake the hands of the preachers who lined the dais with outstretched hands symbolically mirroring the giving process. The large silver bowls, behind which Sister Julie and another lady stood, had silver covers on them to further symbolize the time for giving had ended.

Jamaal looked at Sister Julie and saw that she was wearing her coat and favorite blouse that she wore when she planned to siphon money. And with the cash they were collecting, Jamaal knew, her haul would be... a lot. And Uncle Gerald would get his cut, too, and the bishop would get the rest which still would be considerable and in the thousands.

"Hi, fathead. Why you look so deep in thoughts?"

Jamaal turned when Marie shoved him in the shoulder and grabbed his hand, holding it tight. Jamaal felt excited to feel her hand.

"Why you look stressed, boo-boo?"

Jamaal smiled upon hearing the silly nickname Marie made up for him. He could recall her only using it once but somehow it felt... comforting.

He squeezed back.

"Squeezing my hand isn't answering my question, Jamaal. What is on your mind? You look stressed."

"A lot, I guess."

"About?"

"I'm mad." He felt his body heat increase, his hands begin to moisten, and his words unable to form.

"What are you mad about, Jamaal? Talk to me. You want to go outside and talk?"

In all the years knowing Marie, Jamaal never felt closer to her than now. They had grown up in the church together, fought as kids, played as kids, sang in choir together, and spent countless days and nights in church together. They were friends, church family, and maybe boyfriend and girlfriend. Jamaal felt safe with Marie. She never made fun of him not having a father, like some of the other kids did. She, along with Kevin, were the only ones who never did. They were his best friends and the only ones he would trust with his new knowledge.

"I can't go outside now, Marie. But I do have something to tell you and Kevin. But only you, two, okay? And I want to tell you together and he is not here yet and I don't know if he's coming. He usually won't show up if he's this late so it will just have to wait until we are back at our own church, next Sunday."

"Next week?!"

"Shhhh, Marie! You've got a loud voice. Pipe down. Everyone will hear you."

"I don't care, Jamaal. You can't just drop that big old hint and then tell me you'll tell me what it is all about next week. You know how long a week is?"

"Seven days?" Jamaal said, knowing he was deflecting and knowing Marie would be annoyed. More annoyed.

"Har har har. Oh, so you're a comedian now, is that it? A real clown is more like it, Jamaal. To answer my own question, since you want to make jokes, seven days is so long the Lord made the heavens and the earth." Marie's voice had risen again and the stern looks from multiple nearby women made her quickly look away and back to Jamaal.

"Now who's making jokes?" Jamaal smiled.

"That is not a joke, boo-boo. That's a fact. Look, it doesn't matter, that ages ago. This is right now. Tell me what is bothering you and what is so important you need both of your friends together when you tell us."

"I am still sorting it out, Marie. I need time. Everything is okay, and it is not life and death. It's just information, okay?"

"It's not okay, but I understand, and I will stop pressuring you, even though I want you to trust me and trust I won't say anything to anyone. If you need time then I will have to respect it. But you better be at church early and tell me—us—first thing, you hear me?" Marie had moved closer to Jamaal, closing the seating gap young people were supposed to adhere to while in church and which they only learned after having violated the unspoken and unwritten rule.

"They're looking at us, you know. We're too close and you're too loud." Jamaal rested his hand on top of Marie's, being careful not to make it obvious to any churchperson hoping to catch them doing something inappropriate.

The musical tempo had changed from fast and exciting to slower and more moody, seeming to match the mood Jamaal was feeling.

Jamaal saw concern in Marie's expression which softened her words. He knew she was genuinely concerned about him even when she chastised him for withholding what she knew was important information. He wanted to tell her, but he felt he only wanted to tell it all once and having them together would allow him to do just that and then be done with it once and for all.

"I promise, Marie. I will call Kevin to make certain his butt is early so we can talk before church. Okay?"

"Okay. If you don't, I'll kick your butt, and kick Kevin's ass, just because."

Jamaal laughed with Marie, squeezing her hand this time before she did his. She squeezed back with equal force.

Jamaal and Marie ignored the lone church mother who scowled toward the couple.

CHAPTER 17

CONFESSIONAL

Do homage to the son, that he not become angry ~ Psalm 2:12

"Are you ready to talk, Jamaal? Gerald wants to have a heart-to-heart, and he is saying you don't want to talk with him, even when you two are alone in the car. I believe him, because you won't talk with me, either."

Jamaal had come into the kitchen without Meredith noticing, and now stood behind her, and enough to the side that he could see his uncle.

"Jamaal. I am sorry you—"

"Sorry I know Uncle Gerald is my father? When you're the one who told me, Auntie?" Jamaal lashed out at his Auntie Meredith on instinct, his feelings raging and unformed but needing an immediate target.

"That is not what I meant, and you know it. I know—we know—you are rightfully upset and disappointed in us. That is why I want you and your uncle—"

"Father," Jamaal shot back directly.

"Alright, 'father' then, since that is what you prefer."

“I prefer not to be lied to, Uncle.” Jamaal had turned to face his uncle, realizing he needed to direct his attention to him, first, and then work through issues with Auntie Meredith.

Jamaal was hurting and could see the fact he pointedly called out his uncle-father was making Auntie Meredith uncomfortable.

“Gerald, Jamaal is obviously upset, so we should listen to him, don't you agree?” Meredith's hands were in front of her in the pleading position as her head swiveled from Gerald to Jamaal and back again.

“I am not a priest, but I am trained to hear confessions and offer bible-based counsel.”

“Gerald, that is not what is needed right now, and I think you know that. We need Gerald the man, uncle, and father, not the preacher.”

“We, Meredith? Are you speaking for Jamaal now?”

“I can speak for myself, Auntie.”

“Jamaal, I—” Meredith started to explain herself.

“You need to mind your manners, son. You know better than to speak to your auntie or I with that tone. We raised you better than that, and I won't have it in my house.”

“Oh, okay, Uncle-Father-Pastor-Uncle-whatever.”

“Jamaal Anthony James Andrews, we can have this conversation and still be respectful.” Meredith tried not to raise her voice too loud for fear of pushing Jamaal away, but he still needed to know that he couldn't just talk to either of them any kind way.

“Okay Auntie. Whatever.” Jamaal was standing in the kitchen but still inside door frame.

"Jamaal, your uncle—yes I said uncle because that is what you have always known him as and until you are ready to call him something else, that is what I will refer to him as when I am talking tonight or however long you want me to. I owe you that, Jamaal."

Jamaal felt his face relax upon hearing his auntie's words. His angry and defiant faces had gone away and were replaced by the face his auntie would recognize. And love. The face of her kind, sensitive, sweet nephew who looked so much like his mom, her younger sister, he knew always brought a tinge of pain if she stared at him too long. It had been a long time since she had said those words to him but in this moment that is what Jamaal thought of as he looked at Auntie Meredith.

"Jamaal, I… I did resent you at first because I was deceived by your Uncle Gerald and my sister, for different reasons of course, but deception nonetheless. But you know I loved you the minute you fell asleep in my arms the first time during those first few days following the passing of your mother, my sister."

Jamaal fought his tears but he knew one slipped out and quickly rolled off his cheeks and onto his wrist.

"You slept and I wept. And my love only grew from there. And now you stand here more hurt than I could imagine, and that hurt and pain was caused by me. And your Uncle Gerald."

Meredith looked at Gerald and saw his pallid face that betrayed his in-charge demeanor.

"Jamaal. I am sorry. I have apologized, but I want you to know how very sorry I am that I went along with the lie and held back the truth from you. I have no excuses and, though I can talk about my reasons, they all sound trifling in the face of your real life and your real pain. If you ever—and I do mean ever—want to hear my rationalizations, I will tell you in a heartbeat. I love you not because you are my sister's baby—that is part of it—and a big part. I love you because I raised you. She entrusted you to me, and I never broke her trust or confidence that I would be the parent she didn't get the chance to be. I withheld the truth, and for that I will forever pay penance and will ask your forgiveness for the rest of my days if you want.

"I am not speaking as first lady or pastor's wife or Gerald's wife right now. I am speaking to you, Jamaal, as my authentic self—as Meredith Ferguson.

"Gerald?" Meredith called her husband, looking toward Jamaal after doing so.

"I'm listening, like you told me to, Meredith," Gerald answered.

Jamaal rolled his eyes with great demonstration. And Meredith opened her eyes wide in an exaggerated manner and in that certain way wives do when their partners say obviously and purposeful dumb words.

"Uh, yes. Well. Jamaal, son, I am terribly sorry for what you are going through."

Jamaal could see Auntie Meredith holding her breath. Jamaal knew from all the time he spent around preachers and pastors, that pastors frequently made forgiveness and asking for forgiveness the cornerstone of many sermons, but they themselves frequently struggled to live what they preached. The arrogance was never far away, and Gerald was no different.

"We, uh, we made the best decision we could at the time, Jamaal, and we still believe it was the right thing to do."

"For whom, Uncle-Father? For you? Because it wasn't the right decision for me."

"It was, though. You were spared so much hurt and shame. And even though there is probably some now, of course, you are better able to deal with it than when you were a child or young kid."

"You were spared hurt and shame, not me. I was given hurt and shame. By you. Every time you loudly denied that I am your kid, you gave me hurt and shame."

Meredith caught her breath at Jamaal's words, feeling pride but being careful not to show it to either Jamaal or Gerald.

"You should consider entering the ministry, Jamaal. When you put your mind to it you have a way with words."

"Never."

Meredith looked proud of Jamaal's defiance for once.

"Well, be that as it may, Jamaal, your auntie has apologized with her true heart. I apologize as well. Neither of us can go back in time and change our actions even if we wanted to. Your auntie says I should listen, so I am listening. What do you want me to hear, Jamaal?"

"I don't hate you, Uncle-Pastor Gerald. I thought I did, though. I thought I did for a long time. I never said it out loud or ever told anyone, but I know I did. I loved hating you. And I only took care of you because Auntie couldn't do it. I didn't care if you were in pain. I really didn't. I Don't care. Maybe I will care again one day, but not now. Not for you, your church, or your god.

"Why did you lie to me?"

"I did not lie, Jamaal."

"You did lie, and you are lying. Family shouldn't lie to family. I am only seventeen. You could have told me yesterday, or ten years ago. But you chose to keep a secret. You didn't have to do that. Neither of you thought enough of me to tell me the truth. That sucks.

"How hard was it to tell me you are my father? My mother wanted me to know, I know she did! Why would you do that? WHY?

"What do you mean what do I want you to say? I want you to apologize and admit it. Admit that I am your child. Admit!"

"You are my child, Jamaal. Does that make you feel better, son?"

"NO! I want you to do exactly what you make me, and all the young people do: I want you to admit it to the church and apologize in church. On Sunday. That is what you would make me do for flunking a stupid math test."

Telling his uncle-father that he wanted an apology and he wanted it publicly, just like his uncle-father always made other church members who fell short of the glory of God seemed the most appropriate request, even if doing so changed nothing. But would he do it? If he wouldn't, Jamaal would tell. He would tell!

Gerald visibly recoiled with the sting of Jamaal's words, and then he began to scream and yell and threaten Jamaal. When Jamaal did nothing but turn and leave the room, Gerald had a moment of clarity.

He had been wrong. So very wrong, and he knew it as soon as his nephew-son defiantly talked back and then confidently retreated. The Jamaal that faced him wasn't the quiet and sometimes shy nephew who stayed quiet when in the company of family, preachers, or fellow youth. The Jamaal that faced him was assured, straightforward, and in charge of his demeanor and expressions of emotions. But that didn't mean he would let him be the downfall of his reputation.

CHAPTER 18

EAST CITY CHURCH OF GOD AND CHRIST

Faithful are the wounds of a friend; profuse are the kisses of an enemy ~ Proverbs 27:6

"That's fucked up they didn't tell you, Jamaal. It is. Like, damn." Marie held Jamaal's hand.

Jamaal remained silent. Stewing still, anger unabated but oddly muted in the company of his best friend and girlfriend. He was thinking about how he would tell the community if his uncle-father-pastor didn't.

Kevin sat on the embankment next to Marie outside the church.

"I am so mad and disappointed the pastor… his uncle did that!"

Marie was now standing in front of Kevin who still sat on the embankment, his hands behind him so he had a slight backwards lean.

"I couldn't believe it either," Jamaal said aloud, looking off to the distance at traffic lights and receding fog.

"I ain't." Kevin sounded defiant. "Preachers cheat, lie, steal, and screw around just like everyone else. They are no better or worse than anyone else. It is why my father doesn't come to church. He says the preachers are the worst members and the ones who sin the most so why should he pay them any attention?"

"Well, everybody sins and falls short of the glory of God, we are taught," Marie said, still holding Jamaal's hand, squeezing it as tight as she could.

Jamaal did not squeeze back, running through in his head what he might say about their beloved preacher. Adulterer, liar, protector of child molesters, pimp?

Kevin began to speak, but Marie held her other hand aloft indicating she wanted to continue speaking.

"So, I don't expect any preacher to be perfect. That makes no sense. They need salvation and saving just like everyone else. So, I am not surprised any person—preacher or not—sins. I am just surprised they kept their sin alive for so long and neither of them could anticipate the damage their lie would do once Jamaal found out. And there was no way he would not find out."

"What is that scripture? Things in the dark come out to the light or something?" Kevin was now sitting up straight. He wiped his hands from the grass they had been resting in.

"Whatever it is, it is right, Kevin. And they were wrong."

"Yes, they were both wrong." Jamaal's voice was flat and matter-of-fact. Could he save Auntie Meredith from sharing the shame? Should he try?

"The bible is right, somebody's wrong," Kevin said, repeating one of Pastor Gerald's favorite idioms.

Nobody laughed as the church members did when Pastor Gerald said it.

"His sayings are stupid," Jamaal chimed in as he slid his hand from Marie's without protest.

"Yeah, well. That is right, too. I feel bad though, Kevin. I really do. Jamaal did not and does not deserve any of this. And you know how much I love the first lady, but I can't believe she went along with that lie for so long." Marie moved closer to Jamaal but did not touch his hand. Jamaal remained still.

"It's like those spy movies: she got in too deep. There was no way out I guess, and the fact the lie lasted so long, they just… kept it going, I guess. I'm so sorry, Jamaal. I know I keep saying it, but I just don't even know what else to say or think."

Jamaal's gaze returned to his friends.

Kevin was now standing beside Marie, the old friends looking like they were just two young folks talking about school, movies, music, or the latest peer gossip, and not matters of paternity and a seventeen-year-old lie. Jamaal's seventeen-year-old lie.

"Well, I feel sorry but not for either of them. Fuck them both." Kevin was looking at his phone.

"Your filthy mouth doesn't help anything, and you should have respect for church, Kevin. Cussing like that in front of the church." Marie punched Kevin on the shoulder, causing him to flinch then step out of reach of her attempted next punch.

"Can we not fight today?"

"Stop saying stupid shit then, Kevin."

"Now who's cussing in front of church?"

"Boy, shut UP. Please for once in your life, Kevin, just be normal!"

"Okay, okay, okay. Just don't punch me again. Look, I'm sorry. Being stupid is my own coping mechanism, like Jamaal said his is being a smartass, eh, smart aleck."

Jamaal silently appreciated the normalcy his friends slid into when they were together, no matter the situation.

"I think we need to be there for Jamaal, Kevin. Like, really be there. Do you know what I mean? Like today—right now—Marie's hand found Jamaal's again.

Jamaal welcomed Marie's warm hand and for the first time since they gathered, he squeezed back. Marie instantly smiled but said nothing.

"Friends need each other, Kevin. I think we need to stand together as his friends. Why else are we friends if we aren't with each other when we need one another most?"

"Marie, I know you are right. We all are. Jamaal, too. In fact, I'm always right. The sooner you and Jamaal realize it, the better."

For the first time Jamaal felt his stress pause. Hearing Marie being her usual curt self and Kevin his same irreverent self, felt comfortable and needed. Jamaal welcomed the familiarity. They'd be there for him in the church today, whatever happened.

"Girl, all my good speech wasted on your smart ass." Kevin gently shoved Marie on the shoulder, causing her to smile and pull his arm so that her arm was now entangled within his while she still held Jamaal's hand.

The pull of Marie's hand caused Jamaal to lean toward her as she leaned toward Kevin. Jamaal tried not to smile.

"I love you both and I can't stand you both. But we're family so we have to stick together." Jamaal finally spoke as his friends, happy to hear anything from him, smiled back.

"Family sounds well and good until Jamaal tells me you and he been dry-humping. I don't do that with any of my family, that's for sure. Though I do have that one cousin..." Kevin laughed as he finished talking.

"Eww, shut up, Kevin. Let's go in church and get a seat."

"Yeah. Let's go inside. We may as well continue listening to my uncle-pastor-father's religious crap."

+++

Jamaal fixed his tie. It didn't need fixing but he was fidgety, and his nerves seemed like they were fire, pressing against his skin to break free of his fleshy confines. He sometimes wore his uncle's hand-me-down ties, but today he had chosen one of his own. Even though the tie was too short for his taste, and the pattern was outdated, he felt powerful because it was purple and one that his uncle-father had once demanded he not wear because "a young man shouldn't wear royal purple that is reserved for bishops."

He wanted to send a message to his uncle-father that things were different. Things were different, Jamaal told himself as he habitually re-tied his shoes, then stood and checked himself one more time in the mirror that was too small, old, and was still the only mirror the men's bathroom at his uncle-father's church had.

Jamaal could hear thumping coming from the church upstairs as the choir sang their song before his uncle preached. Marie and Kevin had gone inside when he went downstairs to the bathroom, telling them he would meet them upstairs soon. He was relieved they gave him the space to do so.

Now was his time, he knew, so he confidently walked out of the bathroom and headed for the sanctuary.

He had told his uncle-father the night before what he was going to do, and his uncle-father, always in control and unflappable, had screamed, yelled, and threatened to brand Jamaal a liar, kick him out of his house and, after none of those threats seemed to deter Jamaal, promised he would "drag Deborah's name through the muck and mud."

Jamaal thought the act of apologizing was the punishment Gerald deserved. Jamaal knew that simple action that would have a large impact on his uncle. That is exactly why his uncle had exploded in anger and threats, Jamaal decided. And if he turned it on his dead mother, well, maybe she deserved it, too.

Walking up the stairs of the church felt different. Jamaal thought they were heavy today, and pushing back against his every step, like the stairs knew what was to come and worked to prevent it.

Jamaal pushed on, his mind thinking of Psalm 23: "Yea, though I walk through the shadow of death, I shall fear no evil; for thou art with me; thy rod and thy staff they comfort me. And thy love comforts me."

Entering the sanctuary didn't cause anyone to stare longer than any other time, and everything seemed normal with no one expecting that what would soon happen would forever change how the congregation looked and felt about their pastor.

Jamaal felt different knowing about his mother and uncle-father, but despite feeling like he looked, acted, talked, and walked differently, he knew nothing about him had changed except his knowledge of who he was and who his father—and mother—were. And after today, everyone else would know as well.

Jamaal sat down at the end of the center pew in the middle of the sanctuary. It was a seat seldom occupied by any young person or visitor so the fact he sat there would draw the attention he wanted. Sitting in that seat would ensure that Uncle-Father-Pastor Gerald could not avoid looking at him like he could if Jamaal sat in his usual place at the back of the church with his friends.

The choir's song was coming to an end and the church was full of the large, final anniversary crowd that was expected, one of the largest crowds of the year.

Jamaal watched with interest and disinterest because of what was coming. Looking through the crowd he saw Auntie Meredith fanning herself, eyes closed, and head down in what folk around her would believe was prayer but which Jamaal knew to be deep thoughts.

They'd all have a reckoning together and as much as he wanted to avoid and delay, Jamaal knew it was coming sooner rather than later. Just thinking about what was coming caused Jamaal to feel hot throughout his body.

The choir stopped singing and Dwayne continued softly playing the song's melody as the church transitioned to expecting Pastor Gerald to raise the final anniversary offering. The task of raising the anniversary offering traditionally was the responsibility of anniversary teams.

The church had anniversary teams—Jamaal was on the youth team—and each team was responsible for raising money, but more importantly they were responsible for raising the most money among all the teams. The teams were called up one by one to announce their totals and the congregation cheered each announcement of monies raised.

Jamaal, like everyone, listened to Pastor Gerald review anniversary season with the expectation he would transition to the team captains so they could do their read-out of their earnings. Jamaal was planning to try to relax while waiting for the captains to finish. With eleven teams of ten people each, the read-out could drag on until each team was satisfied they had given as much as they could, including any fundraiser money they had raised since anniversary season had started.

Jamaal listened as Uncle-Father-Pastor Gerald finished his speech and thanked the choir and all the members for the best anniversary season he could remember. Then instead of turning over the service to the fundraising team, Jamaal saw his uncle-father Gerald hold onto the microphone and drop his head, audibly sighing loudly for dramatic effect.

Then, through the church quietness a low murmuring rippled through the congregation as members wondered what the pastor, who had now been standing still for about two minutes, was going to say.

Jamaal looked at Dwayne who looked at the assistant pastors who looked at one another and to Pastor Gerald, no one finding an answer and everyone deciding to just wait to see.

Dwayne's organ music was the only sound, but the volume was so low as to be imperceptible beyond the pulpit. The hush was unnerving because, Jamaal and others knew, silence in church indicated something was happening.

Jamaal watched as his uncle-father-pastor Gerald's head slowly rose and stopped when it was raised ever so slightly. But it wasn't the angle of his head that caused Jamaal to hold his breath and wonder what was happening. It was the tears flowing from his uncle-father-pastor's eyes that rolled down his round cheeks and past his downturned mouth before running-falling to his bleached white shirt where they became one with the sweat that had already dampened it.

Jamaal held his breath, correctly assuming everyone else was doing the same.

Pastor Gerald slowly and deliberately lifted the microphone—still holding it with both hands—and breathed deeply into the head, his whooshing sound reverberating throughout the church and drawing the full attention of the one or two congregants who weren't listening.

Jamaal's mind drifted back to the night before when he unleashed years of pent-up anger, confusion, and disappointment directly at his uncle-father.

Why did you lie to me?

Pastor Gerald held his gaze up to the church and quietly with passion said, "I HAVE A STORY TO TELL. A CONFESSION. FROM ME TO YOU."

I did not lie, Jamaal.

> "I HAVE NOT BEEN COMPLETELY HONEST ABOUT A DARK TIME IN MY LIFE. AND TODAY, GOD IS TELLING ME TO BRING INTO LIGHT THAT WHICH HAS BEEN IN THE DARK."

You never told the whole truth, Uncle.

"GOD IS GOOD AND COMMANDS THAT WE LIVE IN TRUTH. HIS TRUTH. TODAY I AM CHOOSING TO TRUST GOD. AND TRUST YOU, MY CHURCH FAMILY."

(Amen, pastor.)

You did lie, and you are lying. Family shouldn't lie to family.

> SEVENTEEN YEARS AGO, THE DEVIL TEMPTED ME DURING A TIME OF GREAT DARKNESS IN MY LIFE. WHERE LATER IN MY LIFE I KNEW HOW TO CALL ON PRAYER WARRIORS TO HOLD ME UP IN PRAYER AND SURROUND ME WITH CHRIST'S LOVE, BACK THEN I FELT ALONE IN THE WILDERNESS WHEN SATAN ATTACKED ME WITH ALL HE HAD. SOME OF Y'ALL LIVED LONG ENOUGH TO KNOW WHAT I AM TALKING ABOUT.

(Amen! Yes, sir! Say that, pastor!)

Neither of you thought enough of me to tell me the truth.

> I OWE YOU ALL THE TRUTH. AND THE TRUTH IS WHEN I GAVE IN TO THE DEVIL, IT PRODUCED A CHILD. A CHILD WHO HAS GROWN UP RIGHT HERE IN THE CHURCH. A CHILD YOU ALL KNOW AND LOVE. A CHILD OF GOD. I GAVE IN TO TEMPTATION, BUT GOD IS GOOD AND CAN PROVIDE A BLESSING OUT OF TRIALS AND TRIBULATIONS. WON'T HE DO IT?!

(Lord have mercy. Pastor! Lord touch him.)

How hard was it to tell me you are my father?!

> MY LOVELY WIFE AND FIRST LADY, MEREDITH, GOD BLESS HER, IS A WOMAN OF GOD AND HIGHLY FAVORED. SHE HAS STOOD BY ME WHEN SHE COULD HAVE RIGHTEOUSLY WALKED OUT. SHE HAS PRAYED WITH AND FOR ME. AND SHE HAS HELPED ME RAISE JAMAAL AS MY OWN. JAMAAL IS MY SON. I WON'T LIE ABOUT IT ANYMORE NO MATTER WHAT ANYONE WANTS ME TO DO. YOU DESERVE THE WHOLE TRUTH. YOU HEAR ME?! SHE IS A WOMAN OF GOD AND DESERVES SPECIAL RECOGNITION FOR RAISING HER NEPHEW—MY SON—AND HONORING DEAR SWEET DEBORAH, HER SISTER. DEBORAH DIDN'T WANT ANYONE TO KNOW AND SHE—WE—HONORED HER WISHES. WE HONORED HER WISHES. SHE IS RESTING IN THE PEACE OF GOD'S LOVE KNOWING THAT HER SISTER HONORS HER EVEN NOW. GOD BLESS DEBORAH. AND GOD BLESS MEREDITH.

> I HAVE LONG WANTED TO STAND HERE AND CONFESS. I AM A MAN OF GOD AND GOD WORKS THROUGH ME. I HAVE HONORED DEBORAH'S REQUEST AS LONG AS ANY MAN COULD. MY NEPHEW DESERVES TO KNOW THE MAN WHO HAS LOVED HIM, RAISED HIM AS HIS OWN, WHO CARED FOR HIM, FOR EVERY

> BUMP AND BRUISE, AND TREATED HIM WITH ALL THE WORLDLY LOVE GOD HAS BLESSED US WITH. I AM HIS FATHER. FATHERS MATTER.
>
> I WAS A FATHER FIGURE, AND NOW I AM A FATHER. AND IT REMINDS ME OF JOSEPH WHO WAS JESUS' FATHER FIGURE, BUT GOD IN HEAVEN IS HIS FATHER. AND HE IS OUR FATHER. AND HE LOVES US THROUGH HIS SON, JESUS. JESUS! JESUS WHO WAS BORN FOR US, WHO LIVED FOR US, AND WHO DIED AND ROSE AGAIN FOR US! JESUS! WHO SHED HIS BLOOD FOR US ON CALVARY! JESUS WHO TOLD US TO CONFESS OUR SINS! AND BELIEVE THAT GOD HAS ALREADY FORGIVEN US AND WE—YOU AND I—WILL BE SAVED. I'M SAVED. I'M SAVED! I'M SAVED! CAN YOU HEAR ME, CHURCH?! DEBORAH IS IN HEAVEN NOW CELEBRATING THAT SHE NO LONGER HAS TO LIE OR HIDE. HER SINS ARE FORGIVEN. I FORGAVE HER LONG AGO AND JESUS FORGAVE HER, AND GOD RECEIVED HER. SHE CAN KNOW THAT HER BABY BOY IS SAFE, HEALTHY, HAPPY, AND UNDER THE CARE OF HIS FATHER. HIS FATHER! HALLELUJAH!

The church was now on fire, their clapping and punctuating every word out of Pastor Gerald's weeping mouth with shouts of "AMEN" and "GO AHEAD PASTOR" and "LOOK AT GOD." Their shouts were accompanied by Dwayne who played the organ with fervor reserved only for the pastor during his most important sermons. The organ showered sounds from up and down the scales as Dwayne found Gerald's key and pushed him higher and higher, the two synchronized as only experienced preachers and their attendant organists can do.

The rapturous sounds of the organist and preacher danced through the congregation and lifted the church in praise, prayer, and thankfulness. No one talked, no one was left out, and everyone was in those moments in communion and fellowship with their God who loved them, forgave them, and who expected their celebration and glorification. And just when it seemed the church had reached an emotional high, the choir joined in and took the church to the very steps of heaven.

While Jamaal had been watching the church mothers dance and shout, Dwayne had signaled to the choir who then stood up in unison with a praise song on their lips, but now sung at the accelerated pace Dwayne had set. The sounds filled the thick church air with harmonies, melodies, and range, as lead and background singers from alto, tenor, and soprano brought forth the sounds of praise found nowhere else on the planet.

Jamaal watched as the church hung on every word his uncle-father-pastor let flow from his lying, deceitful mouth and now they were celebrating his confession, redemption, and God's forgiveness for and with him.

The rhythmic pounding of the drums shook floors, the meeting of drumstick and cymbal pushed the sounds of shattering glass to the rafters where all the sounds gathered to echo back down and through the sanctuary and into each person.

Jamaal felt an emotion he would forever identify as hopelessness and the feeling of being powerless. He had lost. Uncle-Father-Pastor Gerald had won. Where Jamaal had hoped for him to be ruined, he was being lauded and celebrated. The pastor almost always won, he knew, because he had observed it happen time and time again. He knew he had wrongly calculated that him being who he is would somehow make a difference, but it was not to be. He looked across the church to Auntie Meredith trying to get her attention so he could see her face and expressions. But she did not feel his gaze because she too was in the throes of celebratory ecstasy that although may have expressed itself for different reasons, looked no different than the other church member's expressions of joy and forgiveness.

Pastor Gerald was the shepherd and his flock followed him as they were trained since birth to do. The power of a confession, tears, music and, most of all, scripture, all but assured nothing would come of the revelation about Jamaal's paternity. And if Auntie Meredith went along with it, then the women who were the backbone of any Black church would go along, and the pastor would be safe and would weather the storm that Jamaal thought was a hurricane but turned out to just be seasonal rain that quickly passed and was forgotten.

And Pastor Gerald knew it. He stood solemnly at the dais, soaking in the emotions of his flock.

Jamaal's own emotions got the best of him and with his friends unable to fully understand—they tried—but the whole of it was just too much.

"Fuck me," Kevin whispered, his hand repeatedly tapping Jamaal's hip as they watched Pastor Gerald make a mockery of Jamaal's request that he apologize.

"Fuck him," Marie responded, taking Jamaal's hand in hers and squeezing hard in a feeble attempt to comfort her sensitive friend.

"I hate it here. I hate church and all the lying hypocrites."

"Kevin, not so loud," Marie admonished.

"I am going to the bathroom," Jamaal told them, then excused himself and exited the sanctuary.

+++

"Couldn't take anymore bullshit, could you, Cousin?"

Jamaal was startled to almost walk into Cousin Jean who was standing so near to the door it looked as if she were about to walk into the men's bathroom.

"I thought you'd never come out. Number two, was it? Or just hiding? Either way, you were in there a long time."

"Sorry, Cousin," Jamaal said as he side-stepped Cousin Jean, but she grabbed his arm.

"Follow me, my dude."

Cousin Jean led Jamaal—pulled was more accurate—to one of the small offices where Sunday school was held. Once inside the office, she closed the door behind him, took a seat on the old sofa, causing it to squeak as she plopped down, and patted it where she wanted Jamaal to sit next to her.

"Sit. Let's talk."

"I don't want to sit, Cousin."

"Suit yourself. You will sit before we leave."

"Okay." Jamaal leaned against the far wall, crossed his arms, and looked at his favorite cousin.

"I will always be honest with you, love. When I saw you today, my heart broke. You may not want to hear this right now, but Meredith knew that she broke your heart and spirit, too. I know she did.

"I was watching her in church just now just like you were. Oh, I know you were paying attention to Gerald, but I saw you watching her."

"So?"

Cousin Jean ignored Jamaal and continued talking, her pace steady and her emotions certain.

"Did you see her watching her husband—your uncle-father-pastor, as you call him now? Yeah. I know you call him that."

"So?" Jamaal couldn't find anything else to say.

"We saw him, just like she did, use God, the bible, and his power as pastor to manipulate the emotions of his followers. I know Meredith wanted to comfort and hold you tight, whether you believe it right now or not. But she knew her duty in that moment was to be first lady, wife to the pastor, and leader of the women of the church. She knew everyone would look to her for guidance on how to react to Gerald's confession. And as much as she hated how he did it—and trust me my sensitive cousin, she did hate it—he did exactly what she knew he would do: Turn it around to center himself, demonize your mother, her sister, while painting himself as the man helpless to her sexual advances. It was the oldest excuse men use and most common because despite movements of equality, the tactic still works at home, the courts and at church. And I think you know that, whether you fully understand it right now."

Jamaal felt Cousin Jean looking deeply at him and he tried, unsuccessfully to let her words pass around him but they found their way to his insides and caused him to fight as hard as he could not to cry.

"Toward the end of his speech—let's be clear, it wasn't a sermon by any means. It was nothing more than a self-serving pity-party speech–I saw her, Jamaal. I really did. Meredith had looked away from looking at Gerald to find you again and this time she had tears running down her heavily made-up face, sending that church-lady mascara to stain her lovely blouse.

"That was when she lifted her arms to heaven and looked like she was silently praying for forgiveness. Didn't you see it, Jamaal? I know you did. Everybody did, but I am certain nobody knew like I do that she wasn't crying or praying for herself but for you. She knew that too many eyes were on her, looking for her full support for her husband and pastor. Their church lives depend as much on her performance as his, Jamaal. I know you know that, sweetie, but I also know it was hard for you to stand there and feel like you were on an island."

Jamaal's tears freely flowed now and he didn't care.

"I don't know if you saw, but I slid beside her while she was in her prayerful moment, and I whispered to her to go stand by you. She pretended to ignore me, and I heard her praying. You want to hear what she said?"

"No. I don't care." Jamaal cried and his nose was running now and his sleeve was wet from the constant wiping he was doing.

"Imma tell you anyway because I think you'll like to hear it at some point in the future so I may as well tell you now. She praised God and asked Him to look after your heart and soul, and she asked that she be forgiven for her complicity and lies. She promised God she would never lie to you again and that she would see to it that Gerald didn't either."

Unable to control himself and not wanting to, Jamaal cried aloud now and finally took a seat next to his cousin Jean where she wrapped him in her arms and continued talking straight to his heart and emotions.

"Her arms were raised high, the tears flowing hard, and the hands of other church women were now touching her shoulder, back, giving her support and lifting her up as they believed she needed because of what her husband and their pastor had confessed. Meredith was in a loop of guilt, forgiveness, and loathing, and nothing would pull her out, she knew, until she had made things right with you.

"Once she was finished, she said that talking to you would have to wait until after church when you all got home and if you were ready or would allow it. She said she knew her relationship with you was damaged but held out hope she had time to repair it. Jamaal, honey, she knows it may never be the same but there is hope for growth and that is fueling her."

Jamaal cried and realized that Cousin Jean had lied to him, too.

At just that minute, Jamaal was saved by his friends coming out of the church and grabbing him by his arm. He left Cousin Jean standing in the hallway.

"Jamaal, I am so sorry. I am. He is wrong. Don't let him bother you or see how angry or disappointed you are. Don't give him the satisfaction." Marie felt the inadequacy of squeezing Jamaal's hand, yet she did it anyway hoping against hope it helped Jamaal.

"And look at your auntie and her fake self. I ain't buying nothing she selling. Nothing. Fake ass," Kevin said.

"We know both are wrong, Kevin, so Jamaal doesn't need you to single out his auntie. His Auntie Meredith didn't make a baby with Gerald's brother. HE made a baby with HER sister. HE is most wrong. That is a fact."

"Right," Jamaal said quietly and without energy. There was despair in his voice.

"Come on, Jamaal. Let's get out of here. This shit here is crazy." Kevin pulled at Jamaal's arm, shaking it as he did so. Jamaal didn't protest.

At that minute, Auntie Meredith came out of the church looking for Jamaal. Marie caught her eye and held Meredith's focus trying her best to tell Meredith that Jamaal would be okay because he was with his two friends who loved him and who did not lie to him.

When she was satisfied that her look had communicated what she needed, Marie turned away from Auntie Meredith and followed Kevin and Jamaal out of church.

CHAPTER 19

COUSIN JEAN'S TABERNACLE

Confess your faults one to another... that you may be healed ~ James 5:16

"Stay as long as you need, honey. You know mi casa su casa." Cousin Jean put a bowl of chili in front of Jamaal. Then before he had even picked up his spoon, she placed small saucers with grated cheese, diced onions, sliced jalapeños, and sour cream.

"What did you know, Cousin? And were you ever going to tell me?"

"I knew your uncle had sex with Deborah."

"Why didn't you at least tell me that?"

Cousin Jean took a small scoop of grated cheese and sprinkled some on Jamaal's bowl of chili. Then using a small serving spoon, she scooped onions, then a dollop of sour cream, before finishing with a single jalapeño on top of the sour cream.

"Hon, grownups don't go around telling kids about the people their parents or guardians had sex with. I know other men your mom had sex with. Just like I know other women Gerald had sex with. Hell, I know a man he came close to having sex with. But I don't go around telling you or anyone else. That's not what adults do."

"How do you know my mom and Uncle-Father-Pastor Gerald had sex?"

"Now that is the right question. Because I saw them, that's why."

"What? You did? How? Why would you …"

Even though he was mad and confused, Jamaal couldn't resist Cousin Jean's chili, done up right. As he took a bite, she placed a plate of cornbread muffins that had a scoop of melting butter sitting on the same plate.

"Don't be all morose with me, love. I know what your uncle did is fucked up beyond fucked up. And them both keeping that truth from you is wrong no matter how they justify or rationalize it."

Jamaal seemed to be forgetting to chew before he swallowed. It seemed like he hadn't been fed in a very long time.

"Slow down, speedy. Enjoy my homemade chili and I'll spin you a very short tale."

"Okay."

"I walked in on Gerald having sex with Deborah downstairs in the church. They were in the far office and Gerald was on top of her and she was asking him to get off her. When I walked in, he jumped up just as he was ejaculating—I'm saying that word since I don't think you want to hear me say the other, Cousin, so thank me later for my first time being discreet—so there was his dong sticking straight out and ejaculate still coming out, him trying to put that thing away—it wasn't all that impressive if you ask me—no girth you know—and she was crying and trying to pull her bloody panties up. I screamed bloody hell and rained down hellfire on him for fucking in the Lord's house and he mumbled something like "I'm sorry, I'm sick I shouldn't be here." And high-tailed it out of there so fast all I saw was his backside and the snail trail of ejaculate that followed him."

"Cousin… Jean…"

"Okay, okay. He put his member away and politely left the room, with only his snail trail as evidence he was caught indelicato with Deborah."

"That's… not better but thank you."

"You are quite welcome. Continuing, so finish your chili. I saw to Deborah who remained shocked and in tears about what had happened. She was trying to talk but the words did not really make sense other than she said she hated him but blamed herself for trusting him. I didn't want to question her too hard because of the state she was in, so I got her clothed and took her to the women's bathroom to get her cleaned up. I have been raped and I know a rape victim when I see one."

"He raped her?"

"Deborah said he did not rape her, that their sex was consensual, and I let her know that I supported her whatever she said and … this is important, Jamaal, so put your spoon down, greedy boy."

"But you said—"

"Stop listening to what I tell you and listen to what I say, Jamaal. Gosh." Cousin Jean used her serving spoon to dip into Jamaal's bowl of chili and getting a full spoonful which, she held aloft, added a jalapeño to the top, and then put the entire spoonful into her mouth.

Cousin Jean waved her hands fanning her mouth indicating how hot the spoonful was before she finally swallowed, took a drink of Jamaal's soda, then attempted to finish her story.

"What did she say? Did she tell you anything I need to know?"

"She was adamant she wasn't raped. She said the shame and embarrassment would be too much and she could not live with herself if Meredith thought that. I took her home and we spent all night crying, drinking, laughing, arguing even, until we passed out in bed, me holding her tight as she cried herself to sleep."

The tears coming out of Cousin Jean's eyes were not because of the hot jalapeño.

"When she woke up, she called Gerald despite me telling her she wasn't ready and that if she wanted, I would go with her to press charges. Well, that went over like a fart in church, so she called your uncle, and I recorded the call—I am skipping over the fact she told me not to record but I did it anyway."

"What did she say? What did he say, Cousin?"

"He said he was mad I interrupted them right when he was busting a nut—"

"Oh my god, Cousin!" Jamaal yelled.

"Oh my god, nothing. Look, if you want the deets, then let me be me!" Cousin Jean began singing, "I just have to be meeeee," and danced away from the kitchen and into her living room, where she began rummaging through a stack of albums. After tossing a few aside, she held aloft a Stevie Wonder album and smiled.

"This is the one." Cousin Jean gently placed the old album on her turntable and slowly rocked her head as the song "I Can Only Be Me" began playing. "Butterflies …"

Jean stood and beckoned Jamaal to come into the living room. Jamaal pushed away from the table, picked up his bowl of chili, and sat on the floor in one corner of the living room, staying clear of where Cousin Jean twirled and danced to the song.

She started talking again.

"She told him he needed to apologize. Then she apologized, saying she didn't mean to lead him on—I almost pissed my pants hearing that patriarchy bullshit."

Cousin Jean stopped twirling and stood over Jamaal, her face turning serious, as she spoke directly, looking deep into Jamaal's eyes.

"Don't rape girls, boys, women, or men, Jamaal, you hear me? No one can lead you on, and no one deserves it no matter their mental state, whether they are drunk, naked, or on top of you. No means motherfucking no, you hear me? If I ever hear about your taking sexual advantage of anyone, ANYONE, I will cut your little balls off myself, you hear?"

"Yes, ma'am." Jamaal had finished his chili, thankfully. Otherwise, he might not have been able to swallow.

"Good. Now, where was I?"

"Mom was on the phone," Jamaal responded.

"Yes. Okay, well," Jean began swaying to the record again. "I slapped her ass when she apologized if she had led him on, then after some mumbling, she gently asked Gerald to apologize and from where I stood, it was obvious his guilty ass said no. They argued for a good while, with Deborah telling him she was going to go to the police."

"Did she?" Jamaal asked eagerly.

Jean stopped swaying. "No. You should know that. He wouldn't be pastor right now if she had—and that would serve him right. But that is not how things were or often still are for young girls and women who are raped. Gerald told her no one would believe her because she was young, and it would be easy to destroy her because she had pursued him, and he had friends on the police force who would help make her life a living hell."

"Jesus Christ."

"This don't have shit to do with Jesus, Cousin. But, yes, your 'father-uncle'—is that how you are identifying him now, hon?"

"Uncle-father-pastor," Jamaal said with certainty.

"Nice. That's some truthful but shady shit, Jamaal. Good job. You finally learning from me. They argued but it went nowhere and not even the threat of calling Meredith made Gerald be less of an asshole. After an hour—and I am conveniently leaving out the part I snatched that phone from Deborah and rained hellfire on Gerald. I bet his ass is still burnt from the ass-whopping I gave him that night. Deborah and I spent the next few days together and, really, much of the following few months as she found out she was pregnant and hid from the church and Gerald as long she could."

"How long was that, Cousin? Did she hide it from Auntie, too?"

Cousin Jean paused to look tenderly at Jamaal. She had loved him since he was born. He sat on her floor, young, vulnerable, and needing something to help him get through the most difficult time of his life. She wanted to protect and care for him and surround him with the kind of open and honest love she knew he would never get from Gerald. He would get it from Meredith, bless her heart. Though she would always be loyal to Gerald first, middle, and last.

Jean's heart broke again, like it did when she nursed Deborah to health, tended her wounds that were clearly the result of forced penetration. She could not tell Jamaal about the blood. Or how Gerald had stolen her virginity while leaving her a bruised, battered, crying, scared teenaged girl traumatized and in shock.

She could not tell Jamaal how Deborah had cried in terror for days and nights as she kicked and screamed in the middle of the night reliving the terror Gerald had visited on her body, soul, and mind. Nor would she tell Jamaal of the third night when she had dozed off after making certain Deborah was asleep, only to be awoken by the sounds of Deborah retching in the bathroom after having taken a handful of vitamins. Poor girl thought five B-12 vitamins would send her to heaven and even then, she got scared and tried to make herself vomit. The next night there was anger, then more crying, then plotting to kill Gerald, then plotting to tell the church on Sunday morning right when he got up to preach. Ultimately, they did none of those things. No sense telling Jamaal any of those things.

She could tell him one thing though. "Jamaal, you know what your mama said to me when she found out she was pregnant? She said to me, 'I think I am happy, Jean. I know it doesn't make sense, but I am.'

"I told her that I'd be happy right along with her then. I said, 'I will be your babysitter, partner, and godmother to your baby, you better believe it.'

"We went to the doc at the county hospital for her appointments and just ignored and the looks some judgey folks were giving us. Deborah was radiant, happy, and beyond cute with her growing belly. We window shopped, played around with names, thought about schools, careers, girlfriends and boyfriends, heartbreaks, and even her own eventual grandkids. I really believed carrying you was the best time of Deborah's life."

Cousin Jean had not answered Jamaal's question, but he was relieved to hear that his mother had Jean's company and had enjoyed being pregnant. The situation around his birth had never really been discussed with him, just that his birth mom had died right after his premature birth. He wanted her to keep talking, so he didn't interrupt. Just kept looking at her as the Stevie Wonder album faded into background noise.

"She was a flame that burnt too hot with too much fuel, Jamaal. We were watching Dracula on the video, and she was just six months with you when she started bleeding. She said she was bleeding and I thought she was joking. A few hours later she was in surgery from which she would never wake."

The record had ended, and the needle was thumping at the center. Both Jean and Jamaal were silent for a few minutes in memory of the young lives lost.

"To answer your question, Jamaal, your mom wanted it kept secret, and she did until it was time to go to the hospital to give birth to you, Jamaal. Six months."

"Okay, Cousin. I understand."

"I did tell Gerald she was pregnant, thinking he needed to know and that perhaps he would… I don't know… man up or something. I was stupid, I know. All he said was he wasn't paying for another abortion and hung up. Of course, I never told your mom that. It would have crushed her all over and I knew she could not handle that in the state she had just come out of so, I buried it until this very minute."

"Thank you for telling me. I can handle it, Cousin."

"I think you can as well, and if I could, you can. And, if you need help processing and understanding all I told you, get yourself some therapy from a real therapist, not one of those fake church therapists who quote scripture and tell you to pray."

"Okay, I will."

"You won't, so don't patronize me, big head. But if I notice anything happening with you or your behavior—drugs, drinking, wilding out, I'm going to haul your Black ass to my therapist, you hear me?"

"Yeah. Yes. I do, Cousin."

"Good. The rest of the story you already know and are experiencing right now, I guess. Well, your aunt—and uncle-father-pastor—fuck, that is funny as hell—can and need to fill you in on anything I have left out or don't know. They owe you that, Jamaal, so don't you let either of them off the hook."

"I won't."

"You promise, Jamaal?" Cousin Jean wanted reassurance that the crucial and tough one-on-one conversations between them would happen.

He nodded.

"Good. Then I have one more thing to give you."

Cousin Jean left the living room and walked to her bedroom and then to her closet. She pushed her coats aside and bent to reach an orange hatbox that looked like it had sat in that spot for years because it had done exactly that.

Jean opened the hatbox, tossing the top toward her unmade bed where it bounced and fell to the floor. Jean rummaged for a moment and pulled out a small blue envelope that was sealed with a small green sticker shaped like a heart. The only thing written on the envelope were the words:

"For my baby boy, James."

Jean shook her head. Gerald had even robbed him of his true name.

"Here, Jamaal. This is from your mom. I didn't know she wrote it, and she didn't tell me until she got to the hospital and before they kicked me out before surgery. I thought she was hysterical from blood loss, but she pulled my hand and told me about it. She said to me, she said,

'Jean, I wrote my letter to my baby, just like our grandparents did. For when he turns sixteen. I put it in that ugly orange box in your closet. Don't throw away that ugly box and lose my letter.'

“Read it now or whenever you are most comfortable, Jamaal.”

“James?”

“Yes, she wanted to name you James Ferguson.”

“How did I get named Jamaal Andrews then?”

Jean exhaled.

“Gerald named you. He was happy to hide the fact he was your biological father, and Meredith agreed it was better to have you named Andrews. Meredith fought for you to keep James, but your uncle-father wouldn't budge. I'm sorry.”

“Okay. Thanks for telling me anyway.”

“Are you going to read it now?”

Jean was genuinely curious about what the letter contained but she wasn't going to rush Jamaal.

“I'll read it soon. I promise.”

CHAPTER 20

CONVOCATION, INVITATION, AND DECLINATION

There is nothing better for a person than that he should eat and drink and find enjoyment… this is also from the hand of God ~ Ecclesiastes 2:24

"The anniversaries were very successful this year, everyone." Pastor Gerald sat at the head of the table. It was the Thursday following the final anniversary service and the church's leadership team had just finished providing reports on their fundraising goals.

"Oh, there were some issues—I'm sad about Pastor Carter. We all are. But all in all, things were successful. We raised the most money ever. Sunday's haul alone was the single largest day we've ever had raising money. Seems like confession is good for the soul—and bank account!" Everyone laughed boisterously and then small breakout groups began chattering.

"But Pastor, it really was good that you shared your story on Sunday. Without it, we may have had a good day but with your story we had an exceptional day," the assistant pastor, Johnson, added with a nod, and other leaders began nodding as well.

Pastor Gerald gave a half-smile and looked to the back of his office where Jamaal sat, as he always did, looking as though he wasn't paying attention but clearly gathering in everything that was said.

"Jamaal is a good young man," Pastor Gerald started. "I could not have asked for a better son. I know he will make a good preacher one day. And I know you all will help him become the man he will become. I won't always be here, and now that we all know I have a son, it is time we started preparing him for what is to come—taking over this church in the future."

"But Pastor, he hasn't been called by God to preach," Assistant Pastor Johnson replied, again gaining head nods from the other leaders.

"I will call him until God calls him," Pastor Gerald said with a gusto that generated laughs.

"We will go to our national convention in Tennessee next month with our coffers full and our reputation through the roof. And when we report our offering, I'm looking at a huge promotion, which will mean more national assignments, more visitors from headquarters, bigger offerings, and the circle of life continues." Pastor Gerald sang the "Circle of Life" part of his speech, getting more laughs, and helping to keep the tone lighthearted.

"Let's wrap up. It has been a long anniversary season and we all need our rest. We have a few weeks to prepare for Tennessee. Let's go get dessert. I'm treating." He turned toward Jamaal in the back and gestured with his arm toward the door. "Come on, Jamaal. Let's get that apple pie a la mode we love so much."

"Okay," Jamal replied quietly.

Jamaal inhaled and exhaled before getting up and being the first out the office door.

+++

Jamaal laid in bed awake for a long time as his mind wandered from his mom to Cousin Jean, to Sister Julie, and finally to Marie where it stayed until he finally, and with great relief, began dozing off.

Jamaal's last thought before going to sleep shifted from Marie to what his uncle-father-pastor had spoken about at the church meeting earlier in the evening, and he frowned.

"I am not going to goddamned Tennessee."

Epilogue—Deborah's Letter

Dear James. Mommy loves you. This letter is a tradition in our family, and it will be fun to talk with you about it. I hope you are reading this letter alone in your bedroom in the quiet of your life. Maybe we just fought or maybe you are mad I said no to something you feel you desperately needed. I remember being a teenager so well right now. Maybe you just celebrated your birthday and I want to top it off by sharing some thoughts I had about you before you were even born, and how much I looked forward to seeing you grow up and become who you have become.

Whichever it is, please know that you are my heart and I have and will always love you. It is said that children can't choose their parents, but I don't believe that because I know that somehow someway, you chose me as I did you.

Our lives are forever intertwined as we journey along—finding love, losing ourselves in our hearts, and working to heal each other. You didn't choose your birth father, either. And it is entirely up to you whether and what kind of relationship you have chosen to have with him. Don't let anyone tell you what to do, except your heart. Follow your heart. Protect your heart. And let your heart be open to love, forgiveness, growth, and love from that someone special you will meet. (And may meet a few times!)

If I am gone, I want you to know you were a tough pregnancy so I know that you will be ready for whatever life tosses at you. You are already successful in getting out of my belly so take that success with you into all that you do. Your cousin Jean will be there for you in large and small ways, and she will show you a side of life that is different and unique than the church life you'll be raised in. Her church is nature, fun, and being different and seeing life differently. Embrace it. Except run if she wants to do a séance. Trust me on that.

Oh, and my sister, Meredith—she is more stoic and stuck up than me, but she is the oldest, so her path has always been filled with more responsibilities and expectations. She gives good advice when she's not being annoying, doesn't she?

What I wish for you now, before your birth, is all the wonderful things life offers, all the challenges that build strength and resilience, and I hope you give and receive as much love as your heart desires.

If I am just over in the next room, please don't feel you need to tell me you just read this letter. But if you want to just give your mommy a hug for no reason, I'll have a clue for why. And if I am gone, I am not really gone, am I? Since you are reading my words right now and you are placing them in your heart—where I belong and where I will always be.

Your mother,

Deborah

Acknowledgments

Attending church almost every day from age zero to my twenties, I want to acknowledge the church mothers, deacons, Sunday school teachers, choir folk, musicians, and friends and family to fill the pews and coffers Sunday through Saturday. To all the preachers, pastors, ministers, and bishops in my own family including my brother, Pastor Mark A. Clifton of the East Oakland Church of God in Christ, our late grandfathers, Bishop Martin J. Clifton Sr. and Pastor David Andrews, our oldest brother, Minister Martin (Marty) J. Clifton III (RIP), and all my cousins and relatives who keep the faith and tell the truth: Uncle Bill, Andre, Wanda, and Melissa.

I would also like to apologize to my former Sunday school teachers and all the above for testing their faith with my decidedly ungodly behavior before, during, and after church.

I'd like to acknowledge my friends who forever inspire me to look inward, up, and around. And my editor, Robin Martin at Two Songbirds Press, for all the patience and guidance. Thank you also to my proofreader, Donna Lane.

To those who believe in God, may you find a message that appeals to you in this story. For those that believe in the interesting energies of the universe, may you receive inspiration in the stories. And to those who believe in the Goddess, check out my other book about Her–[winking emoji].

To my daughter who always inspires me to be the parent and role model I need to be for her and myself. I can't wait for the day she reads this and to see the look on her face as she asks me about my experiences going to church as a kid.

To my love, Eliann Marie, who helped push me to finish and gave me the space to do so… and all the late nights going over words, sentences, paragraphs.

And to my beloved mother, Floy, who remains alive in my heart and mind and who would chuckle and shake her head while reading this story.

CPSIA information can be obtained
at www.ICGtesting.com
Printed in the USA
BVHW052140200722
642672BV00004B/34